Encompassed By Darkness

SAVIOR OF THE LIGHT BOOK TWO

A. L. GORDON

Copyright © 2025 by A. L. Gordon

All rights reserved.

No part of this publication may be reproduced, distributed, or transmitted in any form or by any means, including photocopying, recording, or other electronic or mechanical methods, without the prior written permission of the publisher, except as permitted by U.S. copyright law.

This is a work of fiction. The story, character names and descriptions, and incidents portrayed in this publication are the product of the author's imagination. Any resemblance to actual persons, living or dead, or events, past or present, is entirely coincidental. No identification with actual persons or events is intended or should be inferred.

Ebook ISBN: 979-8-9908192-3-8

Paperback ISBN: 979-8-9908192-8-3

Hardcover ISBN: 979-8-9908192-9-0

Cover by Getcovers

Edited by Dr. Michael with FirstEditing

Map and Floorplan by Amanda with Eternal Geekery

Published by Lilabean Lit

Dedication

For all the readers who've been through hell.

And if you're there right now, know that things will get better.

Content Warning

This book contains references to, and scenes that include, captivity, torture, death, violence, and self-harm. Mental health is important, so if you find any of these topics triggering, please be advised.

Playlists

Listen to Brie's Playlist on Spotify

Listen to Michael's Playlist on Spotify

Listen to Lucifer's Playlist on Spotify

THE NINE
CIRCLES OF HELL

THREE - GLUTTONY
TWO - LUST
EIGHT - DECEPTION

ONE - SLOTH

FOUR - GREED
FIVE - WRATH
NINE - TREACHERY
SIX - PRIDE

SEVEN - ENVY

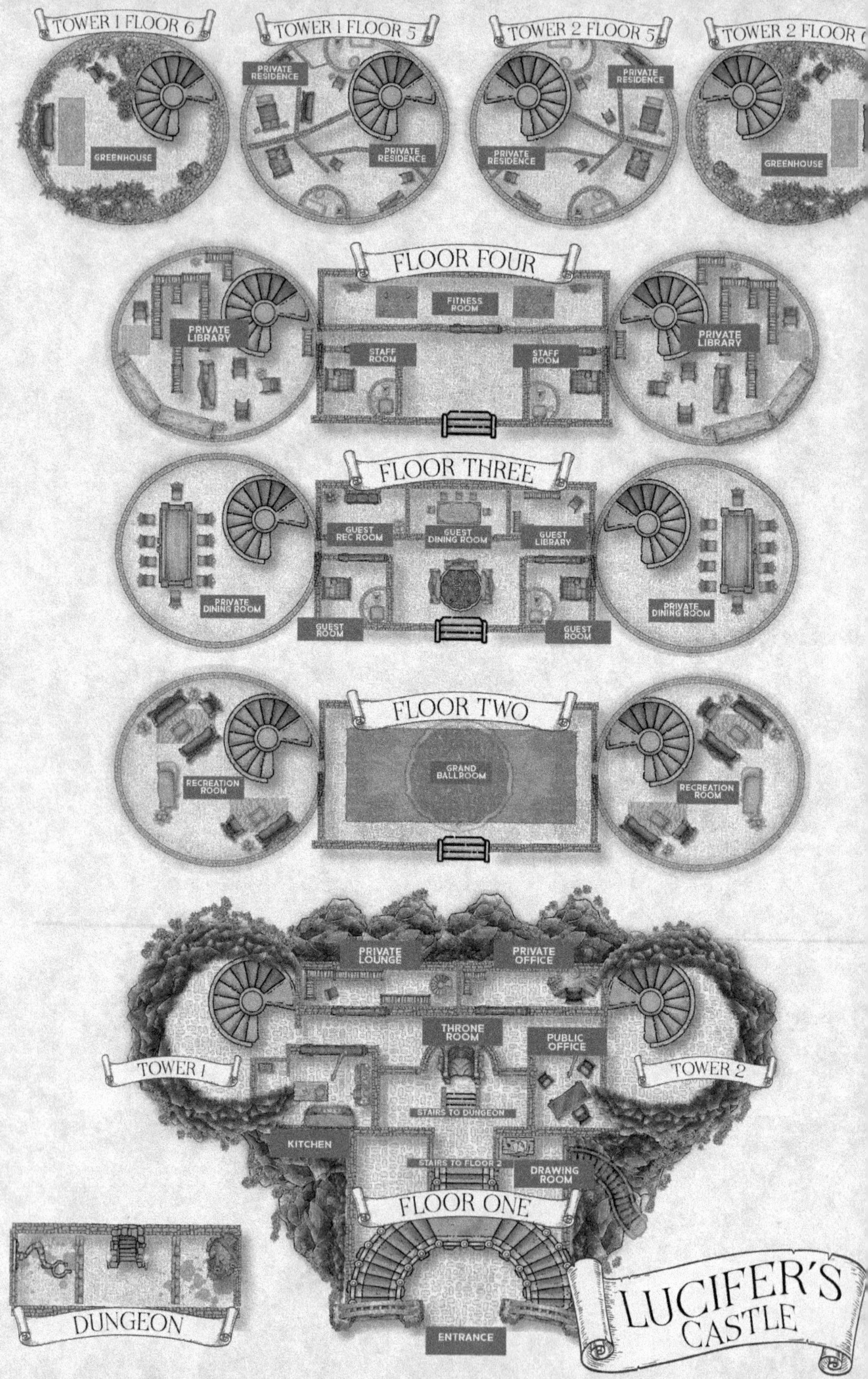

TOWER 1 FLOOR 6
GREENHOUSE

TOWER 1 FLOOR 5
PRIVATE RESIDENCE
PRIVATE RESIDENCE

TOWER 2 FLOOR 5
PRIVATE RESIDENCE
PRIVATE RESIDENCE

TOWER 2 FLOOR 6
GREENHOUSE

FLOOR FOUR
PRIVATE LIBRARY
FITNESS ROOM
STAFF ROOM
STAFF ROOM
PRIVATE LIBRARY

FLOOR THREE
PRIVATE DINING ROOM
GUEST REC ROOM
GUEST DINING ROOM
GUEST LIBRARY
GUEST ROOM
GUEST ROOM
PRIVATE DINING ROOM

FLOOR TWO
RECREATION ROOM
GRAND BALLROOM
RECREATION ROOM

PRIVATE LOUNGE
PRIVATE OFFICE
THRONE ROOM
PUBLIC OFFICE
TOWER 1
TOWER 2
STAIRS TO DUNGEON
KITCHEN
STAIRS TO FLOOR 2
DRAWING ROOM
FLOOR ONE
ENTRANCE

DUNGEON

LUCIFER'S CASTLE

Prologue

LUCIFER

In the edge of my peripheral vision, I notice the face of my Patek Philippe Aquanaut watch fogging over. My lips curl up into a rare smile. To what do I owe this unexpected call?

I'm not left wondering for long. Sabriel's beautiful porcelain face soon appears through the fog. "Sabriel, my darling. How are you?" She smiles in return, but there's a tightness to it. My heart plummets. Something's wrong. Sabriel's smile is never tight. It's always warm and genuine. Something must be wrong.

"Luc, I don't have long." Her head turns to the side. I recognize Michael's voice, though I can't make out what he says. "Yes, I know. I just need two minutes." More murmuring from my traitorous ex-friend. My jaw clenches and my fingers tap on the polished dark mahogany in front of me. This is *my* time with Sabriel. He has her all the time. How dare he infringe on *my* time with her!

Finally, she turns her attention back to me. "Sorry, Luc. I called to let you know that I won't be in contact for a while. I'm not sure how long it will be, but I wanted to let you know rather than just disappearing on you."

My stomach twists. I knew an unexpected call couldn't be good. I feel beads of perspiration forming on the back of my neck. My pulse pounds so strongly I can hear it. Not good. Not good. Not good at all.

"Luc, did you hear me?" Sabriel asks, her melodic voice breaking through my panic and soothing the frayed edges of my tattered soul.

"Yes, my darling. May I inquire as to why I will be required to forego the pleasure of..." I trail off when Sabriel looks to the side again, that infuriating male murmuring muffling my words.

"I'm so sorry, Luc. I don't have any more time. I'll call you as soon as this is over."

As soon as what is over? But she's already gone. I can't even ask. My light has left me. My only light amidst the ever-present darkness. And the darkness encompasses me yet again.

"Where is she?!"

The handcrafted whiskey glass flies out of my hand. It shatters upon impact. Shards of intricately carved crystal rain down. There is a consonance of tinkling sounds throughout the room as they settle atop the smooth stone floor. Rivulets of Macallan 1926 single malt run down the wall, the deep amber liquid pooling on the floor amongst the crystal shards.

"It's been years!"

"I apologize, Your Majesty. We are still unable to locate her." The sniveling hunter trembles, causing his voice to waver. What was his name?

"Leshy, Your Majesty."

"What?" I snap, scowling.

"My name, Your Majesty. My name is Leshy."

Oh, I guess I asked that out loud. I glare at him. He should have known it was meant to be an internal thought. Not that I actually care what his name is. And what a pitiful name to have chosen.

"You had one job. One job! You are supposed to be a hunter, are you not?"

"Yes, Your Majesty. I am the chief hunter."

"And hunters are supposed to be able to track, are they not?"

"Yes, Your Majesty. I deployed all of my best trackers throughout both the hellish and the earthly planes. I have even ventured throughout both planes personally, but we haven't found even the smallest piece of evidence regarding her whereabouts."

Incompetence!

"She didn't just disappear! FIND HER!"

My anger flares higher and the pathetic demon erupts into hellfire. His wails are a melodic backdrop against the blazing red flames engulfing his form. They peter out as his form disappears into ash.

I sigh. That's the third one this year. Nothing to do about it now. On to the next one.

The darkness presses in on me from all sides. It invades my pores and my cells. It steals the breath from my lungs, the light from my soul, and the reason from my mind.

I know I'm losing all reason. I can see the changes, but I can't stop them. The darkness takes over my being like a runaway train. All I can do is watch as my delusions grow and my mental faculties fade.

I'm losing the battle against its control with each day that passes. Without my connection to the light, I'm doomed. And if I'm doomed, Hell is too.

"Your Majesty," the new chief hunter breaks into my thoughts.

"Chief hunter...," I look down at the small yellow sticky note on my desk, "...forty-three. Report."

"We found her."

Chapter 1

BRIE

Empty. Broken. Like the husk of a human being whose soul has fled their body. Except it's the opposite, isn't it? My human body is gone and my shattered soul is all that remains.

I briefly register that Lucifer is still talking, but I couldn't tell you what he's saying if my life depended on it. The words float through my mind like leaves in the wind, never landing long enough to make an impact. My eyes blur and wetness drips down my face, pooling on the smooth, gray stone floor in front of me. Drop by drop, the little pool of tears grows steadily larger, darkening the slate color even further.

My form sags as the weight of my anguish engulfs every particle of my being. My shoulders curl forward, and a thickness clogs my throat, making it hard to swallow. My breath grows thin. Each inhale feels like it could crack my chest apart, each exhale feels like my lungs will collapse in on themselves.

A loud crack echoes through the room and a sharp sting flares to life on my left cheek, bringing with it a modicum of awareness.

Slowly, I raise my gaze. Lucifer's dull, moss-green eyes are filled with a mania I can't comprehend as he lowers his right hand. I lift my own hand, placing the cool extremity on my throbbing cheek in disbelief. I've never been slapped before.

Lucifer raises his arm again, reaching toward me. I flinch and scramble away from him, more and more awareness filtering into my sluggish mind. He lets his arm drop, an intense rage flickering over his face before he schools his features into a more placid façade.

"Sabriel, my darling. I don't want to hurt you. Aren't you happy to see me? It's been so long. So long. It's been so long." Lucifer's smooth tenor is cajoling, but it only makes me more wary of him.

"If you don't want to hurt me, you should help me get to the heavenly plane. Even the earthly plane would be fine. I don't belong here."

Lucifer's expression shutters and his eyes steel. I cringe, knowing I've mis-stepped. I want to get back to Michael, to find safety in his arms and solace in his words, but why would I expect Lucifer to help me get back to him? Lucifer is the one who *set* this trap for me.

He holds his hand out to me again, and this time, I make a conscious effort not to flinch at the motion. "Come." One word. Not a request. A demand.

I slowly rise to my feet, struggling not to curl in on myself again. I refuse to take his extended hand. I'm broken, I'm weak, I'm grieving, but I will not give in to his machinations. I will figure out a way to get out of this place. Lucifer be damned.

I follow Lucifer to a pair of thick, black stone double doors at the end of the throne room. He waves his hand lackadaisically and a smoky darkness drifts from his hand to the doors. The dark smoke pushes the doors open before dissipating into the air. I observe the intricate snake reliefs on both doors as I pass through them, impressed by the level of detail. Too late, I realize that they aren't reliefs, and the movement of the snakes is not the result of the flickering lanterns.

I hasten my steps, still remembering the sting of the snake bites I suffered in Ireland, but in my hurry to flee the snakes slithering atop both doors, I accidentally stumble into Lucifer.

Rebounding off of Lucifer's back, I fall into one of the doors. The snakes hiss at me and bare their fangs, but Lucifer is grabbing my arm and pulling me off the door and into his body before any of the snakes have a chance to strike.

"Shhh...it's okay, you're alright. I've got you. I'll never let anything hurt you, Sabriel. Never. Never. Never."

Lucifer's words sound so sincere, I could almost believe him for half of a heartbeat. But I will never forget how he's already hurt me. I will never forget what he's taken from me. How he's destroyed me. Body, heart and soul—he's devastated every part of me in a way that I don't think I can ever recover from.

I pull away from him and stiffly assert, "I'm fine."

Lucifer rubs my arm gently, then steps away and leads me through the long hallway. I study his form as he walks in front of me. His hair is a sun-kissed shade of auburn, cut into a medium low taper and combed to the side. He's around 6'3" with a bulkier build than Michael's. He walks with an arrogance shaped by years as Hell's ruler and a confidence that hints at the angel he must have been before his fall. Tattoos poke out above the collar of his shirt and below the rolled-up cuffs on his muscled forearms.

I can't say he's not attractive. He is. But with every detail I take in, my heart hurts that much more. My mind compares every aspect of his being to Michael's, as my soul yearns to be reunited with the angel I've fallen in love with.

Michael, I miss you. Dear divine spirit, if you can hear me down here, please help me find a way back to him.

"It took me so long to find you," Lucifer says casually, though the agitation in his body belies his carefree affectation.

"Oh?"

"When you told me you wouldn't be in contact, I tried to be patient, darling. Truly I did. But you know patience is not my forte, Sabriel. I waited and waited. Waited. Waited. I tried to fill my time. I tried to distract myself. Tried to keep the darkness at bay. But my light was gone. She was gone and the darkness seeped in and in and in. And I tried to be so patient, but the darkness... You know how I struggle with the darkness."

Lucifer turns to me, his eyes wide and imploring. I look deeply into his eyes and for the first time, I see a deep pain within them. I'm so distracted by the pain within his eyes that I don't see his arms reaching for me. I startle as his hands close around my upper arms with a vice-like grip. I must wince, because his grip immediately eases.

"Too hard. Too hard. Too strong. Gentle. Gentle. Gentle." I don't think Lucifer realizes that he's speaking the words aloud, but it helps me to understand him just a tiny bit. It shows me the madness that he desperately tries to hide beneath his fancy clothes and pretentious mannerisms. And in this moment, I feel a sliver of pity pierce through the overwhelming disdain I have for the male standing before me.

Lucifer's thumbs briefly glide along my skin before he releases my arms and continues walking. I drag my fingers along the textured black walls as we continue down the hallway, recognizing the stone as obsidian. Obsidian is supposed to be a stone that absorbs and transforms negative energy, but the stone in these walls feels blocked. Instead of transforming negative energy, the walls are filled with it, even emitting it in small amounts. I shudder at the repulsive feel of the darkness brushing against my soul. It's looking for weaknesses in my light that it can penetrate and exploit, but it won't find any. My light is still firmly intact.

Nevertheless, I draw my fingers away from the wall. Torches adorn the wall at regular intervals, the flickering light from their flames dancing along the black stone, creating a theater of shadows performing on the soft material of the blood-red carpet runner under our feet. We pass several closed doors as we approach a spiraling staircase adorned with a matching carpet runner, the soft material muffling our footsteps.

Lucifer leads me up one flight of stairs, then another. He stops on the third landing, which opens into a private dining room, but I can barely take in the details as my mind swirls with regret. Silence is not my friend right now and I fear I have made an irrevocable mistake.

What if I can never get back to Michael? What if I am trapped in Hell for eternity? Why didn't I try to find an alternative solution? I thought that sacrificing myself was the only way to seal the Hell Gate, but I didn't take more than a few seconds to think of alternatives. I was in excruciating pain, my mental capacities diminished. If I had waited just a few minutes and tried to find another way to seal the Gate, maybe I would be with Michael this very moment.

Michael.

The only good thing to happen in my life. My only chance at happiness. Gone. Hurt. All because of me. Because of me and my stupid knee-jerk decision to jump into a Hell Gate. Screw humanity. They let the darkness into their world, they succumbed to the temptations of evil, why am I the one to pay the price for their sins?! I felt that if I didn't sacrifice myself, I would no longer be worthy of Michael, but now it doesn't even matter. I'll never see him again regardless.

I think of his radiant sapphire eyes and his soft brown hair, his solid build and his forcedly stoic demeanor, and I know in my heart that I have just made the greatest mistake of my life. If I could go back in time, I would change my actions in a heartbeat. I would change all of it. I would have told him that I loved him so much sooner. I would have cherished every moment we had together, no matter how brief or trivial. I would have given him every little piece of me I had to give. And I would have found some other way to seal the last Gate.

A tear slips down my cheek and the floodgates open. I cry in heaving sobs. The anguish is uncontrollable, like a runaway train destined for disaster. I fall to my knees, my body jerking with each gasping breath I can muster. I rub the moisture from my eyes—again, and again, and again—until my eyelids become gritty, raw, and swollen. I can barely open them anymore, but the tears don't abate. Until finally, with one last broken wail, I exhaust myself into oblivion.

I wake up groggy, unaware of my surroundings. Fatigue suffuses both my mind and limbs, and for a fraction of a second, I forget. I think I'm back in my little studio apartment in Los Angeles wondering what I did last night that would make me feel this sluggish, but then—then, it all comes back.

I remember. I remember every horrible, agonizing second of what happened, and I feel guilty for forgetting. How could I ever forget what happened? What type of horrible being must I be that I could have forgotten for even a millisecond that I left Michael standing at the edge of a lava lake as I took a running jump into it, destroying both our souls in the process. Maybe I am a wretched soul. Maybe I do deserve to be in Hell.

As if the slight reprieve in my agony were simply an illusion cast over me by the devil himself, I am engulfed by a grief so acute that I could map every fracture of my shattered soul. It steals the breath from my lungs and forces from my throat a keening sound I didn't know I was capable of making. Shivers rack my body until I can take no more and I recede into a despondent numbness.

For the first time since awakening, I peel my sore, swollen eyes open, then jerk in alarm when my gaze is immediately met by a pair of luminescent reddish-brown orbs. Cerberus' three heads are resting on the edge of the bed, two seemingly asleep while the third stares at me intently. Noticing my awareness, the other two heads blink their eyes open and all three heads rise from the bed. Endearing doggy grins, complete with tongue lolling and head tilting, appear on all three faces as Cerberus' tail wags back and forth at the edge of my vision.

Taking a shaky breath, I slowly extend my arm toward Cerberus, caressing the black fur of his middle face. As his head tilts into my hand and he stares lovingly into my eyes, I nearly break down again, the flood of my emotions pummeling against the dam keeping them at bay. Briefly closing my eyes again, I sink further into the numbness and my emotions retreat once again.

I suck in another shaky inhalation and reopen my eyes, keeping them purposely averted from Cerberus this time. Propping myself up, I take in the foreign room. Faint red-tinted light illuminates my surroundings, the ruby glow cast through a large stained-glass wall bracketed by sheer black curtains. The curved wall is a beautiful mosaic of red and black glass, patterned into an elegant floral design.

A black leather sofa with a ruby-red, silk throw blanket spans the length of the room in front of the stained-glass wall. On each side of the bed, intricately carved end tables hold stunning pots of Starlet Velvet petunias, and above me dangles an unlit black crystal chandelier.

I slide over to the edge of the large bed, the smoothness of the satin bedding giving little resistance to my movements. Swinging my legs onto the plush red rug surrounding the bed, my feet sink into the softness of it as I stand and pad toward the two doors to the right of the bed. A shock of cold bolts up my legs as I step from the softness of the rug onto the hard, black-marble floor beyond it.

Opening the first door, I'm met with a large dressing room. Entering tentatively, I'm dismayed to find that the dressing room is filled with women's clothing, shoes, and accessories. Dread replaces the numb feeling and I place a hand against my chest, as if the pressure could still the nervous vibration of my energy. Opening the other door, I find a gleaming bathroom.

Sighing, I turn back toward the bed. Glancing past it into the sitting room beyond, my heart stutters. Lips twisted into a smirk and one arm draped lazily along the back of another black leather couch, Lucifer has been watching my every movement.

Chapter 2

BRIE

"Have you been sitting there the whole time I was asleep?" I ask Lucifer warily.

"I thought it would be better than leaving you to wake up alone in an unfamiliar environment. I didn't want you to panic about where you were."

My hackles rise. That's...oddly considerate...and I don't trust it to be the truth. This is coming from the being that trapped me in Hell in the first place. He probably wasn't worried about me panicking as much as he was concerned that I might escape. And given the opportunity, I would.

"Do you like the room?" He stands from the couch and smiles sheepishly with the question.

"I would prefer to be in my own room."

Lucifer's face falls and his shoulders slump for a moment. He looks toward the large window on the side wall of the sitting room and rubs one hand across the back of his neck before returning his gaze to me with a defeated sigh. "I'm not your enemy, Sabriel. You know this."

"Do I? Because from where I stand, you tricked me into coming to Hell and then trapped me here against my will. Those aren't the actions of a friend, Lucifer."

His nostrils flare and his previously dull eyes blaze. "You left me! You were all I had. My only connection to the light. My only tether to the goodness of Heaven, and you left me. For years! I had no idea where you were. I needed you! I was drowning in the darkness and the only being I could count on to pull me out of it had abandoned me. Vanished from my life with no word of where you were going or how to contact you. I tried to find you. I reached out to all of the archangels, but not one of them replied to my *many* messages. I sent tracker after tracker to find you: they all came up empty. Until finally, after *years* of searching for you, I found out that you were on the earthly plane. And not only that, but you were closing all of the Hell Gates there—cutting off my only means of connecting with humanity and temporarily escaping the darkness. You trapped me here as much as I trapped you here!"

"I was cleaning up your mess! There was so much darkness leaching into the earthly plane from *your* Hell Gates that it wouldn't have been capable of supporting humanity much longer. *You* upset the balance between the light and the darkness on the earthly plane, and I was the one tasked with fixing it. Did you consider that when you opened all of those Hell Gates? Did you want to expand your empire and not care about the collateral damage in the process? Or were you just so selfish that you only cared about your own access to the earthly plane with absolutely no consideration for the beings *living* on that plane?"

He doesn't reply for a beat. We're both breathing heavily, and I don't realize that we're now standing only inches away from each other until Lucifer takes a step back and runs a hand through his auburn hair.

"I didn't...I didn't realize that the Gates had caused an imbalance. I wasn't...it wasn't on purpose. I was, perhaps, a bit neglectful of my duties the past few decades." Lucifer concedes softly, his expression becoming pained. He looks as though he's deflated with the admission, and I feel a small pang of sympathy for him.

"Regardless of your intention, it happened," I say, my own voice softening more than I would like. "And it was my burden to fix it, which I did. I'm sorry that you felt abandoned, but keeping me here isn't the answer. This isn't right. I don't belong here. And if you keep me here, it's going to destroy me. Let me go, Lucifer." I'm not above pleading at this point.

"I can't."

"Why not?!"

"I just can't! Don't ask me again."

My fingernails bite into my palms as my fists clench at my sides. My lips purse and I have to consciously stop myself from finding something to throw at him as my anger overtakes me. But I temper myself. I won't gain anything by lashing out at him. I have to be careful about how I approach this, so I hold myself back.

I look at Lucifer imploringly, silently begging him to understand the damage this will do. But he just turns away from me, his jaw ticking. I feel utterly trapped. Locked in a gilded cage with no escape. Despair overtakes my being and the emptiness returns. Like a drain plug being pulled from a filled tub, what little hope I held onto swirls out of me in a rush.

"You don't care," I whisper. "You'll destroy every piece of me, and you couldn't care less."

Lucifer whips his head in my direction, his eyes gleaming with desperation. "Of course I care!" he roars. "You'll be fine, you just need time to adjust."

I shake my head at him. Resignation constricts my vocal cords, making a verbal response impossible. I'm equal parts numb and heavy as I stare blankly at the polished black marble beneath my bare feet. Seconds pass, or maybe hours, I can't be sure. A gentle touch presses beneath my chin, tilting my head up until my gaze meets Lucifer's green irises.

"You just need time," he repeats.

I don't answer. Don't acknowledge that I even heard him. I blink slowly, staring without seeing. My captor sighs in disappointment and withdraws his finger from beneath my chin.

I don't move. I just stand in place as if I were a statue placed in this gleaming cage of a room. Lucifer moves toward the doors of the lounge, glancing back at me once more before exiting the room. I hear a key turn in the lock and my body starts shaking uncontrollably. I finally move, bringing my arms up to hug myself. I feel like I'm physically holding the broken pieces of my soul together, hoping I can eventually glue them into an imitation of wholeness if only I can keep them from falling to the floor and shattering further.

My eyes well up and I shuffle over to the dark maple bar cart in the corner of the lounge. I grab the closest bottle, not caring what spirit is inside it, and pour myself a drink. I chug the smoky liquid. It burns my throat on the way down, but I welcome the pain. It gives a physical manifestation to the pain I feel inside. I pour a second glass and down that one too. Then, I turn and throw the bottle at the large glass window beside the cart.

The bottle shatters, just like my soul did. Shards of broken glass bounce off the unblemished surface of the window and cut my skin before raining down to settle on the floor. The stings of the small cuts on my skin diminish the numbness within, and a little of my awareness returns. I glance at the mess I've just made, but don't feel the need to clean it. I will destroy everything in this room, just as Lucifer is destroying every part of me by keeping me here.

Like a wave, my anger at the situation returns. I pick up another bottle and hurl it at the window. Then another. And another. And another, until not a single bottle remains, and my body is littered with slices from the broken glass.

I need to find a way out of here. If Lucifer won't release me, I'll release myself. I just need to figure out how.

I let myself settle with this thought for several moments, hardening my resolve. I can't play the role of a damsel in need of saving, just waiting for Michael to come get me. If I want to get out of here, I need a plan of my own. And it needs to be a smart one. If I only get one chance to escape, it needs to be a successful attempt. There is no other acceptable alternative.

I need to gather information about both the castle and the hellish plane that exists outside these walls. I need to look for opportunities to attempt the actual escape. Most of all, I need to lull Lucifer into a false sense of security. I'm not completely sure yet, but I suspect Lucifer doesn't know that I don't have Sabriel's memories. It seems like he trusted the angel me, so I can play off of that to gain some freedom. Let him lower his guard and, as soon as he does... He won't even realize I'm gone until it's too late. Or that's what I hope.

It seems like a valid plan to me. The first step to put into action: reconnaissance. I need to know this castle and Lucifer's schedule inside and out. Standing straighter and pressing my shoulders back, I nod to myself. I can do this.

I let out a long slow breath, let my healing energy seal the small cuts covering my skin, and start toward the locked doors. Luckily, these doors don't have live snakes slithering atop their surfaces like the doors to the throne room. I rap on the door three times, wincing as the thick metal smarts against my knuckles.

Not having expected any answer to my knocks, I feel a rush of nervous adrenaline when I hear the doors unlocking. One of the knobs turns. I take a step back in response. The door pushes open, ever so slowly, but it's not Lucifer who's entering.

"I still don't understand why he insisted on installing such heavy doors," the woman huffs. She's very short, probably not even five feet tall, and portly. Her round belly is clearly the consequence of overindulgence rather than pregnancy, given that she looks to be around sixty or seventy years of age. Her bright pink hair is pulled into a bun on the top of her head and her pitch-black eyes gleam as they focus on the door she's trying to heave open.

Her demeanor is firm but caring as she finally gets the heavy door open far enough for her to enter the room. "You must be Sabriel," she smiles warmly, and it infuses the tone of her voice too. "My name is Deidamia. I know it's a mouthful, so feel free to call me Dee."

I nod, giving her a small, polite smile in return. "It's nice to meet you, Dee."

"It's nice to meet you too, dear. Lucifer has told me so many lovely things about you, part of me feels like I already know you. We are all beyond thrilled that you decided to come visit. We've been eagerly anticipating your arrival."

Her happiness is so palpable, I can't bear to correct her. She also seems genuine. I'll need to learn more about her of course, but from first impressions, perhaps she could become an ally.

"I am here to help you with whatever you need while you're here. Think of me as your one-woman... Oh my goodness, what happened over there?" Her face pales and her hands cover her mouth. I follow her gaze to the mess I've made in front of the bar cart and grimace. What kind of excuse can I make for this? It's obviously not an accident.

"I apologize. I panicked when I heard the doors lock upon Lucifer's departure."

"Ah," her eyes soften in what appears to be understanding. "No matter. I'll get it cleaned up for you right away. Lucifer just wants to protect you. We are in Hell, after all." She gives me a little wink, as though being in Hell is some sort of joke.

She walks toward the mess, stopping a few feet in front of it. Closing her eyes, she murmurs something indistinguishable under her breath and black tendrils of darkness start to extend from her fingers. She starts swirling her hands, and the black tendrils swirl with them, forming a tornado of darkness that sweeps all of the alcohol and glass into its funnel.

Her eyes pop open and she gestures her whirling hands toward the garbage can next to the bar cart, the trash tornado following her movements until it is positioned directly above the garbage can. Then, she throws her hands down, palms flat. The tornado disappears, the darkness integrating into the air around us, the trash it was holding in its swirling funnel crashing into the can below.

Turning back to me, Dee gives me another kindly smile. "All better," she says. But something that I can't decipher flickers across her eyes. An uneasy feeling tries to crawl up my spine, but I squash it back down. I've had a hard day—month—year—and this woman has been nothing but nice to me. I'm probably just uneasy about being stuck in Hell. The feeling probably has nothing to do with her. And all beings in Hell have some degree of darkness, so that would make me uneasy as well. I'm overreacting. But in the back of my mind, I hear the memory of Michael telling me to always trust my instincts.

Chapter 3

MICHAEL

"Michael! Michael!" I ignore the haughty yell, continuing to focus on the maps before me while palming the engagement ring in my pocket. I'd been carrying it when Brie sacrificed herself, planning to propose to her as soon as the Gate had been sealed. Even though Sabriel and I have been married for eons, since Brie didn't have those memories, I thought she would like to experience the first-time feeling of a wedding again.

"Let me in there you flaming hot hunk of a man. I will *not* be distracted by your very large and defined muscles, sir. You let me through!"

Raphael chuckles lowly and crosses the shimmering white marble floor to take care of the disturbance.

"Look, you are obviously very committed to your job, and well done on that, but I really need to talk to Michael."

"And what exactly do you need to speak with Michael about?" Raphael asks, leaning against the polished archway.

"I heard that Michael returned yesterday and I would like to know why my best friend didn't come with him. Because I've been asking around about Brie, but no one has seen her. So Michael better get his angelic behind out here right now and explain to me where my best friend is!"

Her voice has gotten louder the longer she's spoken, and I cringe at the commotion she is causing. Sighing, I stand from my chair and head toward the entrance of the Angelic Army Command Center.

"Brie? Brie is *my* best friend and you don't have the clearance to—"

I cut off Raphael by placing a hand on his shoulder.

"Michael." The girl's chocolate-brown eyes settle on me with a glare, and my own eyes widen in recognition. I take in the short, light brown hair that's shaved on one side of her head and her slim build. Sometimes a soul's angelic form differs slightly from their last human form, but she looks identical to how I remember her.

"Callista."

"Where is Brie?"

Her voice is hard as stone and it twists the knife that has been embedded in my heart since Brie's sacrifice. I run a hand over my face. How am I going to explain this?

"Let her through."

The guard, who had been physically blocking Callista from entering the Command Center, steps aside with a small nod, but Raphael simply narrows his eyes at the girl. I tap his shoulder and, with a huff, he finally lets the girl pass through the threshold.

I lead her to the center of the room and retake my seat, gesturing for her to sit as well. She doesn't. Instead, she crosses her arms and starts tapping one foot. Its tap, tap, tap echoes on the gleaming marble, magnifying the sound.

"Brie—she..." I shake my head. "She's not here. She..." Just rip the Band-Aid off, Michael. You have to say it out loud at some point. It's real and it happened, whether you speak the words aloud or not. "She's in Hell."

Callista gasps.

"We were quite busy planning her rescue when you interrupted us," Raphael adds unhelpfully.

"You're going to Hell?" Callista confirms.

I nod.

"Let me come with you."

"Absolutely not!"

"She's my best friend!"

"You are untrained. You are not a member of the Angelic Army. As I said before, absolutely not. Brie wouldn't want you to put yourself in harm's way, not to mention that having someone untrained on a precision mission could put the entire operation at risk."

"But, Michael, I have to do something." Her voice breaks and tears well in her eyes. She quickly swipes them away, refusing to let them fall. Without her tough girl bravado, I see Callista as she truly is. I can see her fear, but I can also see her resolve. I worry that she might try to rescue Brie on her own if I deny her participation in our rescue operation.

"Fine, but you will do everything I tell you, without question. You are not trained for this and I will not allow you to put yourself or anyone else on this mission at risk."

Her eyes light up. "Agreed!" she shouts quickly.

Raphael turns to me in bewilderment. "You can't be serious!"

"Would you rather her go on her own?"

"Of course not, but—"

"I know and I agree, but I also understand her desperation, and I am not going to fail Brie a second time in regard to her friend."

Raphael's lips turn down as he considers my words. "Understood," he finally responds.

Our failure to prevent Callista's death when we were on the earthly plane still haunts all of us. I owe it to both myself and Brie to keep her safe this time around.

"Now, as I was saying, Lucifer will likely know that we have entered Hell quite soon after our arrival. He has many beings vying for his favor, and they will be eager to report our movements to him. Do not trust any being that you meet down there, no matter how benign they may seem."

I pause, looking each angel in the eye, before continuing.

"While it is of course a good thing that Brie and I managed to seal all of the Hell Gates on the earthly plane, it also means that the only remaining entrance to the hellish plane is through the astral plane. Therefore, we will enter Hell here." I point to the location at the edge of the first circle of Hell, where the Gate from the astral plane is located.

"Brie is most likely being held in Lucifer's castle, here." I point to the small circle within the large map that denotes the location of Lucifer's castle. "Each of Hell's circles is accessible through a single checkpoint. We will need to be prepared to meet large numbers of beings at all points in our journey, but particularly at each checkpoint. They will not want us to progress in our journey, and the checkpoints are the most obvious points of weakness for our side."

I swipe my hands through my hair, gently pulling at the ends. A nervous gesture, but only Brie knows me well enough to pick up on that. The small bite of pain from my scalp keeps me centered.

"Questions?" Each of the angels respond in the negative. I pull a more detailed illustration of the first circle of Hell to the top of the pile of maps in front of me and continue.

Fourteen hours later, I dismiss my subordinates, instructing them to be ready to leave at first light tomorrow. I hate to wait even an hour more, but I know that if they don't get sufficient rest, they'll be sloppy, and that could put the mission at risk. A successful outcome is the only acceptable outcome, so I need to be patient and make smart decisions, not emotional ones.

With only Raphael and I remaining in the Command Center, I slump in my chair. "What if we don't get her back?"

"That won't happen. We'll get her back."

"But what if we don't?" I say, desperation filling my words.

"Then I guess we'll all be moving to Hell." I whip my head up to study my brother as he joins us in the Command Center. Though the comment sounded flippant, I can tell by his expression that he is dead serious.

Gabriel swipes his dark honey-blonde hair out of his baby blue eyes as he leans on the back of Raphael's chair.

"You really mean that," I say in disbelief.

Gabriel nods as Raphael replies for them both. "We're family, Michael. We'll do whatever we need to keep this family whole. If that means moving into Lucifer's castle because we can't extract Brie, so be it. It would be entertaining to see how he would react to all of us living with him. He'd probably decide to let her go just to get rid of us."

I chuckle for the first time since losing Brie, my heart swelling that Raphael and Gabriel would be willing to do something so drastic for Brie and me. Sometimes I feel like I don't deserve them.

"Thank you. For helping me, for standing by me. I don't know what I'd have done without you two."

Raphael's whole face lights up with his grin, as Gabriel comes over and squeezes my shoulder gently, murmuring, "I love you, big brother."

As dawn lights the skyline in beautiful hues of pinks and purples, I zip up the hydration bladder compartment of my rucksack and heft it onto my shoulders. I verify that I'm able to easily draw my swords from their scabbards, even with the pack on my back, and set off toward the Heavenly Gate. Raphael and Gabriel fall into step with me almost immediately, but I don't yet acknowledge their presence, lost in my thoughts. They know that this is part of my pre-mission process and won't take offense.

I mentally review each of the terrain maps I laid out yesterday, along with the routes we will need to take to get to each checkpoint and to move through the circles surrounding Lucifer's castle. I revisit everything I learned about Hell during my last trip to the hellish plane and think through as many of the scenarios we might encounter as I can imagine. I also take stock of the strengths and weaknesses of each member of the rescue team.

I hand-picked every angel that will be a part of this mission, with the exception of Callista. Raphael has been by my side on nearly every mission I have undertaken in my long history as the commander of the Angelic Army, so his inclusion was a no-brainer. Gabriel rarely accompanies us for missions, but he is battle-trained and insisted on joining this one. It meant more to me than I let on. I will repay him for this gesture until my last day in existence.

Haniel and Kemuel are two of my most-trusted warriors. They have been in my command unit for eons and I can count on either of them to make the hard decisions and complete the mission if I am unable to. The last member of our extraction team is Ariella. She is a young, eager angel with incredible potential, and has moved up through the ranks quickly. Her fighting style is elegant yet brutal, an embodiment of the lion within her soul.

And then there's Callista. She shouldn't be coming on any mission, let alone a precision mission, but I couldn't leave her to do something reckless. She will be a liability at best, and likely a distraction during our battles as well. I'm currently questioning my decision to include her, but the moment I lay eyes on her determined expression, I know I've been backed into a corner.

The group is assembled beside the Heavenly Gate in silence, patiently waiting for my ruminations to cease so that we may embark. After glancing at each angel, checking their uniforms and weaponry, I nod to myself. Everything seems in order. Even Callista is equipped and dressed appropriately, which surprises me. I'm guessing that's Ariella's doing. Her forethought is one of the qualities that has contributed to her rapid ascension within the Angelic Army. It helps that Brie mentored Ariella, so she understands how important this mission is.

"Is everyone ready to move out?"

I receive affirmation from each of them and my throat thickens with emotion. Although I hand-picked each of these angels, they had the right to refuse the mission. Every one of them accepted, even knowing the potential consequences.

"I'm reminding you that if your energy is damaged beyond repair while in Hell, your soul will cease to exist. You will not regenerate or return to Heaven. This is your last chance to back out."

No one leaves. They all simply stare at me with resolve in their gazes, and a sliver of my heart mends from their support. I don't know what I did to deserve the amazing beings surrounding me, but I will forever be grateful. I imprint this moment into my memory to keep me going when the long nights try to pull my thoughts toward negativity.

Speaking specifically to Callista, I ask, "I know you haven't been in your angelic form long. Have you learned to manipulate the density of your energy yet?"

She nods in affirmation and a bit of my stress about letting her join our group dissipates. "And you can manipulate the energy of the angelic objects you possess as well?" I confirm.

Again she nods, and I breathe a small sigh of relief. "Good. Let's set off."

The group allows me to take the lead. Raphael and Gabriel fall into step a pace behind me, and I hear Haniel instructing the girls to follow Raphael and Gabriel. The generals take the rear, prepared to defend our backs in case of ambush. I'm grateful that my generals are able to take such initiative, so I don't have to give such elementary instructions. My focus lies elsewhere, as it should.

I feel the shiver of protective energy as I pass through the Heavenly Gate and announce my arrival to the garrison protecting it. They part without delay and stand at attention as we pass by. The gate itself is covered in angelic runes of protection, preventing unauthorized access to the heavenly plane, but those runes could be overpowered if hit by a large enough deluge of darkness, so the garrison provides extra protection in keeping our plane pure.

Erelah, the garrison commander, wishes us a safe and successful mission when we pass by her. Her eyes linger on Kemuel for a moment longer than the rest of us, her worry for her soulmate shining through, though she remains professional. Seeing her concern, knowing that her soulmate is risking his life to save my soulmate, brings a tightness to my chest and I quickly turn my gaze away from her.

As I enter deeper into the astral plane, I spread my energy so my form and gear become incorporeal. Pumping my wings, I shoot through the astral plane toward the Hell Gate, soaring above all the souls awaiting sorting. The air thickens as I approach it, quickly becoming oppressive. I condense my energy into my corporeal form to counter the heaviness of it and land just before the Gate.

A group of three demons are casually chatting in front of the Hell Gate. They don't even look our way as we approach, engrossed in their inconsequential conversation about which bands they hope will be lured toward Hell. Without saying a word, I move to step around them, but one of the demons seems to finally remember that he is here for a purpose and shifts into my path, blocking me from accessing the Gate.

"Name?" he asks, boredom infusing his tone.

I quirk an eyebrow at him. He should know who I am on sight. The fact that he doesn't speaks volumes about the state of Lucifer's leadership.

"Michael."

He doesn't react to my name, only drawling, "The purpose of your trip?"

I debate how to answer this. I could be frank and tell him that I'm here to rescue my soulmate, but I decide on a more ambiguous answer.

"I have some issues to discuss with Lucifer." *Discuss*. More like drive a sword through his being and rip his soul apart piece by piece so he can never threaten my soulmate again.

"Sure. Whatever. Do you acknowledge that there is a high likelihood of your death and / or torture if you decide to continue into Hell? And do you take responsibility for your likely death and / or torture if you pass through this Gate? If you accept that Hell bears no liability related to your potential death and / or torture, please place your palm on this tablet."

He pulls a flat slab of smoky quartz from his pocket. I place my palm on the brownish-gray crystal and feel a prick in my energy as the stone absorbs a sliver of it as proof of my binding agreement. The rest of the group follows my lead, and once Haniel has completed his oath, the smoky quartz disappears back into the demon's pocket. He and his companions step away from the Gate, waving us forward. As my foot crosses the threshold of the Gate, I hear a monotonous, "Try not to die." Then, the darkness of the portal engulfs me.

Chapter 4

BRIE

"I'm so glad you accepted my breakfast invitation, Sabriel."

I'm sitting across from Lucifer in the private dining room he tried to lead me to before my epic breakdown. I gave myself the rest of the day yesterday to settle with my plan to gain intel and come to grips with my situation, but today I'm in full recon mode.

When Dee greeted me this morning, she was carrying a black wooden tray holding only a ruby-red envelope. My name was scrawled on the front in black ink. I turned it over to find a black wax seal with an image of a flame. The red cardstock inside matched the red of the envelope, and the chaotically penned message on it invited me to breakfast with Lucifer. It took me a while to figure out what it said, given the messiness of the handwriting, but once I had deciphered it, I relayed my agreement to Dee. She seemed surprised at how readily I agreed, but enthusiastically launched into a speech about how amazing Lucifer's private dining room is.

I have to admit that Dee was right about the room. It is incredible. The entire exterior wall is made of large panes of glass. Since the tower is circular, that means we have a 270-degree unobstructed view of the hellscape surrounding the castle. There is a little bit of open land between the castle and the sprawling city beyond it, but I'm still able to look out over the cityscape clearly. The sun gleams off the glass of the skyscrapers in the distance, complementing the reds, yellows, and oranges of the skyline.

"Sabriel."

The timidity of Lucifer's voice pulls my attention away from the massive windows. I've seen a few sides of Lucifer, and timid is not an affect I ever would have predicted he'd display. He gives me a sheepish smile as he continues, "I..." He clears his throat, then starts again. "I wanted to apologize for slapping you yesterday."

My draw drops. I probably look like a gaping fish right now with my mouth opening and closing in astonishment, but an apology is the last thing I expected to come out of the devil's mouth.

"I honestly can't believe I did it. I'd never want to hurt you. You were just so despondent. You weren't acknowledging me or reacting to anything I was saying, and I panicked. My arm moved of its own accord, and I didn't even realize I had done it until I heard the sound. By that time, my arm was already withdrawing. You know me. You know that's not who I am. I've never been violent with you before and I never will be again. You're my light. I know you'll forgive me, but I still need to apologize regardless of your benevolence. It was a stupid, stupid mistake...stupid, stupid, stupid..."

The madness that I caught glimpses of before briefly engulfs his eyes, but his eyes are clear again in the next beat. He clears his throat a second time.

"Anyway, I hope you will accept my apology. I do feel genuine remorse for my action."

He trails off, looking at me like a lost little boy. I'm not sure that I trust him when he says he's remorseful or when he says he won't raise his hand to me again, but it serves my interests to tell him that I forgive him. He'll trust me more if he thinks I've forgiven him.

"Of course I forgive you, Lucifer. It must have been quite a shock to see how I was reacting. I don't blame you for forgetting yourself in the moment." I hope that was believable. I don't really have experience with lying, and I do blame him one hundred percent for everything he's done.

He sighs in relief, so I guess my lie was convincing. I turn my gaze to the polished ebony wood of the dining table. The golden light from the chandelier overhead glitters on the shiny surface of the table and makes the room feel cozy rather than creepy, despite the black ceiling and walls.

I absently run my hand over the dark red wine-colored velvet of my high-backed dining chair as I try to think of what I should ask Lucifer. I need to take advantage of this opportunity, but I don't want to sound like I'm prying. Arousing his suspicion is the last thing I need. I wish I had Sabriel's memories. This would be so much easier if I knew how much she knew about Hell.

"Would you tell me a little bit about the castle?" Lucifer gives me a confused look and my heart drops into my stomach. Shiznits, I've messed up already. "I mean, I assume you don't expect me to sit in my room and stare at the wall for days on end," I quickly amend.

Lucifer's confusion immediately dissipates, and I breathe a silent sigh of relief. "Of course not, darling. I remember how much you love to read, so I thought you may want to spend some time in the library. I think you'd also be happy to spend some time in the greenhouse, given how much you love working with plants. And, of course, the gym and the recreation room are always available to you as well. I want you to be happy and to feel at home here."

His last sentence hangs heavy in the air between us. How can he think I would ever be happy here? He pulled me away from both my home and my soulmate. I could never be happy here.

I don't say that though. In my quest to build rapport with Lucifer, I decide to answer, "Thank you for your generosity. That all sounds fantastic."

A relaxed smile crosses Lucifer's face and he leans back in his chair, just as Dee enters with a beautiful cherrywood rolling cart filled with domed platters and pitchers of drinks. I smile as Cerberus trots in excitedly behind her. Dee gives me a cheeky smile and a little wink as she positions the cart at the head of the dining table, and Cerberus crawls under the table to lay at my feet.

Dee removes the sterling silver dome covering one of the platters, placing it on the empty lower shelf of the cart, before picking up the loaded plate. It must be heavy, considering how much food is piled on top of it, but she doesn't struggle or waver under its weight. Dee moves to place the dish in front of Lucifer, but he raises his hand to stop her. "Please serve our guest first."

It's a gentlemanly move that I, once again, didn't expect from Lucifer, and I briefly wonder if I've been too harsh on him. Perhaps I've misjudged him. But no, he's holding me hostage. No manner of gentlemanly kindness can compensate for such an egregious act.

Dee quickly reroutes, placing the platter in front of me as Lucifer requested. "Thank you, Dee," I say. I don't know if Lucifer will have a problem with Dee and I talking. I hope my gratitude won't get her in trouble, and thankfully, Lucifer doesn't seem bothered that I have addressed her directly.

Dee beams at me in response, though a shadow moves behind her gaze. "It's my pleasure, dear." It makes me uneasy that she seems to hide some sort of darkness any time she smiles at me, but I am quick to disregard it. I don't know her past or what type of inner demons she might be battling. She's been nothing but pleasant to me so far, and that says all I need to know about her. It isn't fair to judge her inner turmoil.

Dee returns to the cart, picking up a pitcher of orange juice in one hand and a champagne bucket in the other. She places the champagne bucket to the side of Lucifer and I, so it doesn't obstruct our views of each other. "Would you like a mimosa?"

I'm so tempted—it would make this situation slightly more bearable—but I know I need to keep my wits about me. I can't have my reactions delayed or my judgment compromised. "No, thank you. The orange juice is fine. Coffee would be great if you have it."

Lucifer's brow knits and his lips purse. His head tilts fractionally as he examines my face, like he's searching for something. Eventually, he says, "We don't have coffee on this plane. The beans spoil from the toxins in our air. The closest thing to coffee on this plane is boiled licorice root."

Wait, toxins in the air? This keeps getting worse and worse. I bite my bottom lip to keep from lashing out again and instead say, "I'd love to try the boiled licorice root." Lucifer gives me another indecipherable look as Dee retrieves the carafe from the serving cart and pours the steaming light amber liquid into the teacup in front of me. The cloying smell of it wafts over to me and I grimace, already missing the nutty caramel scent I'm used to.

It seems silly, but coffee has always been like a comfort blanket for me. No matter what happened in my life, coffee always reminded me of home. My dad used to brew it in the mornings and I loved the smell. The taste took some getting used to, but the smell—that always reminded me of my dad. Or Brienna's dad, I guess. But he was my dad to me.

Dee serves Lucifer and then quietly wheels the cart out of the room, leaving us alone again.

"When did you start drinking coffee?" Lucifer asks me casually. I freeze like a deer caught in headlights, my fork halfway up to my mouth, yolk and hollandaise running off of it and dripping down onto the plate below.

"Um, a few years ago, I guess. While I was on the earthly plane." Not a lie. Best to go with the truth whenever possible.

With a noncommittal noise of acknowledgment, Lucifer continues slicing his steak and eggs in the most elegant manner possible. Then he says, "I'm surprised. You've always been such an herbalist. You were so proud of your teas; the Sabriel I know would have considered asking for coffee a form of blasphemy."

There's a sparkle in his green eyes, but I can also see a hint of suspicion. How is it possible that I've already triggered his suspicion twice in a handful of minutes when I've barely said anything? Did he really know angel me that well?

"Things change," I answer with a shrug. Another truth.

"Hmmm." Lucifer slips Cerberus a piece of his steak while he stares at me with a penetrating gaze, musing. "What else changed while you were on the earthly plane?"

I have no idea how to answer this. I don't really know what Sabriel was like, so how can I know what's different between us? I shift uncomfortably in my seat but decide playing coy is the best way to avoid answering Lucifer's question. "I guess you'll need to spend some time with me and decide for yourself." I smirk at him, but inside I want to vomit. I feel dirty talking like this to anyone other than Michael. A bitter taste fills my mouth as my words play on a loop in my mind.

It's not technically cheating, but that's what it feels like. Am I being unfaithful by flirting with Lucifer and leading him on? It sure feels like it, and I worry who I'm becoming. If this is how I'm acting after only one day in Hell, what kind of being will I be a month from now? A shudder of disgust rolls through my body as fear overtakes my mind. I can't stay here long enough to find out. I need to get out of here as soon as I have a plan of escape and the opportunity to execute it.

Lucifer, oblivious to my internal meltdown, raises his fork to his mouth and licks some of the juice off of the speared steak lasciviously. He slowly closes his mouth around the plump piece of meat and slides the fork out of his mouth, his eyes pinned on mine the whole time. He savors the meat as he chews it, like it's the best food he's ever tasted. I watch his Adam's apple bob as he swallows and finally, he says, "I think I like that plan."

Chapter 5

MICHAEL

When I step out of the portal into the first circle of Hell, I'm immediately hit by a wall of warm humidity. Sweat begins to bead on my brow, but I swipe it away before it can fall into my eyes. The combination of the heat and humidity is oppressive, clogging my lungs and weighting my limbs.

I step away from the Gate, providing space for the rest of my team to come through. I raise my legs quite a bit with each step, so my feet don't end up ensnared in the knee-high, orange grasses. My eyes catch on a tall sign directly in front of the Gate that reads, "Welcome to Sloth. The faster you run, the less tortured you'll be." An empty, rickety wooden bar stool sits next to the sign, but judging by the amount of dirt covering the seat, it hasn't been occupied for a long time.

As my team appears on this side of the Gate, I pan my gaze across the landscape surrounding us. The first circle of Hell was designed to punish those with the vices of sloth and neglect. The landscape is covered by tall grasses. There are mountains, and a volcano stands proudly in the distance. Large predators are as plentiful as the souls being punished here. Everything about this circle is designed to keep the souls inhabiting this circle as active and vigilant as possible. It's one of the most dangerous circles of Hell, from a survival perspective.

"Keep your eyes open and be ready to run in an instant." A single moment of distraction can lead to death in this environment. Raphael and I have been through Hell before and know what to expect, but none of the others have, and I want to be sure they will take every threat seriously.

We start trudging through the tall grasses, each of us scanning our surroundings for threats. It doesn't take long to realize that things are quiet. Too quiet. A few vultures speed past us, flying low overhead. The air seems to swell, becoming heavier and denser. The humidity doesn't decrease, but my nose starts burning as if the air were dry. And then, a deafening crack rends the air.

We all look up when a blindingly bright flash splits the clear red sky. My adrenaline spikes. The violence of the lightning storms in this circle are legendary, and as another bolt of lightning crashes toward the dry plains, I know we're about to see that violence and destruction firsthand.

"We need to run!" I call as I pick up speed. I don't even look back to see if my team is following. I simply trust that they are.

Lightning bolts crash out of the sky in every direction, setting the dry brush around us on fire. The air quickly fills with smoke and a smell similar to burning plastic, making it even harder to breathe. I pull my neck gaiter up to cover my mouth and nose as I swerve to avoid a lightning bolt that crashes down much too close to us.

I dodge and pivot as hacking coughs fill my lungs. The grasses all around us ignite, leaving us small paths to swerve through in our attempt to escape the deadly flames. We're slower on foot, but with the lightning, it's too dangerous to take to the sky.

Strong winds whip across the plains, fueling the fire. It roars to life in a way I've never seen and spreads across acres in the blink of an eye. A wall of yellow and orange chases us as dark plumes of smoke block the light of the sun. The heat encasing us intensifies, scalding every particle of my being, but still I run. As fast as I can, I sprint this way and that, narrowly avoiding flames at every turn.

My lungs burn as carcinogens pass through the gaiter. Ahead of us, souls of the damned appear from the brush, fleeing the flames just as we are. I leap over a small, ignited shrub and I can feel the fire licking at my heels. Heat scorches my skin as I sprint as fast as my legs will allow.

But even so, we're lagging. The wildfire is too close for comfort. I push through the burn in both my nose and my chest as I race to avoid the roaring flames. All around me, souls are engulfed by the blaze. A desperate type of wailing that I will never be able to forget echoes from every direction.

Finally, the lightning ceases. The fires still rage and the winds still fan their flames, but without the lightning, we can now take to the sky. I pump my wings. The denser air makes each movement harder. I'm expending more effort than I ever have before to leave the ground. But I'm a warrior. If I can't do this, I might as well relinquish my position within the Angelic Army.

Pushing off the ground with all the power I can muster, I rise into the air. It's slower than I'd like, but I grit my teeth and focus on each flap of my wings. And I rise, bit by bit, until I am high enough that the flames no longer lick at my legs. Looking over my shoulder, I'm relieved to see everyone in my group is still with me. I'm surprised that Callista was able to keep up, considering how new she is to flying, and it increases my respect for her.

Before I can let the relief of our escape filter through my mind, though, I notice our next threat. Flying above the fire, snatching up the souls that don't get caught in the flames, are harpies. Suddenly everything clicks. Harpies have the ability to create windstorms. These high winds that are whipping the fire into a frenzy are stronger than the natural windstorms that typically follow lightning storms here. No, these winds are much more powerful. And the harpies are the cause.

The vulturine women are terrifyingly beautiful. Their human torsos are clothed in black-feathered corsets, the feathers preserved from their own molting. Their long hair billows out behind them as they coast on the wind currents, their jet-black wings splayed wide. Intermittently, one of the harpies will dive down to capture one of the souls below, their thick, sharp talons digging into the captured soul so there is no chance of escape. One by one, each harpy that has captured a soul disappears into the billowing smoke of the fire, retreating to their nest.

Still, there are dozens of harpies remaining. And they don't seem to like us being in their airspace. Instead of continuing their hunt of the souls, most of the harpies reroute their focus to us once they notice us in the sky ahead of them. I pump my wings harder, pushing myself to fly even faster, but I know it's a lost cause. Harpies can fly as fast as the wind. We have no chance of out-flying them.

Desperate for a solution, I train my gaze on the landscape below. We need to find someplace underground where we can wait out the fire without the harpies following us. Think, Michael, think.

This circle produces coal. If we can find an entrance into the mines, we can hole up there. It's still risky, since coal ignites so easily. The entire mine, including the underground shafts, could ignite once the wildfire hits it, but I can't think of anything else. We don't have time to search the tall grasses for a burrow large enough for us, we can't outrun the fire, and we can't continue flying for much longer. There's no good answer.

I scan the area ahead of us, hoping against hope that we have covered enough distance from the Gate to be close to one of the mines, when I hear a blood-curdling scream. My head whips around to see Haniel in the clutches of one of the harpies. Kemuel tries to fight her off without catching Haniel with his sword, but it's not going well. The harpy is old and experienced. She dodges Kemuel's sword with ease while simultaneously using Haniel as a shield.

Ariella joins the fight. She tries to assist Kemuel by attacking the harpy from the left while Kemuel attacks from the right, but several other harpies have caught up to them as well and Ariella finds herself in a fight of her own. Callista isn't far behind Ariella in joining the battle, and I'm shocked to see that she is actually adept at swordplay.

Raphael, Gabriel, and I rush into the fight as well. We alight our swords with our angelic energy, just as the others have done. The harpies screech when our swords catch them, the light energy tearing at the foundation of their being with every glancing blow.

I catch one harpy straight in the heart and she detonates. Her being explodes from where my sword pierced her body, feathers and fragments of darkness flying everywhere as she ceases to exist. Her obliteration gives the other harpies pause, and the tides turn.

While the harpies are frozen in shock, Kemuel and Raphael land direct blows as well. The harpies they struck explode just like the first. Haniel, released when the harpy holding him was obliterated, starts to fall to the ground, but Kemuel swoops down and is able to grab hold of him .

Smithereens of darkness and feathers cloud the air and land on all of us. The harpies shriek in both anger and terror as bits of their comrades float around them. The sight of what kind of death awaits them if fatally struck with our angelic weapons is enough to convince the harpies to give up the fight, and they retreat into the wildfire's dark plume of smoke.

We're safe from the harpies for the moment, but the wildfire is still raging below us and we can't fly forever. We still need to find a haven. Haniel also needs healing, his arm shredded from the harpy's talons, but it will need to wait until we are back on solid ground.

"Haniel will now fly in the middle of our formation. Ariella, move back," I direct before resuming my forward flight. I don't turn back again to check that my instructions were followed, I simply trust that they were.

We fly for another fifteen minutes before I finally spot an abandoned open-pit mine up ahead. I scan the walls surrounding the pit, hoping the inhabitants of Sloth mined underground as well. I fly the perimeter once, twice, three times as the untamable blaze creeps closer and closer. On my fourth pass, my heart leaps: I see a small crack in the ground of the pit.

I send up a prayer to the divine spirit and dart toward the crack, hoping it's big enough for us to pass through. I land just next to the crack, and hear the light footfalls of my team landing behind me milliseconds later. Walking up to the crack's edge, I tuck my wings in close, and jump into it feet first.

Rough rock and compacted dirt brush my body as I fall through the fissure. The light above me disappears as I fall deeper and I conjure angel light in my palm to temper the darkness. The fissure starts to narrow, but before any panic is able to fully form, the walls around me disappear as I pass through the ceiling of a large mine shaft and land in a crouch.

I quickly step to the side, not wanting the next angel through the crack to fall on my head, and scan my surroundings. Though the abandoned shaft is fairly wide, I'm still able to make out the rough-hewn rocky walls. I shiver as the cold, stale air penetrates my uniform. It's a very noticeable difference from the scalding air I just left.

Raphael drops into the shaft from the crack in the ceiling, his landing the only sound other than a soft drip, drip, drip coming from somewhere down the tunnel to my left. I watch as he gets his bearings and steps aside just in time to avoid Gabriel dropping in on top of him.

"You couldn't have waited a few seconds longer?" Raphael asks sassily, coupling it with a huge eye roll.

Gabriel looks a little chagrined as he says, "I like being close to you?"

Raphael melts at his response, pulling my brother into a tight hug as he whispers, "I like being close to you too."

I turn away from them, my eyes burning. My chest tightens as their moment reminds me of all that I've lost. I don't want to be hurt by their display. I should be happy that they have each other. Instead, witnessing their devotion to each other feels like salt in my wounds. I try to hide my reaction under the guise of further examining the mine shaft, but I'm staring, not seeing.

It takes me a moment to refocus my thoughts away from my loss. In that time, the rest of my team has gathered in the shaft. I turn back to the group just as Raphael focuses his attention on Haniel.

Haniel doesn't have healing abilities, so Raphael will need to heal his arm. And it looks like it needs a lot of healing. The thing is completely shredded. I'm honestly not sure how he's still functioning given how much pain he must be feeling.

I look closer at Haniel for the first time since he was injured. The warrior's jaw is clenched, his lips pressed tightly together. His skin has paled, and his eyes are glassy, but he makes no sound. His good arm is cradling the injured one gently, and he winces when Raphael lays his own hand atop Haniel's injured arm.

I watch as Raphael's powerful healing energy pours into Haniel's injury. The fibers of his arm start knitting themselves back together. Haniel shakes from the pain of it and his breath rasps in and out, his first audible reaction to the injury since it occurred. But after only a few minutes, his breath changes to a sigh of relief. His arm is healed.

Haniel claps a hand on Raphael's shoulder. "Thank you, my friend."

"You're welcome," Raphael responds with a fond smile before turning to me. "He's fine to continue."

I tip my head down in acknowledgment. "I heard water dripping down this tunnel," I explain, pointing to the tunnel on my left. "I think we should move in this direction. The coal is highly flammable and if the mine ignites, we want to be as close as possible to both water and a way out."

The others give words of agreement and we start walking down the tunnel. The scuffs of our boots on the uneven, rocky ground echo off the stony walls. Small animals flee our path as we progress and the dripping sound grows slowly louder. The ceiling seems to lower the farther we go, until we reach an intersection.

I listen closely, trying to determine the direction of the dripping water. The sound of loose stones raining down comes from the right, drowning out the sound of the dripping water. Comparing the shafts, I see that the tracks in the one to the right look more recently used, so I take a chance on the left one.

It seems to be the right call. As the sounds from the shaft we passed up recede, I can once again hear the drips of water, and they seem to be growing louder. We pass several caverns off the main shaft as we continue along it. The ceiling rises and the shaft widens as we progress. Soon, the rocky floor becomes wet. Then, that wetness increases to standing water. The smell of the standing water is reminiscent of a sewer, but there is less than a centimeter of it, so it isn't a problem to walk through.

I briefly wonder if we should have taken the other mine shaft when we reach another fork in our path. The water seems to emanate from both shafts. I can hear creaking and muffled sounds from the tunnel on the left this time. I assume these are sounds from outside and, with a heart full of hope, I continue into the leftward shaft.

There's light up ahead and I know I've found an exit from this underground maze. Relief sweeps through me when I smell fresh air and only a faint odor of smoke. I think we'll be able to exit away from the fire.

As I step further into the shaft, a silhouette peels away from the shadowed wall. And then another does the same. And another.

And another. And I now know I've made a mistake, because a den of serpopards stands in front of us. And they are ready for battle.

Chapter 6

MICHAEL

The knobbly-kneed creatures tower over us, standing proud and alert. The expansive size and height of the shaft, much larger than a normal mine, gives them just enough space to stand at their full height. They stomp their cloven hooves in warning when they see they have our attention.

Serpopards are notoriously smart. They are also absolutely ruthless, completely unpredictable, stunningly fast, and incredibly strong. The perfect predator. And their sights are set on us. I peer up at the dragon-like face of the serpopard in the front of their group, assuming he is the leader of the den.

By my calculations, we have three options: one, we can try to reason with them; two, we can retreat through the mine shafts until the ceilings are too low for them to follow; or three, we can battle our way through them. I'd prefer one of the first two options, but as soon as I open my mouth to try to reason with the massive beasts, an ear-shattering boom sounds from one of the distant tunnels behind us.

The serpopards interpret the noise as a declaration of war and launch into attack mode before I can say a single word. They hurl themselves at us. Their long serpent-like necks extend and their strong maws open to show sharp teeth dripping with venom. I swipe out with my sword, my movements slower than normal—I'm still exhausted from battling the harpies. Still, I manage to dodge the vicious teeth aimed at my face and nick the bottom of the leader's neck.

He comes at me again, even more enraged than before. I dodge, but he's stepped closer and is now trying to kick me with one of his hooves. It's a smart move. One well-placed kick could prove lethal. Thankfully, I manage to avoid the weapon by swinging my body weight to the side.

His head comes at me again and I just manage to block. He brings his long neck in a wide circle behind me and I have to duck and roll to avoid him wrapping it around me. Their necks have crushing strength, and that too would have been lethal. If I wasn't trying so hard to survive this battle, I would be impressed by the tactical intelligence of this serpopard. His method of fighting interests the warrior in me. But given the circumstances, I don't let my fascination distract me.

It's not until he rears up on his back legs, trying to kick me with both front legs, that I realize I can see him more clearly now than when this fight started. If I couldn't pick up on the lightening orange glow, I would think my eyes had simply adjusted to the darkness. With a jolt of alarm, I understand that's not the case. The muted whooshing sound my ears pick up not long after confirms my supposition.

Terror engulfs me and my movements stutter just long enough for the serpopard to clamp its jaw around my left shoulder. I grunt in agony as the serpopard's venom mixes with my light energy. Still, I manage to use the position to my advantage, landing a deep blow to its neck. It releases my shoulder with a roar, snapping at my sword hand. I'm able to dodge again, and scramble to think of a way to end this battle. I need to warn my team of the other danger. The greater danger.

I run around the serpopard in a wide circle to gain distance, and once I reach the front of it, I slide underneath, holding my sword high. The tip of my sword carves into the serpopard's fleshy underside, but it's not deep enough to be a killing blow. The serpopard stomps its back hooves, trying to catch me underfoot at the end of my slide. I place one hand on its knobbly knee and swing around to the side, just barely avoiding the trampling.

I take the moment after my swing to yell a warning to my team. I don't know if they'll be able to hear me above the echoing sounds of our battle and the growing roar from the shafts behind us, but I have to try. We only have seconds left to leave this death-trap.

"IGNITION!" I bellow as loud as I can.

"IGNITION!" I hear in return, my soldiers acknowledging my warning and amplifying the call for anyone who didn't hear it.

The serpopards are intelligent enough that they understand the word, much to my relief. Their blocky heads snap up. Then, with admirable coordination, they each sweep their necks at us. I think their aim is to knock us off our feet so they have time to retreat, but they don't need to worry. As long as they're no longer attacking us, we won't be attacking them.

The serpopards turn away from us and flee deeper into the shaft that we're currently in. "I don't want to follow them and end up in another battle for survival," I tell my team. "Backtrack to the last shaft we passed and take that one. Run as fast as you can."

Before I even finish my last word, my team is following my instruction. They are all sprinting toward the newer shaft that we passed. I take up the rear, running like my life depends on it because, well, it does.

Just as we turn the corner into the new shaft, the roaring wall of flame flashes around the far turn in the maze of tunnels and barrels toward us. The fire consumes what little oxygen these shafts hold and my breathing becomes more labored. I assume the boom we all heard was the pit igniting and I'm thankful that the fire took a while to enter the underground portion of the mine. Otherwise, we'd already be dead.

I try not to look back as I sprint through the mine shaft, but I can't help myself. I glance over my shoulder to see the rapid fire chasing us at a much greater speed than our poor attempt to escape it. Is this my end? Is this how my light will be extinguished—fleeing a mine shaft ignition in the first circle of Hell? Dear divine spirit, please don't let this be my end. Please don't let me perish without seeing my soulmate one last time.

Light filters in ahead of us. The brighter yellow hues battle with the orange glow from the fire behind us. If this weren't such a dire circumstance, I might marvel at the beauty of it. Instead, I focus on reaching the source of that yellow-tinted light.

I'm steps away from the opening now, flames once again licking at my heels. The others burst out of the mine shaft ahead of me. The fire is too close though. It's going to engulf me before I make it out. But then I spot a red button embedded in the wall of the mine shaft, just next to the opening.

In a last ditch effort, I push the button as I run through the opening of the shaft into the world beyond and a heavy metal door slams down behind me. The flames try to escape through the cracks on the door's perimeter, but there isn't enough oxygen flowing through to fuel it anymore. Just as fast as the fire chased us, the glowing embers are snuffed out. I bend over and place my hands on my knees. My breaths come in forceful gasps. My limbs are shaky from adrenaline. But I'm alive, and that's all that matters. We made it out.

I send a quick ping of gratitude to the divine spirit before straightening up and recomposing myself. "How did you learn to wield a sword?" I ask Callista, who looks surprisingly unruffled by everything that has happened.

"Oh, I've been fencing since I was seven. I was actually on track to compete in the Olympics before I died." Her tone holds a note of sorrow. I can't imagine how difficult it must be for her to be joining in this mission so soon after her death.

Our typical 'Death Acceptance Program' in the angelic realm is several years long. I can't imagine grappling with your own death while journeying through Hell to rescue your best friend, but Callista is doing it almost effortlessly. The more I learn about her, the more respect I have for her. I understand now why Brie values their friendship so much. Callista is a good soul.

Finally taking note of our surroundings, I start, realizing we're not completely alone. A group of souls stands a few yards away from us. As I peer at them more closely, I realize the souls are waiting in a scraggly line.

I know I can't trust any being in Hell, even the souls, but I'm curious what they would be waiting in line for. If we ask them directly, they could purposely mislead us, or they could run to one of the demons with our location, hoping to gain Lucifer's favor in return. But information is a valuable commodity, and it's been centuries since I was last in Hell, so my current intel is outdated.

Learning more about our environment could be the difference between life and death in this journey.

I sigh. There are no good options for anything to do with Hell, but something has to be done. "Gabe, I want you and Ariella to go stand in line behind those souls. Listen to everything they might say, but don't engage. Report back before the situation becomes precarious."

Gabe nods at me and Ariella falls into step with him as they walk over to the line of souls. The rest of us inconspicuously sneak glances. We watch their backs, hopefully without making the souls near them feel uncomfortable.

It doesn't take long for Gabriel and Ariella to return. "They are talking about getting fresh water," Gabriel tells us.

"Water would be amazing," Haniel says with longing. "I finished the last of my water bladder after Raf healed me."

A few of the others nod. I'm thirsty too. Between the running, the fighting, and the heat, we've all needed to hydrate more than we've been able to, and Haniel isn't the only one to have used up the last of his water. But this is Hell and I know there will be a catch.

I decide to skirt around the waiting souls to see if we can glimpse this water source and gain more information on the requirements to receive it. If it's as simple as bartering, we can do that, but I have a feeling it won't be so straightforward.

As soon as we clear the group of souls, I realize exactly what is going on. The line curves around a glittering playa lake. Unfortunately, the water in playa lakes is typically salty, alkali, or both. Since this is Hell and almost everything is acidic, it makes sense that the lake is filled with saltwater. But sitting patiently between the salty playa lake and a lake of hellfire, is the one and only Ammit.

She catches sight of me just as I catch sight of her. Her upper lip curls up at its ends in a semblance of a smile as she lifts one paw and beckons us toward her.

I cautiously accept the invitation, walking over to her but leaving a wide berth between us. Her V-shaped snout opens wide, showing a mouth full of gleaming teeth. The scales of her head and neck gleam in the dimming daylight as she turns her crocodile head toward me.

"Angelic one," she hisses in greeting. I dip my head to her in a show of deference. Ammit is one of the more respected hellish creatures, even among the angels.

"Would you like to weigh the purity of your souls in exchange for fresh water?" Ammit asks in a steady tone. The briny scent of saltwater follows her every word, and I get another whiff of it as she motions to a large pot of water behind her and the golden scale beside her.

Ammit raises her hindquarters onto her stocky back legs and takes a few steps toward the large pot. "I made it myself," she tells me with pride, and I have to hold back my gag. With her crocodile mouth and throat, Ammit has special glands that can remove salt from water—meaning she drank the saltwater from the playa lake and regurgitated that water, sans salt, into the pot to tempt the souls into playing her game.

Fresh water is scarce in the first circle, so I can understand the souls' desperation for it. Still, drinking regurgitated water is disgusting. And risking almost certain death and eternal torture for it makes this charade even worse.

"Thank you for the offer, Ammit. Unfortunately, we both know you occasionally devour souls for their purity as well, so we will have to pass on your generosity."

"Your loss," she says, raising her hackles in a non-aggressive way—her version of a shrug. Then, she turns her attention to the soul at the front of the line.

Ammit beckons the soul forward. The poor soul is shaking like a leaf. "Step onto the scale so your heart can be weighed against the feather of Ma'at," Ammit instructs in a bored tone. Judging by the line, she must say those words at least a hundred times a day. I would be bored of saying them too.

The soul steps onto the scale, a hopeful expression on her face. The side of the scale on which the soul is standing drops and the soul falls. Whether her fall is from the movement or the judgment is unclear to me, but it doesn't matter either way.

"Your heart has been deemed impure," Ammit declares. Faster than lightning, she launches at the soul, seizing the soul in a vice-like grip. With cold detachment, Ammit bites into the soul's essence, gulping it down. Then, opening her mouth wide, Ammit launches the now flaming soul into the darkening sky above us.

I follow the soul's progression until she settles into place among the other flaming souls that make up Hell's skyscape. Her flame will burn for eons, her soul trapped in a constant state of torture—all because she gambled on a purity she could never have possessed, given that she was sorted into Hell in the first place. I lower my gaze from the sky to find Ammit watching me closely.

"Always a pleasure, Ammit," I tell her respectfully.

"You flatter me, angelic one. I will look forward to our next encounter."

And with that, I turn away from her. Ammit isn't the type of being to strike when someone has their back turned.

Chapter 7

MICHAEL

I lead my team around the hellfire lake, the fire inside bubbling and jumping. I glance back and catch them giving each other uneasy glances as they process the implications of what they've just witnessed. Night is fast falling upon us, and with the growing darkness, the twinkling of the blazing souls forever bound to suffer in Hell's sky becomes more apparent. Like millions of tiny pinpricks, they shine as beautifully as a brilliant star on the clearest of nights. It's such a tragic juxtaposition: that something so magnificently gorgeous can be born of everlasting torment.

But I've known this truth for nearly as long as I've existed, so I don't spare too much thought on it as we continue to round the hellfire lake. The red glow of the fire illuminates our surroundings and I'm grateful for it as I look for a place where we can hunker down for the night. Night is the most dangerous time in this circle, so I don't expect that we'll get any sleep, but we do need to rest before entering the second circle.

As we continue around the hellfire lake, I see the outline of a large tree amidst the darkness. I direct my group toward the majestic baobab tree, its gargantuan size indicating that it has stood guard here for centuries. When we finally reach it, night has fully fallen.

I run my hand over the rough bark, thanking the tree for its gifts before I pull a spile and a small hammer out of my pack. I gently tap the spile into the baobab's large trunk. Excited exclamations come from my team as the water it holds comes trickling out of the spile. I step back, motioning for them to fill their water bladders first.

It takes a few moments of prodding, each of the angels too selfless to want to get their water before the others, but eventually Haniel acknowledges he's in the worst shape of all of us following his injury. He steps up to the dribbling spout and fills his bladder just enough to take a swig before stepping back and motioning for Callista to do the same.

As the newest angel amongst us, she has the worst endurance of the group. Still, she has impressed me at every turn. I think she will end up being a welcome addition to the Angelic Army once this is all over. Brie would probably love to have Callista in our unit.

Before I know it, Kemuel is motioning me forward to take my swig of water. I fill my bladder just enough for one mouthful before stepping back so the rotation can start again. I pull the bladder up to my dry lips and tip the liquid into my mouth. Its taste is glorious—slightly sweet from the stored water mixing with the tree's sap, it dances on my tongue. It feels cool and slick as it slides down my parched throat, providing much-needed relief from the burning feeling that's lingered since my first breath containing the fire's smoke.

I think this may have been the best mouthful of water I've ever had in my many, many years. The relief it provides is so complete that even my taut muscles are relaxing from the sensation. When my turn in the rotation comes up again, I eagerly return to the tap to fill my water bladder completely.

Now that our thirsts are quenched and our water bladders are full, I use the back of the hammer to pry the tap from the tree. Although I'd love to leave it for the souls that live in this circle, the smell of the sweet liquid would attract predators, and I can't endanger my team like that.

"I hope you're all ready to climb. We're going to make camp on the branches above us." My men remain expressionless at my declaration, likely having already assumed as much, but the two women peer up at the wide branches. Their reactions are so different that I can't help but feel amused. Ariella's face lights up with excitement, as though I've just given her the best gift of her existence. Callista, on the other hand, scowls at the branches like she'd prefer to camp anywhere but here.

Tightening the straps of my pack, I leap off the ground and fly to the lowest branch of the grand tree. Even this branch is about seventy feet above the ground, giving me a comforting—albeit false—sense of security. The air is cooler up here, though no less humid.

I settle into the curve where the branch meets the trunk and watch as each member of my team chooses a branch to make their own. For a moment, no one speaks as we all relax into the sturdy wood. It's the first taste of peace we've had since leaving the heavenly plane.

Seconds pass in blissful silence before Haniel's voice cuts through it. "Do you know which angelic gifts you've been blessed with yet, Callista?"

"No, not yet. I started the testing but haven't completed it yet. I'll find out after we return to the heavenly plane," she says with complete confidence, as though there's no possibility we won't all make it back. I wish I shared her optimism, but I've fought in too many battles to be so naive. The truth is, it's very likely that not all of us will return. That's just the way of war, and thinking otherwise only leads to disappointment.

"You must be so excited to find out!" Ariella exclaims. "I remember when I learned I have some of the warrior-descended powers. I was beyond happy. I always knew I had a fighting spirit." She laughs with genuine joy, and it makes my heart hurt that much more. I wish I could share in her joy, but such a feeling isn't possible—not until my soulmate is back by my side.

"That's one of the highlights of my angelic existence as well," Kemuel agrees.

"Do you have any suspicions, at least?" Ariella presses.

"Not a clue," Callista admits. "I wish I did, though. It would make things so much easier. At least my flying lessons went well. Being in the air is so much fun! It's like being on a roller coaster that you can control."

"Yes!" Ariella shouts, but she's too loud. My stomach sinks as I see several predators that had been hunting below us glance up at our tree. It's already too late to remind her to keep her voice down. While we may be seventy feet above the ground, we're far from safe up here.

As though Ariella's shout were a dinner bell, predators of all kinds slink toward our tree. Some fight among themselves, while others flee when they see the competition. But two groups stand out: a clan of lyonas and a colony of snallygasters. Both are ferocious hunters. With the lyonas climbing from below and the snallygasters approaching from above, we're trapped.

I hesitate, unsure of the best course of action. Lyonas are agile hunters capable of scaling great heights, while the snallygasters' tentacles can easily reach between the branches to capture us. Neither option is good. Even the most vicious monsters steer clear of the lyonas, and now they're heading straight for us.

"Michael," Kemuel hisses. "Make a decision. What's the call?"

This is the hardest part of being in charge—knowing that any decision you make could lead to someone's death. Knowing there's no perfect answer but you must act regardless.

"We should take to the sky," Gabriel says confidently, and I don't question it. If he's stepping in to make a tactical decision, it means he's had a divine vision, and we always trust his visions. Always.

"Take to the sky," I repeat, and we all leap from the branches into the glowing night sky. The snallygasters caw with glee. Now that we are no longer amongst the branches, we are easier prey for them.

We dart toward the gate, and the snallygasters alter their route to pursue us. A loud rumble suddenly shakes the branches of the baobab tree we just left, rustling its leaves. Is it an earthquake?

Another loud boom echoes behind us and Ariella lets out a piercing scream. I whip around to see one of the snallygasters coiling its long tentacles around her waist. She struggles desperately, but she can't break free of its hold. I start in her direction, but two of the snallygasters intercept me.

They whip their tentacles toward me, baring razor-sharp teeth in a clear omen of what awaits if we fail to best them. I slash my sword, spinning mid-air, and manage to slice straight through one of the snallygasters' tentacles. The severed piece spirals to the ground as the snallygaster shrieks in fury. Another boom echoes, and the sky lights up as a stream of lava shoots from the distant volcano in a merciless orange fountain.

The volcano isn't far enough away to keep the lava from reaching us, making it imperative that we finish this battle quickly. All of my comrades are engaged in their own skirmishes, their movements growing more frantic as they register the eruption.

Lava bombs explode in all directions, several hurtling toward us. I jab my sword at the two snallygasters I'm fighting, forcing them back step by step. Another strike drives them farther away. And with one final thrust, I push them into the path of a falling lava bomb.

The bomb is massive, colliding with both snallygasters and igniting them instantly. They spiral in opposite directions, their scales catching fire, the slimy coating atop each scale acting as an accelerant. Flapping their webbed wings in desperation, they try to extinguish the flames, but the fire spreads too quickly. Within seconds, they both plummet to the ground in charred heaps.

The remaining snallygasters press their attack, swooping and darting, tentacles sweeping and grabbing. They show no signs of mourning their fallen kin. They don't even falter. The loss of their clansmen seems to have no impact on the survivors' ferocity.

More lava spews from the mouth of the volcano, and growing streams of the deadly substance rush down its sides. We need to reach the Gate—and we need to reach it now.

I rejoin the fray, assisting Gabriel and Raphael, who are fighting back-to-back against three snallygasters. The way they move together is an artform. Watching them is like witnessing a well-rehearsed dance: their movements perfectly synchronized. I know that when I join them, we'll continue to move as one—eons of training and fighting together have ensured it.

Spotting an opening, I plunge my sword into one snallygaster from behind, skewering him. He collapses, his form going limp. I push his lifeless body off my sword, grimacing at the wet, squelching sound.

Raphael swings his sword in a clean arc, severing the neck of another snallygaster. With the remaining snallygaster outnumbered, I know Raphael and Gabriel won't have any issue disposing of it. I scan the battlefield for others in need. Callista and Ariella are fighting side by side. Ariella, having freed herself earlier, is holding her own, and I'm pleased to see their teamwork.

Haniel and Kemuel are also paired up, facing two snallygasters. However, Haniel is clearly struggling. Though Raphael healed his injured arm, his energy is still diminished from the ordeal, his usual precision giving way to sloppy movements.

I fly over to them, thrusting my sword between Haniel and the snallygaster, forcing her back. Predictably, the beast shifts her attention to me. I give as good as I get, meeting her attacks head-on. Every strike she attempts, I parry, frustrating her more with each deflection. Frustration breeds mistakes—a principle I've relied on in countless one-on-one battles. It never fails, and this time is no different.

The snallygaster hits her limit and finally lashes out recklessly, leaving her rib cage exposed. It's the moment I've been waiting for. I seize the opportunity, jabbing my sword into the vulnerable spot between her shoulder and ribs, aiming the blade toward her heart. The sword sinks deep, piercing its target. The snallygaster locks eyes with me for a fleeting moment before her tentacles droop, her wings falter, and her body begins to drop out of the sky.

Unfortunately, her corpse is still impaled on my sword, and the weight drags me down with it. I grip the hilt tightly—I can't afford to lose my weapon in the bright orange lava pooling below. Bringing up both feet, I kick the lifeless body off my blade and flap my wings furiously to regain altitude. The heat of the lava scorches my legs as I ascend, but I manage to block out the pain.

I reach my group just as Ariella delivers a killing blow to the last of the snallygasters. Without exchanging a word, we all turn and fly toward the Gate. I don't know what awaits us in the second circle, but it can't be worse than this.

Chapter 8

BRIE

I watch Lucifer out of the corner of my eye as I flip to the next page of *A Demon's Field Guide to Hellish Monsters and Brutes*. I'm curled up in the reading nook of the private library, my shoes discarded on the polished wood floor. A plethora of soft pillows supports my body, and the warm orange glow streaming through the window behind me reflects off the pages of the massive, thousand-plus-page bestiary I'm pretending to read.

I probably *should* be actually reading it so I can learn about the creatures I might encounter during my escape, but over the past few days, observing Lucifer has become a compulsion. I can't figure him out. I'm fascinated by him, but I'm also horrified—and guilt-ridden—by that fascination.

At the moment, Lucifer is stretched out in a large, brown leather armchair. Even while relaxed and reading Jane Austen's *Pride and Prejudice*, he looks effortlessly dapper in his Tom Ford suit. Every now and then, he runs his fingers through his sun-kissed auburn hair. I follow the movement with my eyes, and the sudden urge to run my own fingers through those strands shocks and alarms me.

Lucifer is my enemy. He tried to choke me. He's holding me captive. Why am I having these feelings? *How* can I be having these feelings? What's wrong with me?

My inner turmoil must have crept onto my face because Lucifer looks up from his book, his piercing green eyes locking onto mine. I quickly shift my gaze back to the large bestiary in my hands, flipping another page.

"Are you alright?" he asks, startling me. His voice is calm, laced with what almost sounds like concern—and maybe even a little sympathy. But that can't be right. I must be misinterpreting his expression.

"Sabriel?" he prods gently.

"Why did you choke me?" I blurt out. The words are out of my mouth before I even realize I asked them. I've been doing such a good job of keeping my cards close to my chest and maintaining my composure, but this question has been gnawing at me, refusing to stay buried.

Lucifer frowns, his gaze turning distant. He looks toward the beautiful red-backlit, two-story aquarium in the corner of the room, and his eyes lose focus as his hand runs through his hair again.

"I didn't mean to," he says at last. His voice is quiet, tinged with something resembling shame. "The darkness held me tightly in its grasp, and I became desperate to reach the light. That was always you. When I was cast out of Heaven, you and the archangels were my only connection to the light. The five of you helped me keep the darkness at bay because you were all so full of goodness. But one by one, they all stopped speaking to me. They refused my calls and then, it was only you. You were the only one who still spoke with me. You became my only tether to the light."

He takes a deep breath, sorrow flickering across his features. "When you left, my connection to the light disappeared with you. It was...difficult. When I learned you were on the other side of one of our Earth Gates, I rushed there. But I was already so consumed by the darkness. All I could focus on was getting to the light. My mind didn't process that you were the source of the light I was chasing. When I arrived, I didn't see *you*—I only saw the light you embody. I needed it. Desperately. So I reached out and grabbed it. I couldn't let go. I had to hold it. Had to keep it. I *needed* it. I didn't realize it was *you* I was grabbing until the portal forced me to release my grip. Only then did I recognize that it was you on the other side of the Gate. I'm sorry. I never wanted to hurt you."

I'm getting more used to his apologies—and his excuses. He's a good actor. His face looks truly remorseful, but this is the same being who refuses to release me as he speaks those words. If he truly felt remorse, if he genuinely regretted his actions, he would let me go. He'd allow me to return to the heavenly plane. But I'm still here. Talk is cheap, and his actions undermine his words.

Still, I know I have to play nice for now. Let him think I've accepted my situation, lull him into a false sense of security. Let him drop his guard. Only then will I have the chance to escape. So I force a neutral expression and respond, "I guess I can understand how that could happen. Desperation can drive anyone to do crazy things."

Little does he know how desperate I am.

Lucifer returns to his book, and I set the bestiary aside to wander the library. It's a breathtaking space, bathed in golden light that washes over row upon row of books. This library would be any Belle fan's dream. Between the reading nook where I had been sitting and the aquariums, large windows showcase the immediate landscape of Hell in all its glory.

Opposite the windows are intricately carved oak double doors and a staircase that curves up to a balcony. The room is adorned with dark wood, brilliant artistry, and thousands upon thousands of books. In addition to the reading nook and Lucifer's leather armchair, there are two additional chairs and a sofa, which Cerberus appears to have claimed for himself. The space is surprisingly homely and inviting, though it puzzles me—Lucifer is the only one who uses this room, so why is there so much seating?

I climb the stairs to the nonfiction section of the library, scanning the shelves for a book containing maps of Hell's circles. If I'm going to escape, I need to learn as much as possible about this place.

I eventually find an atlas, and grab a few other books off the neighboring shelves without paying much attention to their titles, using them to camouflage the atlas so Lucifer doesn't realize that I'm plotting against him. Carrying the stack of books to the lower level, I place them on top of the bestiary.

"Do you mind if I bring these to my room so I can read at night as well?" I ask.

Lucifer gives me a fond look. "Of course. I remember how much you love reading."

I smile back at him. I guess that's one thing angel me and human me have in common.

"I'll take them to my room now if you don't mind. I've been feeling more exhausted than usual since I arrived and would like to nap before dinner."

"Of course," he says again, though this time his eyes narrow the slightest bit. Something in my statement seems to have sparked his suspicion. Hoping to avoid further scrutiny, I pick up the heavy stack of books and leave the library, making my way back to the suite where I've been staying.

I jerk awake, heart pounding forcefully in my chest. A light knock sounds at the main doors of the suite. Groaning softly, I flop back onto my pillow and throw an arm over my eyes, giving my poor, racing heart a chance to settle.

One of the doors creaks open, and I hear a familiar voice grumble about how heavy it is. "Hi, Dee!" I call from my spot in the bed. I wasn't lying when I told Lucifer I'd been feeling exhausted. A deep weariness has weighed down both my body and soul ever since I arrived in Hell.

"Hi, dear," Dee greets in response, stepping into the room with the air of a mother inspecting her child. "You don't look so good. How are you feeling after your nap?"

"Exhausted," I admit. "The nap doesn't seem to have helped."

"Well, maybe some food will do you good. Lucifer asked me to fetch you for dinner."

I groan again—not because I don't want to eat, but because I don't want to leave the bed. Nevertheless, I drag myself up and out from underneath the cozy comforter. Dee has already marched into the closet and is selecting something for me to wear.

She returns holding an elegant silk column dress with an off-the-shoulder cut in a stunning dark green. I slip it on, marveling at how perfectly it clings to my curves. The rich color makes the green flecks in my hazel eyes stand out.

Dee smiles in approval and ushers me over to the dressing table to do my hair and makeup. Why I need makeup for a dinner attended by only Lucifer, myself, and Cerberus is beyond me, but I don't argue—it's not worth the effort.

I sit on the cushioned stool, trying not to fidget as Dee sections off strands of hair to frame my face. I'm still not used to seeing the darker hue of my hair. Lucifer once commented that it looked slightly more golden after my time on Earth, but even so, I now resemble Sabriel far more than I do Brienna.

Dee sweeps the rest of my hair back, maneuvering it into a complicated braided updo. I seize the opportunity to start gathering information. "How long have you worked for Lucifer?" I ask casually.

"Oh, not long. He hired me shortly before you arrived."

"Really? You seem so comfortable here, and you're so skilled at everything. I would have thought you'd been working here for decades."

"Aren't you sweet," she coos. "No, I think Lucifer wanted to bring in a female you'd feel comfortable with to help ease your transition. He didn't say as much, but that's what I gathered from my conversations with the castle manager."

"Did you do similar work before this?" I probe.

"Somewhat. I've always had a nurturing nature, and I enjoy taking care of others however I can."

I notice that she doesn't actually reveal what she did before this, but I decide not to push. My main goal is to keep her talking and glean as much information as possible. "How did you learn about the position?"

"Well, there was a general call for interviews across all the inner circles. The Demon Guard put up notices everywhere. So I attended an interview, and they decided I was a good fit for the job. It was such a rare opportunity—I still can't believe they chose me out of everyone who applied!"

"I'm thankful they did," I say, offering a smile. "You mentioned you're from one of the inner circles?"

"Oh, yes. I'm from the eighth circle. I've lived there since I descended. Coming here was my first time passing through the ninth circle and seeing the castle. As you probably know, we're only allowed to move freely within our own circle once we arrive to it. The barriers only let us pass through if we are granted special permission, and that's exceptionally rare."

I file that tidbit of information away to research later. I need to find out if I'll be able to pass through the barriers or if they'll block me from even reaching the ninth circle. If it's the latter, it could be the largest obstacle in my escape plans.

"Do you miss your circle?" I question.

"Yes and no. It's what I'm used to, so of course, a part of me misses it. But life here in the castle is much easier—and much more glamorous," she adds with a wink, brushing translucent green eyeshadow along my lower lash line. She directs me to close my eyes, then applies more to my lids with a precise hand.

Dee makes a noise of approval, and I reopen my eyes to see her smiling face in the mirror's reflection. "Done," she announces with satisfaction. Her work is stunning, and as I gaze at myself, I have to admit—I feel beautiful.

Dee hurries back into the closet, returning with a pair of strappy gold heels. I slip them on and stand. My gait is unsteady at first but as I adjust to the height of the heels, the wobble fades, and I'm able to walk confidently.

I descend the stairs slowly, reflecting on our conversation. I wish I'd managed to gather more information from Dee, but it's a start. I know more now than I did before the conversation began, and that's progress.

Just before entering the private dining room, I turn back to Dee. "Thanks for talking with me. I'm really grateful to have a friend here."

Her responding smile is blinding. For a fleeting moment, I notice a reddish hue creeping into her black eyes, but it disappears just as quickly while she shoos me into the dining room with a gentle gesture.

Chapter 9

MICHAEL

A deeply penetrating cold envelops me as I crash land on the other side of the Gate—the change in temperature is jarring. There's no sign to greet me this time. No "Welcome to Lust." No tips on how to survive the second circle of Hell. Only a cold so savage that it chills me to the bone almost instantly.

My teeth chatter as I fumble to grab my cold-weather gear from my pack, pulling it on as quickly as my shivering limbs will allow. Relief washes over me once I'm fully covered, my breath forming a cloud of condensation that lingers in front of my face before dissipating. I rub my gloved hands together, waiting for the others to finish donning their own gear.

I never knew cold like this existed until my first trip to Hell many years ago. It bites through my clothing, even the thick outerwear, sending sharp pinpricks of pain through my fingers and toes.

We trudge across the treeless plain surrounding us, heading toward the river in the distance and the snow-capped mountains beyond. The movement does little to temper the cold, which slices across my face like a blade, snapping against my balaclava-covered cheeks as the wind gusts viciously.

We skirt short, moss-covered boulders and small, low-lying shrubs, carefully watching where we place each step on the soggy ground. I want to camp soon; we haven't slept since arriving in Hell, and the exhaustion is making us sloppier than we should be. But camping here isn't an option. With only ankle-high rocks and sparse shrubs for cover, we're too exposed—easy prey for whatever lurks nearby.

Fortunately, the river crossing isn't far from the Gate. Once we pass it, it will be a straight shot to the next Gate. That doesn't mean our trek will be easy, though—just direct.

When we reach the bank of the sparkling river, my team members let out a few exuberant exclamations. Drinkable water was so scarce in Sloth it was practically nonexistent. But here, in the alpine tundra of Lust, clean freshwater is abundant, and the river before us glitters with it.

We each take our time refilling our water bladders for the journey ahead. Even so, we maintain the vigilance necessary in this environment, though the absence of immediate danger is a small luxury we savor. Moments of peace like this will be rare in the days to come.

"We're crossing the river, correct?" Gabriel verifies.

"Yes. We'll fly over and land on the other side, then continue on foot until we find a place to rest," I confirm. Walking uses far less energy than flying, especially in Hell, where the air is heavier and denser.

Gabriel nods and pushes off the ground. The silver and sapphire feathers of his outstretched wings gleam beneath the harsh light of the four suns circling in the clear sky above us. You'd think with four suns, this circle wouldn't be so cold, but they offer no warmth—only a harsh, unyielding brightness that never dims.

As in Sloth, this circle punishes souls by countering their primary vice in every way. Lust, associated with dark, warm intimacy, is punished here by unrelenting brightness and bone-chilling cold. Everything the souls avoided during their mortal lives, they now endure for eternity.

As Gabriel glides above the river, I realize it's wider than it appeared at first glance. An illusion or just a trick of the light? My brother is just about to reach the halfway point when a glimmer below catches my eye. I shift my gaze toward the distraction, and dawning horror seizes my body.

A maelstrom pushes up from the water. Whirlpools typically pull downward, but this one rises as though controlled by a supernatural force. That tells me everything I need to know about it.

"Gabe!" I shout.

He glances down at me, and I see the tension enveloping his body when he notices the swirling water reaching for him like a grasping hand. He pumps his wings harder, but it's not enough—he won't be able to escape in time.

Raphael is already flying toward Gabriel at top speed, but he's too slow as well. The powerful vortex swallows my brother, dragging him into its unrelenting grip and pulling him down into the freezing depths of the river. Without hesitation, Raphael dives after him, plunging into the frigid water like an arrow seeking its mark.

Seconds pass, then minutes. We all stare at the water in expectation, but with each passing moment, my hope dwindles, and my worry grows. Just as I'm about to dive in myself, Raphael resurfaces with a gasping Gabriel in one arm and a writhing nguruvilu in the other.

The nguruvilu thrashes violently, its long body twisting in an attempt to escape Raphael's grasp. Its fox-like face contorts with rage as it yowls loudly, baring sharp teeth. Raphael tightens his grip around the creature's neck, tilting his head away from its snapping jaws. The nguruvilu claws at Raphael, but he's holding it in such a way that it can't land a blow.

Raphael gently lays Gabriel on the opposite shore before turning his full attention to the nguruvilu. He traps its spiked tail between his legs as the creature flails its long body even more violently, its desperation plain to see. Raphael draws his sword and points the tip between the nguruvilu's eyes, instantly stilling the beast.

When Raphael speaks, his voice booms with a fury I've never seen from him. "I will hunt down your entire skulk if you so much as think about harming one of my companions! Not even your kits will be spared my wrath. Make one more move, and you'll see how seriously I take my vows."

The nguruvilu goes limp in Raphael's grasp, signaling its compliance. Raphael releases the river guardian, dropping it to the moist ground where its fur quickly becomes caked with dirt. Dismissing the subdued creature, Raphael rushes to Gabriel's side.

Gabriel is shivering uncontrollably, his entire body trembling with the force of it. Raphael, though trying to mask his discomfort, is clearly struggling as well. Both of them are soaked, and dangerously cold. The nguruvilu, looking slightly abashed, inches toward Gabriel in a submissive posture. The rest of us rush across the river and land on the opposite shore without incident. We gather around Gabriel as the nguruvilu wraps its body around him, attempting to share its warmth.

Gabriel's teeth chatter so loudly that I fear they might shatter, and Raphael is visibly fighting the same cold, though he hides it better. It's obvious they'll both become hypothermic if we don't get them out of their wet clothes and warmed up. Despite my earlier hesitation to camp in an area this exposed, I recognize that this is no longer a choice.

"Set up camp," I order. "Gabriel and Raphael need to warm up. The rest of us will guard the tent until they've stabilized."

Haniel and Kemuel move quickly to erect a tent, while Ariella starts a fire. Callista sets up the small camping stove and begins heating water atop it. Once the tent is securely in place, Kemuel and I carry Gabriel and Raphael inside. The nguruvilu unwinds itself from Gabriel's body, lingering nearby as if reluctant to leave.

I dismiss Kemuel to stand guard outside and start removing the wet garments from my brother and his soulmate, determined to warm them up before it's too late.

It's a little uncomfortable stripping the clothes from my brother's soulmate, especially considering he's still awake and alert. We've been dear friends for eons but that doesn't mean I want to see the guy naked. Still, it has to be done. I cover each of them with an emergency blanket and call Kemuel back in to help me move them onto the dry blanket we've laid out inside the tent.

Once they're both settled, I pull dry hats onto their heads, place warm compresses on their necks and chests, and cover them with an additional blanket. Raphael manages to stutter out a thank you through his blue lips and shifts closer to Gabriel, trying to share more body warmth. That's when I realize how stupid I've been.

Shaking my head at myself, I start stripping off my own clothes, leaving only my boxers.

"W-w-what...a-are...y-you d-doing?" Raphael stutters out.

"I'm lending you both my body heat. Stop talking. Save your energy for warming up."

I slip under the blankets on Gabriel's other side. His breathing is even, which brings me some solace. I'm less worried about Raphael, whose self-healing abilities as the angel of healing are far superior. My brother, however, is a different story.

"Can I come in? I have warm water," Callista calls from outside the tent.

"Enter," I reply.

She unzips the tent flap and ducks inside, bringing a rush of colder air with her and I immediately regret allowing her entrance. She hands a camping mug to Raphael, who props himself up just enough to sip the warm water. Then she hands another mug to me.

"In case he wakes up soon. We shouldn't open the tent too often," she says.

I nod, and she slips back outside, zipping the flap shut behind her.

It takes Gabriel four painstakingly long hours to wake up. When he finally does, there are no lasting signs of hypothermia. I'm sure the healing energy Raphael funneled into him during those hours played a significant role, but I still send up a silent prayer of gratitude to the divine spirit for seeing Gabriel through.

Since the tent was already set up and we all desperately needed rest, I instructed the others to sleep in shifts while we were waiting for Gabriel to recover. Now that everyone's had a chance to rest, we've resumed our trek toward the next Gate. We make good time reaching the mountains and begin ascending the lightly worn path that winds into the range.

We're nearing the summit of the first mountain when a fierce wind tears through, whipping up the thick snow cover that blankets the higher elevations. Strong winds are normal in the second circle—expected, even—but this is no ordinary gust. The sheer force of it is unnaturally powerful.

I nearly lose my footing as the wind slams into me. My muscles tense as I push against the blast of glacial air. I try to shout for my team to link up, but my voice is swallowed by the howling wind. Another powerful gust sends snow swirling so thickly that my vision is completely obscured. The world becomes a blinding cloud of white.

I inch backward, trying to feel my way toward Raphael. Unable to see even vague shapes through the whiteout, I cautiously toe down the path a few feet, arms outstretched in the hope that I'll make contact with him. I'm effectively blind, and without any visual references to anchor me, I'm almost certainly disoriented. Still, I press on, seeking.

I trust that Raphael is doing the same to find Gabriel, and that Kemuel and Haniel have managed to link up—they're seasoned warriors with sharp strategic instincts. But Ariella is new to the army. Will she realize the importance of anchoring with the group? And Callista...she's not even a member of the Angelic Army. She has no training and is the most vulnerable among us.

As though Hell itself can hear my thoughts, a muffled scream cuts through the howling wind. The gusts abate, the snow begins to settle, and my vision clears just in time for me to see Callista teetering on a rocky ledge carved into the edge of the mountainside. She flails her arms wildly, trying to regain her balance, but the motion only destabilizes her further. Her foot slips, her body tips back, and before any of us can reach her, she's tumbling down the treacherous cliff face.

Chapter 10

MICHAEL

Time seems to slow as I watch Callista bounce off the rocky cliff face. Her mouth opens in a cry of pain, but the sound is muffled by the distance as she falls farther away from us. Raphael gestures wildly, shouting for her to extend her wings, but she's too lost in her panic to look up at us. And just as her cries are muted by her descent, Raphael's shouts fail to reach her. She's too new to being an angel, too unaccustomed to having wings, to instinctively think of using them.

I don't think—I just act. Diving off the protruding ledge of the precipice, I fold my wings tight against my body to streamline my descent, striving to overtake Callista in her uncontrolled fall. She tumbles violently, bouncing repeatedly against the harsh rock face. Each impact must be excruciating for her, but the repeated collisions slow her fall, giving me an advantage.

The distance from the mountaintop to the ground is vast, granting me precious time to reach her. Small mercies. But the downside is stark: if she hits the ground before I can intercept her, she will certainly meet a permanent death.

As angels, we are more durable than humans, but even our resilience has limits. A fall from this height would destroy her energy completely, erasing her soul from existence in any realm.

I can't let that happen. I've already failed her once—failed to save her life on the earthly plane. The weight of that regret is unending, and I refuse to let it happen again. I won't fail Callista. I won't fail Brie again.

I'm closing the distance when Callista tumbles into the craggy rockface once again. Except this time, she collides with the rough stone headfirst. The impact is sickening, sending pebbles tumbling after her. Her neck bends at an unnatural angle, and her head lolls as she loses consciousness.

Her limp body spirals downward, gaining speed, as I finally reach her. I unfurl my wings, catching the air in a painful jolt, and glide beneath her torpid form. Wrapping my arms around her waist, I pull her flaccid body into my own, holding her tightly against me. With a sharp adjustment, I shift direction, climbing upward and scanning for a level place to land. Flying in Hell saps energy quickly, and despite the adrenaline coursing through me, I can feel my strength waning.

The weight of Callista's limp body in my arms makes the ascent even harder, but I manage to hold her securely. After several agonizing minutes, I spot a flat area amidst the rugged terrain and descend. Raphael is already on his way, descending toward us at full speed. His urgency gives me hope, but I worry his haste may have drained his energy—energy we desperately need to save Callista.

Raphael lands beside us, his expression grim. He kneels immediately, his face a mask of deep concentration. I carefully lay Callista on the loose scree between us, her body limp and unnervingly still. Raphael places his hands on either side of her head, and bright green healing energy surges from him. The light infuses her body, spreading through every cell of her being in mere seconds.

Raphael's body slackens as the fatigue of performing such a rapid healing overcomes him. "I've done all I can," he says, his voice low and tired. "The rest is up to her."

"Do you think she'll make it?" I ask, unable to hide the fear in my voice. Callista still hasn't regained consciousness, and I have no way of knowing how much damage remains.

"I honestly don't know," Raphael admits. "But I can't give her any more of my energy. I was already partially depleted from healing Gabriel."

Many assume Raphael's healing abilities are limitless, like a bottomless well, but they're wrong. Some of us have more power than others, but if any of us deplete too much of our energy, there will be nothing left to sustain our being. It's a fragile balance. We need time for our energy to regenerate after expending any quantity of it. And given how much energy Raphael was feeding to Gabriel during his four hours of unconsciousness, it doesn't surprise me that he hasn't recovered yet.

"We should make camp while we wait for her to wake up. You need rest as well, and we'll have to hike all the way back up the mountain to rejoin the group." We landed not far from the base of the mountain, so there's a significant climb ahead of us to regain our position at the summit. I'm certain the others will make camp until we reunite, so we might as well do the same.

Raphael nods in agreement, and I begin setting up the tent. He moves to help, but I wave him off. I meant it when I said he needed to rest—I'm not taking any chances with him depleting his energy further.

I've nearly finished erecting the tent when a thunderous rumble echoes from higher up the mountain. I look up instinctively but quickly avert my gaze as a shower of pebbles rains down on us. Once the debris settles at our feet, I tilt my head up once again. This time, my body freezes at the sight before me.

Sucking in a sharp breath, I feel the freezing air pierce my lungs like tiny needles. The pain jars my immobilized body back to action—a good thing, considering what I see above us. Barreling down the slope of the mountain at an impossible speed is a massive avalanche of shale and snow, and it's heading straight for us.

The ground quakes from the avalanche's force, unsteadying my balance. Abandoning the tent, I rush to Callista's unconscious form and sling her over my back in a fireman's carry. I shout at Raphael to leave without me, but the stubborn angel ignores my order, staying close.

Pumping my wings is awkward with Callista draped over my shoulders, but I manage to slowly lift off the ground. She isn't heavy, but the added weight doesn't do me any favors as I fight to gain altitude and escape the avalanche's deadly path. Raphael flies beside me, both of us heading toward the side of the next mountain. I can only hope the rockslide that triggered this avalanche hasn't caused similar events on the surrounding peaks.

We need to ascend higher to avoid the plume of snow that will erupt when the speeding mass collides with the flat ground at the base of the mountain. I pump my wings harder, but exhaustion quickly sets in. We haven't had time to rest, and with each beat of my wings, my energy wanes further. I glance at Raphael: his wings are slowing, his altitude dropping—he's nearing his limit.

"Grab onto my legs!" I shout. I don't think he'll make it otherwise.

"It's too much weight for you. You can't carry both of us," he argues.

"I can!" I snap, determination burning through my fatigue. *I will.* I'll use every fiber of my being, every last drop of energy, to ensure Raphael survives this ordeal.

I see doubt flicker across his face, but after a moment's hesitation, he reaches out and grabs onto my legs, swinging himself into position. The added weight pulls me down sharply, but I grit my teeth and fight to regain control. My wings strain as I pump harder, driving us closer to the mountainside.

For a fleeting moment, uncertainty grips me. *Have I taken on too much?*

By sheer resolve and strength of will, I force my wings to keep beating until we are safely away from the danger zone. Soon enough, Raphael is releasing his grip on my legs and dropping down onto the mountainside that is now beneath us. We're a bit further up than we were when we left the previous mountain. It will help us traverse the mountain more quickly and keep us away from the fallout of the avalanche's collision with the ground.

I land deftly and settle Callista on the ground softly. She's still not moving, but she is breathing, so I know she hasn't yet succumbed. It's a good sign.

I look around, hoping to spot the rest of our group. They weren't running ahead of the avalanche, so they must have taken to the sky—or they were caught in the torrent of snow and rock. No. I can't let my thoughts go there. I have to believe they escaped, just as we did. But they're nowhere in sight.

Neither Raphael nor I have the gift of telepathy. Gabriel can communicate with others through visions, but only with angels capable of receiving them, which excludes both Raphael and me. I pull out the scrying crystal Gabriel and Uriel created, silently praying it works. The celestite crystal allows angels without scrying or visionary gifts to communicate across distances, but it requires light energy to function.

In Heaven, where light energy is abundant, it's effortless to use the crystals. Here though, surrounded by dark energy, I'll need to channel my own light energy into the crystal and hope I have enough reserves to activate it.

Tracing the angelic rune for communication on the crystal's smooth surface, I focus my energy. Bright white light flows through my finger, etching the rune into the crystal. As the glowing symbol absorbs into the shard, it lights up from within. A circular projection of white light emerges above the crystal, forming a shimmering screen. The crystal buzzes lightly in my hand before an image of a frazzled Kemuel appears in the glowing projection.

"Michael, thank the divine spirit you're safe. Is Raphael with you?" Kemuel asks, his expression taut with worry.

Raphael steps into view behind me, and I see Kemuel's face relax with visible relief.

"Where did you end up?" I ask.

"We headed toward the next summit over, due west," Kemuel replies.

"Okay, we're on the neighboring mountain, due east. We're only about a third of the way up, so we have some climbing to do, but Raphael needs to rest, and Callista is still unconscious. Make camp if it's safe to do so. Rest and replenish your energy stores. We'll aim to meet on the backside of the mountain range. If you head toward the eastward mountain and we head westward, we should spot each other and reunite without difficulty."

"Understood," Kemuel responds.

"Stay safe."

Kemuel nods just before his image flickers out. I slip the scrying crystal back into the side pocket of my pack for easy access, grateful that Gabriel and Uriel had the foresight to create such a device.

Behind me, Raphael is already setting up the tent, his movements sluggish and deliberate. He's clearly exhausted and needs rest. With one tent lost to the avalanche and Callista still unconscious, I carry her into the tent Raphael has erected. "I want you two to share the tent. I'll stand guard and rest once you're recovered," I instruct.

Raphael accepts my directive without protest. He knows his condition demands immediate rest, more so than mine. I rifle through Callista's pack, pulling out her sleeping bag and tucking her carefully inside. I leave her pack beside her still form, then glance at Raphael. He's already passed out in his sleeping bag, his chest rising and falling in a steady rhythm.

Quietly, I step out of the tent and take up my position as guard. *Divine spirit, I know I've asked much of you already on this journey, but I have one more plea. Please...don't let them die.*

Chapter 11

MICHAEL

One good thing about being in the army is that you learn to fall asleep quickly in any environment. Even in times of peace, we still ran drills and simulations that involved sleeping in less than pleasant conditions. It works to my advantage in times like these. Despite the blazing, unrelenting light of the four suns circling the second circle, I was able to fall asleep within minutes once Raphael was up and took over guard duty.

I'm not sure how long I slept, but I wake to rustling within the tent. Instantly on alert, I jerk upright and scan the interior of the tent. I breathe more easily when I see that the rustling was caused by Callista. She has regained consciousness and is trying, and failing, to quietly escape the confines of the sleeping bag I had settled her into.

"I'm glad to see you awake." Callista startles at the sound of my voice, but I continue, pretending not to notice when a blush spreads below her cheekbones. "How are you feeling?" Even though she has risen, there's still a possibility that she sustained brain damage from the blow.

"I'm alright. My nerves are still a little jumpy from the adrenaline, but I feel okay physically."

"Do you have any lingering pain?"

She pauses, taking stock of her body. "No, I don't think so." Raphael must have done a better job of healing her than he thought.

I shuffle out of my own sleeping bag, rolling it up and shoving it into my pack. I unzip the tent and slip out into the bright, icy day. Callista also manages to disentangle herself from her sleeping bag and exits the tent behind me.

"Have your energy stores fully recovered?" I ask Raphael, getting straight to business. Between Raphael's need for recovery and Callista's unconsciousness, we've already rested longer than the other portion of our group. While I don't mind giving the injured time to recover, the longer it takes us to reunite, the greater the danger we'll face. A larger group is always easier to defend than a smaller one.

"I'm at about eighty percent. The rest will return in time," Raphael replies.

I nod in acknowledgment. Raphael nearly depleted his energy, and he needs more time to fully recover—time we don't have. Even so, he walks over to Callista to scan her for any remaining damage.

"Take it easy until you're back to one hundred percent," I say.

Raphael gives me a look, but we both know it needed to be said. He's too empathetic for his own good, often neglecting his own well-being for the sake of others. As his friend and commander, it's my responsibility to ensure he takes care of himself too.

After finishing his scan, Raphael confirms that Callista is clear of any lingering injuries. With that, we pack up the tent and begin our ascent toward the summit.

The climb is arduous. Invisible patches of ice threaten to turn the mountain path into a treacherous slip and slide. Small shrubs catch at our feet, trying to trip us. Glowing eyes and camouflaged fur stalk us from the shadows, though our unseen predators don't attack—yet. Despite these challenges, we reach the summit without disaster or delay.

And walk straight into an ambush.

Just as we crest the summit, an electric whirring sound cuts through the stillness, disrupting the rhythm of our heavy breathing. It's followed by a cacophony of clicks, clunks, and mechanical whirs. The sounds seem to come from all directions, making it impossible to pinpoint their source.

Then, the snowy peak to our right shifts, revealing a hidden passage. The same happens to our left. And behind us. The animals that had been stalking us scatter with cries of fear, their furry and scaled forms fleeing down the mountain as fast as their legs will carry them.

A flicker of unease passes through me, but I shove it aside. Whatever this is, we'll handle it. I motion to Raphael and Callista to start descending the mountain on the other side. My priority is to move us out of range of whatever creatures emerge from these hidden passages.

But before we can take more than a few steps, massive fingers—each as thick as my arm—curl around the edge of the opening to our right. Long fingernails, sharpened into dangerous points carve through the icy layer coating the snow around the passage entrance. The fingers curl, the fingernails dig in deeper, and the top of a head comes into view, crossing the barrier separating the passage from the mountain's surface.

Spiky hair emerges inch by inch. The monster moves with a deliberate slowness that unnerves me even more: to be so unhurried suggests he thinks we don't stand a chance against him.

"Move!" I urge Raphael and Callista, quickening our descent. We slip and slide on the icy slope as we rush, but I temper our speed—we can't afford carelessness. The last thing we need is another accident like Callista's fall.

Glancing over my shoulder, I see the giant pulling his torso free of the passage. At the same time, three of his comrades emerge from the other openings. One of them catches my gaze and grins, revealing teeth the size of my neck, each sharpened into fangs. The grin is deeply menacing.

"Can you both fly to the summit of that mountain?" I ask, pointing to the peak ahead. "Is it too far? Do you have enough energy?"

"I have the energy, but I'll be low again. If anyone needs healing immediately afterward, it'll be questionable whether I could provide it." That answer is pure Raphael—always thinking of others before himself.

"I think I can make it, but I'll probably be slower than you both," Callista replies tentatively. She's so new to being an angel that she's still uncertain about her capabilities. That's normal, but far from ideal in a situation like this. Still, I need to trust her instincts. If she thinks she can make it, I have to believe she can.

"Alright. Let's go." I launch into the air, speeding toward the summit. Behind me, I feel the air ripple as Raphael and Callista take flight as well.

We've only traveled a short distance when I sense an additional disturbance in the air. Glancing back toward the summit we just left, my stomach drops at the sight of a massive boulder hurtling straight toward me. I huff in irritation.

"Boulder incoming!" I yell.

Raphael and Callista both whip around at my words. Raphael remains calm, completely unbothered by the projectile, but Callista's face turns a sickly white as she pumps her wings harder.

The boulder narrowly misses her, and she lets out a cry of fear. A second boulder soars through the air, and I again give warning. The second boulder overshoots us, slamming into the mountain we're heading toward and dislodging several snowdrifts, which tumble down the slope and crash to the ground below. Swinging my head around again, I watch as Raphael gracefully dodges yet another boulder.

Behind us, the giants on the summit are whooping and hollering as they heave boulders out of the passages, launching them in our direction. It's a game to them. They must have a stockpile of stones ready for such occasions.

This time, it's my turn to dodge. A boulder whizzes past me, missing by mere inches, but I manage to avoid the blasted thing. A few minutes later, I land on the summit, followed closely by Raphael.

We turn back just in time to see another boulder aimed directly at Callista.

She wasn't wrong about being slower than us. In my haste to avoid the boulders, I hadn't realized how far behind she was. Now I see she's only just past the midpoint between the summits. As the only angel still in flight, she's a prime target for the carnivorous Laestrygonians.

"Incoming!" I shout again, pointing toward the projectile. Callista follows my gesture with her eyes, spotting the boulder just in time to dodge it. She dips and swerves instinctively, her movements defensive despite her lack of formal training.

Regret briefly grips me. I wish I'd refused her demand to come on this rescue mission. She's already been seriously hurt, and I'd never forgive myself if something worse happened to her. Realistically, I know the danger is far from over. We're only in the second circle, and she's already narrowly avoided death. But deep down, I also know that if I'd said no, she likely would have followed us on her own. At least this way, I can try to protect her.

"Push higher!" I yell when another boulder comes dangerously close to clipping her feet.

She obeys, climbing higher and avoiding the blow. Finally, she lands beside us, bending over to catch her breath.

But I can't give her time to recover. We're still in danger.

Now that we've all landed on the other mountain, the giants are throwing their boulders with even more force, aiming to hit us despite the increased distance. "Let's go," I say, starting down the mountainside, knowing the others will follow.

It seems the summit is just beyond the range of the Laestrygonians' throwing capabilities, but that doesn't deter them. I can still feel the impacts as their boulders slam into the side of the mountain. One particularly strong hit shakes the ground so forcefully that I nearly lose my balance, but I manage to stay on my feet.

Unfortunately, the snow and ice behind us don't hold against the impacts. A familiar groaning sound punctuates the air. I don't need to turn around to know what's happening—we're about to be caught in another avalanche.

Sure enough, a whooshing sound follows, accompanied by the trembling of the ground beneath my feet. "Run!" I yell. I start sprinting downhill, but the speed of my descent quickly spirals out of control. My feet stumble, and I trip over the uneven terrain, barely able to steer myself.

Callista must have lost control of her feet as well because she collides into me from behind, knocking me off my feet. I tumble into a snowbank, which absorbs most of the impact. Shards of ice within the snowbank tear at my clothing but, thankfully, the thick material keeps me from being injured.

I try to push myself up, sliding my knees under me, but a heavy mound of snow crashes down on top of me, pinning me back into the bank. My face is buried in the freezing powder, and I manage to lift it just enough to suck in a gasp of air before another surge of snow engulfs me entirely.

The avalanche sweeps me into its relentless grasp. Snow surrounds me on all sides, crushing my body and suffocating me. The force of it presses the air from my lungs, clutching me in its icy embrace as it barrels downhill at an impossible speed.

I can't breathe. I can't move. My vision begins to blur, dark spots creeping in from the edges. My body temperature plummets, and the cold seeps into every fiber of my being.

Is this the end? The thought barely registers as darkness overtakes me. Am I still moving?

Then, suddenly, a hand punches through the snow, gripping my arm with an unyielding strength. I feel myself being pulled upward, through the suffocating layers of snow, and into the open air. I gasp desperately, my lungs flooding with the sweet relief of oxygen.

Dots of light punctuate the haze in my vision, and gradually, the world comes back into focus. Pure joy wells up within me as Raphael's concerned face comes into view. With trembling limbs, I throw my arms around his neck, hugging him tightly.

"Thank you, brother." My voice is raw as I push myself to my feet, my limbs shaking from the effort. "Callista?"

"I'm right here. I'm fine." Callista's voice is filled with relief. "I bounced off you, and it pushed me onto the surface of the snow. I just skidded along the top of it. I'm so sorry I pushed you down into it." She wrings her hands, her worry evident.

"It was an accident," I reassure her. "You didn't do it on purpose. We're fine."

Callista hesitates but eventually nods, though the worry lingers on her face.

The only silver lining of that avalanche is that it brought us much closer to the bottom of the mountain. Now, we have only a short distance left to cover before reuniting with the rest of our group.

Sure enough, I spot Kemuel waving at us in the distance. We head toward him, calm washing over me as we approach. The moment we're together again, the tension I hadn't fully realized I'd been carrying melts away. Our group being whole again feels like a balm to my frayed nerves.

As we venture through the hollow at the base of the mountains, we encounter a rare stroke of luck. The avalanche didn't extend far enough to disturb the sparkling freshwater lake at the center of the hollow. Approaching the lake to refill our water bladders, I can't help but feel a deep sense of gratitude that it remains untouched.

We reach the mountains on the other side of the hollow and our luck continues. A mountain pass winds between the mountains on this side of the lake, something the mountains on the other side of the lake lacked. We won't need to climb up and down these mountains to reach the gate: we simply need to follow the pass through. Small mercies. I smile, knowing the divine spirit is watching over us—even in Hell.

Chapter 12

BRIE

The more time I spend with Lucifer, the more I enjoy his company. And I don't want to enjoy his company. I want to hate his company. But I don't. And I don't understand how that's possible.

This is the man who tricked me into sacrificing myself. The man who is holding me captive in Hell. The man who is refusing to let me leave, refusing to let me reunite with my soulmate. He's selfish. He's evil. But is he?

I groan into the empty room, staring at the shiny black ceiling above me. Shadows blanket the space, but the dim city lights from the ninth circle filter through the stained-glass window, reflecting faintly off the glossy surface. It never ceases to amaze me how relentless light can be—how, even in the dead of night, it still finds a way to shine.

The air feels heavier with each passing day, my muscles aching more and more. Lucifer says the pain will lessen with time. He explained that it's caused by the toxins in the air and that, eventually, I'll acclimate. He said the darkness of the beings in Hell helps them metabolize the toxins, and while I lack that protection now, it can build within me. But I'm not sure it's a protection I want. To be light in a world consumed by darkness is a painful existence. If the pain disappears, will I still carry the light?

It's a question that circles endlessly in my mind as I lie here, unable to sleep. I feel myself slipping further each day. I don't know if it's the influence of the darkness surrounding me, of Lucifer, or of my own choices, but I'm worried.

What began as half-truths and omissions to conceal my lack of memories has morphed into outright lies. I'm spiraling, my misdeeds gaining in both scale and momentum. And I'm terrified that if this continues, Heaven won't let me through its gates—even if I do manage to escape Hell. I'm afraid I'll lose myself. That I'll become a being who *belongs* in Hell.

Soft taps at the suite door pull me from my thoughts. The door cracks open, a sliver of light spilling into the room.

Lucifer's face appears through the gap. "Sabriel?"

Everything in my body tenses, intrigue and loathing warring within my mind.

"Yes?"

"Are you alright? I thought I heard a noise and wanted to make sure you weren't having a nightmare."

And this is why my feelings are so conflicted. How can the being holding me captive also seem so thoughtful? The concern in his whispered voice sounds genuine, even heartfelt. Yet he still won't let me go. He still won't do what's best for me—only what's best for himself.

"I'm in pain. Everything aches." I hesitate, then push forward. "I'm hurting, Lucifer. Maybe...maybe it's time for me to leave Hell? I don't think I can endure this much pain for much longer."

Are my words manipulative? Yes. Do I feel ashamed about that? No. *Should* my lack of shame concern me? Absolutely. But even though I've been agreeable toward Lucifer lately, it doesn't mean I want to stay. I still firmly believe I don't belong here. And everything would be much easier for me if he would just release me rather than forcing me to find a way to escape on my own.

"I'm sorry, Sabriel," he says, his voice soft with regret. "I promise it will get better. I'll call Dee to bring you some painkillers."

It's not the response I wanted. Not the response I'd hoped for. But it is the response I'd expected.

I turn away from Lucifer, rolling onto my side so my back faces him. Tears slip silently down my cheeks, soaking into the silk pillowcase beneath me. I sniffle. I don't mean to, but I'm unable to hold it back.

Lucifer sighs, and footsteps cross the floor toward me. The mattress dips under his weight as he sits at the edge of the bed. A smooth hand rubs gently up and down my arm.

"Please don't cry, darling," he whispers. "I promise the pain will get better. I promise."

His voice is filled with such anguish, so thick it feels like it could drown me. But still, the agony in his tone isn't enough for him to release me. So does it really matter?

Another knock sounds at the door. Lucifer must have left it ajar, as there's no grumbling about its heaviness this time. When he rises from the bed, his weight leaving the mattress, I shiver at the unwelcome sense of loneliness that washes over me. I shouldn't feel this way. I don't understand what's wrong with me.

More tears slip down my cheeks, the self-loathing I feel only amplifying my distress. These feelings feel like a betrayal of Michael and our bond, and I hate myself for having them. I know I can't control my emotions, but it doesn't feel right. I shouldn't be feeling this way, and the fact that I do fills me with disgust. I hate myself for it. It makes me question whether I even deserve Michael. Maybe I do belong in Hell.

But no—I can't let myself think like that. I don't belong here. I know I don't.

I hear Lucifer whispering his thanks to Dee, followed by the soft sounds of two pairs of feet moving in opposite directions. The door clicks shut, and moments later, Lucifer rounds the far side of the bed so he can see my face. He places a glass of water and a pill packet on the bedside table before sitting down beside me again.

"Sit up, darling," he says softly, brushing a strand of hair away from my face. The unwanted touch stirs a confusing mix of emotions in me—a cringe of discomfort mingled with an undeniable pang of longing.

I sit up as instructed, and Lucifer hands me the pills and water in turn. I hope the medication will make me drowsy, dragging me into a peaceful oblivion where I won't have to feel or process the conflicting emotions that churn within me at every touch, every word. Right now, all I want is nothingness.

I lie back down, waiting for the pills to take effect. I turn onto my other side, once again giving Lucifer my back. But he doesn't leave. Instead, I feel him curl up behind me, his warmth chasing away the chill that has settled in my bones since arriving in Hell. And like everything else about him, I don't *want* to like it. But I do.

I wake alone, and disappointment pricks at my heart. I immediately chide myself for the feeling. I shouldn't be disappointed that Lucifer isn't here. I should feel relief, joy, a sense of opportunity—not this unwelcome pang of loss. I really need to get my head on straight if I intend to make it out of here.

The dim light filtering through the stained-glass window tells me a new day has dawned. I expect Dee will arrive soon to help me start my day. I instantly feel guilty when I think of how her sleep must have been disturbed last night because of me. I'll need to apologize to her.

As if on cue, a sharp knock cuts through the silence of my room, followed by Dee's mutterings about the heavy door as she enters the room. Cerberus slips in behind her, his tail wagging and tongues lolling. He's quickly become a light amidst the darkness for me. His presence fills me with so much joy that I can't help but love him, and the thought of leaving him deepens the ache in my soul.

I wonder if this is how Lucifer feels about me. He's said before that Sabriel was his light. Is it possible that I give him the same sense of comfort and solace that Cerberus gives me? If so, maybe I understand his desperation a little more. I can't imagine enduring this place without the little moments of happiness Cerberus brings me.

Dragging myself out of bed, I kneel to pet and kiss Cerberus, his cheerful energy lifting my spirits. But Dee is quick to usher me into the bathroom, her tone brisk. Apparently, we're running late today. For what, I have no idea—my movements are confined to the castle, after all.

I leave the bathroom after a quick shower to find Dee bustling about my room. She doesn't seem to realize that I'm in the room yet, as she mutters under her breath. I can't make out what she's saying but her harsh, rapid tone, coupled with her jerky movements tell me that she's angry about something. I step further into the bedroom. Dee stiffens and swings around, plastering a smile on.

"I'm sorry dear. I didn't realize you had finished your shower. How are you feeling today? It seemed like you had a rough night."

"A little rough," I tell her honestly. "Thank you for bringing up the pain medication. I'm sorry Lucifer woke you to do it. Hell doesn't seem to be agreeing with me all that well."

"It was no bother. That's what I'm here for," Dee replies warmly.

I smile back at her. I was wary of Dee at first, but I think that's just because she lives in Hell. Everyone here carries some degree of darkness, so it makes sense that anyone I encounter here would put me on edge. But the more time I spend with Dee, the more I find myself liking her. I even think there's a chance she might be able to help me when I make my escape.

"Um, what are we running late for, by the way?" I ask, genuinely curious. I've never seen Dee so frantic before.

"I can't believe I forgot to tell you!" she exclaims. "Lucifer felt terrible about how upset you were last night, so he planned an outing for the two of you today. Isn't that so sweet of him?" She gushes like this is the kindest gesture she's ever witnessed.

I quirk an eyebrow in response. "Where is he taking me?"

"He's going to take you into the ninth circle! I think he hopes that seeing more of your favorite places in Hell will make you happier here. And I'll be honest, the ninth circle is the best. Even though I'm from the eighth circle, I can admit that each circle gets better as you go deeper. There isn't an area of Hell better than the ninth circle—well, except the castle of course, but it seems like you're getting a little stir-crazy being trapped here all the time. I think an outing will do you good."

I think so too, though not for the reasons she imagines. A tour of the ninth circle is an invaluable opportunity to gather more intel. Escaping won't just be about leaving the castle—once I'm out, I'll need to navigate my way through Hell itself. Knowing more about each circle will make that infinitely easier.

I don't even try to hide the smile that spreads across my face. Dee will assume I'm excited about the change of scenery, but in truth, Lucifer's decision has just brought me one step closer to reuniting with Michael. And I couldn't be happier. When opportunity comes knocking, I'll slam the door wide open and fly right through it.

Ninth circle, here I come.

Chapter 13

BRIE

I push eagerly through the entrance hall doors, unable to contain my excitement at finally leaving the castle. Lucifer follows closely behind, with Dee and a demon named Boagdan trailing after him. I stop abruptly, overwhelmed by the scent of the hellfire moat—warm toasted marshmallows mingling with cedar embers, like a campfire. Lucifer grips my shoulders to avoid colliding with me, but I barely notice.

Pain prickles behind my eyes, and I quickly blink back the tears threatening to form. I can't allow myself to cry over something so seemingly trivial. If Lucifer decides I'm too fragile to leave the castle, it could derail the entire outing. But dagnabbit, that smell! It reminds me of evening bonfires on the beach with Callie, before all this angelic drama began.

I miss those days. I don't regret getting to know Michael in his corporeal form, and I don't regret accepting the challenge to seal Earth's Hell Gates. But I do miss how things were before—when Callie was alive, and when I was blissfully ignorant of the struggle that lay ahead. My life wasn't exactly peaceful, but it was simpler. I miss that simplicity.

Shaking myself free from the melancholic train of thought, I ignore the soft caress of Lucifer's hands along my shoulders and his softly uttered, "Sabriel?" Instead, I lift my chin and stride forward, heading toward the wide bridge that crosses the hellfire moat into the ninth circle. The heat from the hellfire radiates a comforting warmth as I purposefully step onto the bridge. Lucifer walks beside me now, waving casually to the bridge's guards as we approach.

When Dee first mentioned this outing, I expected something very different. I imagined a battalion of demon guards flanking us, their eyes scrutinizing my every move, ready to pounce if I made a break for it. What I *didn't* expect was the sphinxes atop their black-marble watchtowers simply nodding at Lucifer and resuming their silent vigil. Nor did I expect that only Dee and Boagdan would accompany us, with no additional guards in tow.

I know what they say about assumptions, and it seems I'm guilty of falling into that trap repeatedly when it comes to Lucifer. He surprises me at every turn, and, more often than not, those surprises are unexpectedly...considerate.

Perhaps I need to reassess my biases toward him. The lack of guards suggests he trusts me, even when I don't trust him. Yet, I can't shake the nagging suspicion that his caring demeanor might be part of some grand illusion. Lucifer is a master of deception. While he seems more stable now than when I first arrived, I can't rule out the possibility that much of what he shows me is a carefully constructed act to gain my empathy—and compliance. How quickly would that mask fall if I tried to escape?

As we cross to the other side of the bridge, my gaze drifts upward to the sphinxes stationed at this end. Majestic and terrifying, the creatures constantly scan the area below their towers. Their sleek leonine tails swish lazily back and forth, but their arched backs and raised fur signal predatory anticipation.

Their expansive wings are spread behind them, ready to launch them into the air at a moment's notice. Their human-like heads swivel sharply, watching for the slightest disturbance. The intelligence gleaming in their eyes only amplifies their menace. These are not creatures to be trifled with.

A shiver runs down my spine as I remind myself that while this outing may offer me opportunities, it also carries immense risks.

Thankfully, these guards simply dip their heads toward Lucifer in recognition as well. I step over the threshold of the bridge. Gleaming gold lettering on a sign of shiny black marble reads, "You are now entering Treachery."

The campfire smell of the hellfire moat diminishes as we walk further into the ninth circle. I have a moment of relief as the homesick feeling deep in my gut abates with it, but just as quickly, the feeling returns as I get my first glimpse of the bustling outdoor market we're approaching.

My throat tightens, and my breaths grow heavier. This is yet another reminder of the life I lost. One of my favorite parts of living in Southern California was the abundance of farmers' markets. Every Saturday, before our bonfire on the beach, Callie and I would start the day at the market.

There was a large, multi-street market just a few blocks from my apartment. Callie and I would walk over around ten in the morning to buy groceries for the week. Then we'd drive to Beverly Hills, stopping at one of the cafes there before spending the rest of the afternoon and evening at the beach. Every week—it was our Saturday ritual.

The only time we deviated was when it rained, which was rare. On those days, we'd have a cozy movie day instead. My chest tightens with the pang of fond memories, and my eyes prickle with tears as the weight of all I've lost sinks in deeper.

Like before, I blink the tears away. Breaking down now, on my first trip outside the castle, would not be wise. I need to encourage further outings, and more importantly, I need to stay focused on gathering as much information as possible. I can't squander this opportunity.

The market before me is large and bustling with activity. Excited conversations buzz in the air, mingling with the mouth-watering scents of cooked meats, savory dips, and sweet treats. Vendors call out to the souls passing by, offering free samples or advertising their wares. To my delight, the market offers much more than food.

Rows of neatly arranged booths display everything from fine jewelry and silks to portable misting fans and serving robots. One stall in particular catches my eye—a rose gold pendant adorned with aquamarine gemstones and diamonds shaped like a cresting wave stands out among the other delicate necklaces. It reminds me of home.

Before I know it, my feet carry me to the booth. My fingers brush against the breathtaking pendant, and I lose myself in its beauty until the clinking of coins pulls me from my stupor. I glance at the merchant, whose beaming smile shows he's just made a sale. Confused, I turn to Lucifer, who takes the necklace from my fingers and clasps it around my neck.

Leaning in, Lucifer brushes his lips against my ear, his velvety voice sending a shiver down my spine. "A beautiful necklace for a beautiful angel," he whispers. His warm breath rustles the loose strands of hair around my face as he presses a soft kiss to my temple before pulling back.

I'm breathless. Speechless. Engulfed with desire despite my best intentions. Guilt washes over me—this is crossing a line. Michael is my soulmate. I *shouldn't* be feeling this way, but Lucifer has a way of muddling my mind so easily, it's terrifying.

I clear my throat to regain composure. "Thank you, but you didn't have to. I was just admiring it." Reaching up to unclasp the chain, I turn to the merchant and offer him a sincere compliment. "It's incredible work!"

The vendor's smile falters as he realizes I'm about to return the necklace and he'll have to part with the coins Lucifer just gave him. Before I can finish unlatching the clasp, though, Lucifer stills my hand.

His fingers thread through mine, gently pulling my hand back down to my side. His other hand cradles my jaw, his dark green eyes shimmering with restrained intensity. "It's a gift, darling," he says softly. "We both know it's rude to refuse a gift. Don't insult me by doing such a thing."

His words give me pause. I meet his gaze, and the sincerity in his expression is disarming. My resolve falters, and I lower my eyes, murmuring quietly, "Thank you."

Lucifer's thumb brushes along my jaw before his hand drops away, though he keeps his other hand intertwined with mine. "It's truly my pleasure," he replies, his voice low and warm.

We continue down the row of stalls, examining the wares displayed at each booth. Boagdan remains exactly two steps behind us at all times, his posture rigid, while Dee flits from stall to stall, exclaiming over various items. She points out dresses, jewelry, sandals, and even a crown, loudly announcing each find to Lucifer with enthusiastic declarations like: "This would be just perfect for your Sabriel!"

I shoot Dee a few pointed looks, silently willing her to shut it, but she studiously pretends not to notice. I briefly consider telling her aloud to tone it down, but I don't want to risk angering Lucifer or doing anything that would cut this trip short. To my dismay, Lucifer graciously buys every single item Dee points out, as well as a few items he chooses himself. I consciously avoid lingering on any item for too long, fearing that he'll interpret my interest as a desire and buy it too.

Boagdan begins to resemble more of a walking shopping cart than a demon as he carries the growing mountain of packages. Dee, meanwhile, is practically glowing with joy. Her excitement, coupled with the lively energy of the market, gradually lifts my spirits. Without realizing it, the ache of homesickness begins to ebb, and I find myself enjoying the outing as we meander through the bustling space.

Lucifer looks surprisingly lighthearted and happy in this moment. There's a carefree boyishness about him that I've never seen before. My heart warms as I watch him and Dee playfully debate over which color silk is best. In the end, Lucifer throws up his hands and declares, "We'll take them all," much to Dee's delight.

I laugh. I can't help it. Lucifer glances over at me and smiles, and my breath catches—for once, in a good way. He looks...angelic. The golden sunlight bathes his face, giving him a halo-like glow as his expression radiates pure joy. How is it possible that

Lucifer—the devil, the being who once slapped me, who once choked me—keeps surprising me in the best ways? Did I misjudge him? Or did I misjudge myself?

At the far end of the market, Lucifer gently steers me to the side. A large sign reading "Petting Zoo" comes into view, and I actually squeal. I love animals. I'm pretty sure Cerberus is the only reason I've managed to stay sane since arriving in Hell, and the thought of petting more animals can only help.

Lucifer greets the manager of the petting zoo, a soul named Harold, like an old friend. "We were worried about you, Your Majesty. It's good to see you well and back to visiting our animals," Harold says warmly.

"I'm glad to be back," Lucifer replies with a soft smile. "I've missed my visits here."

I glance at Lucifer curiously, caught off guard. I didn't expect him to be an animal lover. Michael's story about how Lucifer acquired Cerberus had always seemed like an exception—a bond with a like-soul to stave off loneliness. But now I realize I misjudged him yet again. He obviously harbors a genuine love of animals.

With every new tidbit I learn about Lucifer, I'm forced to see him through a new lens. As we step into the petting zoo, the animals immediately flock to him. Their excited squeals and squawks are piercing as he lavishes them all with attention. His gentle care and their obvious adoration for him are undeniable.

My heart stutters. My breath stalls. I stand frozen, staring as he interacts with the animals with such affection and kindness.

My mouth goes dry. My pulse quickens. I bring a hand to my lips, trying to process the overwhelming emotions swirling inside me. I can't stop staring.

Lucifer turns to me with a brilliant smile and beckons me over, seemingly unaware of my inner turmoil. I walk toward him in a daze.

I reach down to pet an animal that resembles a goat, but with six horns and tiny spikes along its spine. "Hello, little one," I coo softly. "What kind of animal are you? You look like a goat, but you're something else, aren't you?"

Lucifer freezes. His jaw drops. His eyes widen. Shock and disbelief are written all over his face. Then, so softly I can barely hear him, he breathes, "You don't remember."

Chapter 14

BRIE

"You don't remember."

Lucifer's words echo relentlessly in my mind. My breath catches, panic spreading through every cell of my being. He's suspected something was different about me for a while—I've seen it in the probing looks and furrowed brows that follow my words. But now, I've inadvertently confirmed his suspicions. With six simple words, I've put myself in more danger than I've ever been in before.

My gaze drops to my sandaled feet, tracing the intricate gold cloth and diamonds woven into them. I have no idea how Lucifer will react to this revelation, and I'm scared. More scared than I've been since arriving in Hell. His lucidity seems to have improved during my time here, but he's still a loose cannon—unpredictable, volatile.

"We should return to the castle," Lucifer says stiffly. I look up just in time to see him turn his back on me. His body is rigid, his movements jerky, but his chin remains high as he strides toward the castle.

Dee loops her elbow through mine, sabotaging any fleeting thought I might have had about running in the opposite direction. Her face is tense, her lips pursed, and her grip on my arm is nearly bruising as she all but drags me behind Lucifer. Boagdan falls into step behind us. He might want to appear as though he's accompanying us for protection, but I know the truth—he's another obstacle between me and freedom.

I keep my head down, quickening my steps to match Dee's brisk pace. My mind races, running through the possibilities of Lucifer's reaction and how I might respond to each. Anger seems inevitable.

As soon as the castle's thick doors slam shut behind us, Lucifer whirls on me. "Leave us," he commands. Dee unhooks her arm from mine and pats my back twice before she and Boagdan slink out of the entrance hall without a word. Their sudden absence leaves me feeling alone. Exposed. Vulnerable. Prey before the predator.

Lucifer exhales a heavy breath. I lift my gaze, bracing myself for the storm—but instead, I'm taken aback. His head is tilted downward, his eyes closed, and his hands are gripping his hair. He doesn't exhibit the anger I had anticipated. No, his posture and expression radiate something far more disarming: pain. No, not just pain—anguish.

It's an emotion I've come to know well during my time here. The same gut-wrenching sorrow that engulfs me every time I think of Michael. And now, Lucifer...is feeling it in connection with me. What does that even mean?

Lucifer raises his head, opening his eyes, and immediately pinning me with a probing stare. His normally smooth voice is rough when he finally speaks, and he utters just one word: "Explain."

I hesitate, unsure of what to say. I don't know how much to reveal or how much he's already deduced. Showing my hand now could be a grave mistake. Tense silence stretches between us before I settle on the safest response I can muster: "I don't know where to begin."

Lucifer starts to pace the hall, his hands balled into fists at his sides. I reach up, playing with the necklace he bought me at the market, absentmindedly rubbing my fingers over the rough gemstones and smooth rose gold. The contrasting textures ground me.

"Do you remember anything?" Lucifer spits, his tone laced with venom.

My eyes widen at his hostility, but I force the rest of my expression to remain impassive. "I remember you choking me," I say acidly. "I remember my best friend being murdered because of you. I remember you manipulating the Hell Gates to trap me here. Is that enough memory for you?"

Lucifer halts mid-pace, his gaze snapping back to mine. His mouth opens, then closes, as if searching for the right words. Finally, anger twists his features, and I see the fight brewing within him. "I don't even know what you're talking about! Raphael is alive and well, to the best of my knowledge. He wasn't murdered—and certainly not by me."

"I'm talking about *Callie*, you piece of cow dung!" I shout, my whole body shaking with rage.

"I don't know who that is!" Lucifer roars back.

I march up to him, jabbing my finger into his chest. "She was my best friend, and she was murdered! Because. Of. You. One of your corrupted sycophants shot her right between the eyes, trying to win your favor. The great Lucifer, king of frickin' Hell."

"I never ordered that. I don't even know who she was." His tone has softened, but it only fuels my rage further.

I bark out a caustic laugh. "Don't even know the humans murdered in your name. How surprising."

"Sabriel..." he begins.

"That's not my name!" I scream, my voice so shrill it sounds like it could shatter the towering windows of the entrance hall, but I can't even bring myself to care. "My name is Brie. *Brienna.* I am not Sabriel, and I am most certainly not your darling."

Lucifer staggers back a step, as if he's been shot. But there's no wound—or, at least, no physical wound. Only the wound caused by my words. The pain, however, is etched into his face, raw and unguarded.

Before my eyes, his expression hardens into a mask of stone. "I see," he says quietly. "So, you remember nothing before your most recent trip to the earthly plane?"

I cross my arms tightly over my chest, glaring at him, refusing to reply.

"Which means you don't remember me at all," he continues, his voice slow and deliberate, as if he's struggling to process the implications of his own words.

The anguish radiating off him sparks a cruel, vindictive satisfaction in me. I almost smile—a mean, a smile of retribution. He's hurt me in countless ways; doesn't he deserve to feel some of that pain himself?

A little uncertainty breaks through my rage. It's enough for my thoughts to shock me. Who have I become that I would wish pain on another being? This isn't who I am. I believe in justice, in swift and righteous vengeance when wrongs are committed, but I have never relished the idea of someone else's suffering. It makes me realize just how much darkness I've absorbed during my time here.

I take a step back, and Lucifer's eyes narrow slightly, as if he senses the change in my demeanor. "How did you lose your memories?" he asks.

"They were removed by the angels. I volunteered to go to the earthly plane without them to combat the darkness your Hell Gates created." Bitterness creeps into my tone with those last words. If Lucifer had managed those Gates properly—or better yet, not created them at all—none of this would have happened. I have every right to be angry with him.

"I didn't realize," Lucifer says, his tone edged with regret. "I didn't intend to hurt you—or anyone else. I didn't know the darkness had caused an imbalance on the earthly plane. I was, perhaps, remiss in my duties, but I didn't purposely try to disrupt the balance between light and darkness."

"Regardless of your intentions, it happened under your watch. That makes you responsible. And I was the one who had to clean up your mess—a mess I didn't create. So if you're angry about my missing memories, you have only yourself to blame. *You* are the reason I don't remember you."

His gaze drops to the floor, the weight of my words sinking in. "I'm sorry," he whispers.

I remain silent, unwilling to give him the comfort of my forgiveness. When his eyes rise to meet mine, I see tears pooling in their depths. He blinks quickly, looking up at the ceiling as if to force them back, and takes a steadying breath.

"I can't undo anything that happened," he says, his voice firm yet sorrowful, "but I will find a way to make it up to you. I promise."

His sincerity is undeniable, and I seize the moment, knowing it may be my best chance to appeal to his guilt. "If you want to make it up to me, you can start by sending me back to Heaven so I can reclaim the memories that were taken from me. It's an easy solution."

"No." His response is solid, decisive, devoid of hesitation. There's no waver in his voice, no turmoil regarding his decision.

"Why not?" I cry, frustration rising like a tide. "You said you wanted to make it up to me. This is how you can do that! Why would you refuse?"

"Because I need you." His answer is so simple. So straightforward. And there's no way to argue with it, it's utterly irrefutable.

"Why? Why do you need me?" I demand. I can't understand why he's being so stubborn about this.

"Because you were the only one who ever cared about me. You were the only one who stood by my side after I was cast out of Heaven. You are my light. And I love you. That's why."

My mouth falls open. I can do nothing but blink. Words fail me, my mind emptied by the shock of his confession. I stand frozen in the middle of Lucifer's grand entrance hall—motionless, breathless, speechless.

Lucifer holds my gaze for a moment longer, as if waiting for a response. When none comes, he slips his hands into his pockets, turns on his heel, and strides out of the room.

I want to stop him. I want to call out, to ask him not to leave, but I don't know what to say. I don't know how to respond, how to react.

Michael is my soulmate. My heart belongs to him, and I am faithful to him. But deep down, I can't deny what I've been trying to ignore. As much as I hate Lucifer, I've also developed feelings for him. And that is a very dangerous truth.

Chapter 15

MICHAEL

You don't know cold until you've traveled through Gluttony. The third circle of Hell is a polar desert—but much, much colder than any polar desert on Earth. Everyone knows about hellfire, even humans. But most beings have never heard of *hell-ice.* Most who encounter it don't survive long enough to talk about it.

While the second circle was cold enough to bite into your bones, the third circle will freeze you solid in seconds. It's a cold that exists nowhere else. And it's the reason Gluttony is my least favorite circle. Beasts and monsters I can dispatch easily, but I can't fight the elements.

I pull my hood tighter around my head. Our cold-weather gear is designed for this extreme climate, but it's still miserable. Every inch of my body is covered, yet we must keep moving constantly to stave off the inevitable death of exposure.

My boots sink into the sparkling black sand as I trudge toward the rocky terrain looming ahead. Despite being the deadliest of Hell's circles, Gluttony is also the most beautiful—a stark reminder that the most enticing things in Hell are often the most dangerous.

The sunlight reflects off the glittering sand, creating a hypnotic, mesmerizing dance beneath my boots with every step. I can't tear my eyes away. It's enchanting. A deadly trap, just like everything else in this cursed place.

The crunch of gravel beneath my boots jolts me out of my trance. I shake my head, annoyed at myself for falling into it in the first place. I should be alert, scanning for danger. Allowing myself to be distracted was reckless—a lapse in self-control I can't afford.

Grateful that nothing attacked us while I was momentarily vulnerable, I slow my pace to walk beside Callista. "How are you feeling?" I ask.

"Fine, mostly. A little tired," she admits.

"That's expected," I reassure her. "Your energy is still recovering. That injury took a lot out of you. Even though you look healed, your energy is still restoring itself. It'll take time before you're fully back to normal."

"I know. I just don't want to slow the team down. I don't want to be a liability," she says, her voice tinged with worry.

But she *is* a liability. She has been since the moment I agreed to let her come with us. I obviously can't tell her that though. I'm not aiming to hurt her feelings, and it was my decision to allow her to join. I won't burden her with my regret. "If you need a break, let us know," I say instead.

"I will," she promises quietly, then hesitates, opening and closing her mouth a few times before she finally asks, "Do you think Brie will be okay when we find her? Do you think he's hurting her?"

My jaw tightens. The mere thought of Lucifer laying so much as a finger on Brie ignites a rage in me like nothing I've ever experienced before. The intensity of it burns through me, chasing away the unimaginable cold of this circle. Steam rises from my outerwear in a visible display of my fury as my light energy writhes violently within the confines of my corporeal form, urging me to mete out justice against any being who would dare harm my soulmate.

I force myself to take a few deep breaths, and when I finally manage to unclench my jaw, my voice emerges sharp and unforgiving. "If he is, I will *revel* in his demise." Bright white angelic energy crackles at my fingertips, and Gabriel's head snaps toward me. His blue eyes, shades lighter than my own, swirl with concern. He knows this reaction is unlike me, given my usually even temperament.

Gabriel's concern is enough to trigger my own alarm. Taking another moment to calm myself, I recompose my thoughts and address Callista. "Brie is strong. No matter what she's experiencing, she'll be fine."

"You're right. Brie's the strongest person I know. I'm sorry I doubted."

"Angel, not person," I correct gently, reminding her of what she is too.

"Angel," Callista repeats with a small nod.

I refocus on my steps, carefully leading us through an area filled with snow dunes. The group falls into a single-file line behind me, following my path.

The wind picks up, blowing clouds of glittering snow from the dunes' surfaces. Like the sparkling black sand and shining dark rocks we left behind, the sight is mesmerizing. But as I glance up at the red sky, darkening with black and gray clouds, unease settles over me. This breathtaking phenomenon feels like another deadly façade.

Within minutes, my fears are confirmed. The blizzard starts subtly, with just a few glittering snowflakes drifting around us. But the wind grows stronger, and the snowfall intensifies quickly, obscuring the landscape in sparkling white.

The wind whips against my clothing, probing for gaps to sneak through and chill me further. Snow piles higher around my legs, and the storm continues to gain strength, showing no signs of relenting. We need to find shelter—and we need to find it quickly.

I push forward through the thickening snow in the direction I think we should go, though visual landmarks are gone. The snow dunes are harder to distinguish now, and I have a few close calls but manage to pivot just in time. While we can still see each other, the white-on-white terrain makes navigation nearly impossible.

I'm so focused on the ground directly in front of me that I don't notice the distant brownish blobs until Raphael shouts jubilantly, "Yes! Shelter!" Following his pointing finger with my gaze, I find the shapes and hasten my stride. As we draw closer, the blobs take on the distinct shape of conical huts.

Relief and gratitude start to unfurl within me—until we reach the huts, at which point my heart sinks. The lack of accumulated snow around the structures is a bad sign. I approach the nearest hut and tentatively push the door open, my hand trembling with anticipation. The door resists slightly but swings open easily enough. Inside, my worst fears are confirmed: snow has piled high through gaping holes in the roof, blanketing the single room.

I close my eyes, disappointment washing over me, threatening to drag my thoughts in a negative direction. But I didn't rise to lead the Angelic Army by giving up after a single setback. "Check the other huts," I order.

My comrades fan out, each inspecting a hut. With every report of failure, my heart sinks further. The storm rages around us, the wind growing stronger with every moment. As I focus on one of the huts that hasn't been checked yet, its roof is ripped away completely, vanishing into the tempest.

We can't stay here. Being in or around the huts will put us in more danger than being in the open would. "It's too dangerous. We need to keep moving."

I scan the whiteout around us, trying to orient myself, but it's hopeless. I turn to Gabriel. "Do you have any divine wisdom for us?"

His eyes swirl silver momentarily before he shakes his head, his gaze dropping to the ground. "That's okay," I say with a weak smile. "I knew it was a long shot."

The snow continues to fall harder, and the wind grows fiercer as we trudge forward. My goggles fog up, and I rub them with my gloved hands. When they clear, I notice a dark shape looming in the distance. I want to temper my hope, but it flickers to life despite my better judgment. Maybe—just maybe—this could be our salvation.

I quicken my pace, my team hustling to keep up. As we approach, I gasp. The dark shape sharpens into a stunning ice cave. The brilliant white ice forms sturdy striations, welcoming us in. *Shelter*.

"Let's go! Everybody in!" I call back, my excitement unmistakable.

My team races into the spectacular ice formation. "Let's head a little deeper into the cave, then we can rest and sleep," I suggest, still marveling at our luck.

"Rest," Raphael sighs dreamily, throwing me a cheeky grin. It's the first time I've seen even a flicker of his old self since Brie was taken. His jovial demeanor has been dulled by the weight of her absence, as has all of ours. But seeing this glimmer of his former self gives me hope. Perhaps, in time, we can find the angels we were before this trauma and recover those parts of ourselves.

As we venture deeper into the cave, the light diminishes. I extend my hand, letting soft, white angelic energy glow from my palm. The light shines on the ice, making the walls seem even more magnificent, like a crystalline palace carved by divine hands.

"I think this is the most beautiful thing I've ever seen," Ariella whispers, more to herself than to anyone else. A few others murmur their agreement, but a quiet voice in the back of my mind whispers, *"In Hell, beautiful is deadly."*

A chill skitters up my spine. I don't have visions or premonitions like Gabriel, but the thought feels foreign, not entirely my own, and I can't help but worry that it wasn't my imagination. A gnawing sense of foreboding settles deep in my gut. I don't try to dismiss the warning. Instead, I force myself to become even more vigilant, straining to hear any sound, see any flicker of movement or light that might suggest danger. But there's nothing to indicate that my wariness is warranted. Nothing except the serene quiet of the ice.

Perhaps it really is my imagination. We've ventured far enough into the cave that the howling wind no longer reaches us. The air is surprisingly warm, given the icy walls surrounding us. For the first time in hours, my body begins to relax.

Exhaustion claims me as my adrenaline fades. I slide my pack from my shoulders and prop it against the wall. Settling down next to it, I lean back, tipping my head against the cool surface. My eyes droop, and sleep beckons.

Then a jarring sensation yanks me awake. A shiver of energy leaving my body sends alarm surging through me. My eyes snap open, and I jolt upright.

My gaze darts to Raphael, then Gabriel, Kemuel, Haniel, Callista, and Ariella. They're all sprawled across the floor or against the walls, heads propped on packs, eyes closed. No one is standing guard. No one is even alert.

This is wrong.

This goes against everything we've trained to do—against everything that's kept us alive for eons.

This...isn't natural.

This is the work of vampires.

Chapter 16

MICHAEL

I can't see the vampires, but I know they're here. The steady drain on my energy is proof enough. I rouse the others as quietly as possible, gently shaking and squeezing shoulders until each member of my team is awake and alert. The vampires already know we're here, but that doesn't mean they need to know that we're assembling for battle.

The fatigue they are pushing onto us by sapping our energy is all-encompassing. My reactions are sluggish. My mind is foggy. My judgment is compromised. Regardless, we have no choice but to fight if we want to make it out of here alive. Running would simply encourage a chase.

I stealthily draw my sword and motion to the others to do the same. I creep further into the cave, keeping my back toward the wall and my sword at the ready. The draw of energy the vampires are stealing from me is steady, indicating that the nest we've discovered is substantial.

I peek around a natural curve in the cave's formation. The chamber I find has a flatter ceiling than the peaked ones we've seen here thus far, and hundreds of bats hang from it. Bats may avoid areas of extreme cold in the human realm, but that's simply because it's the climate they're forced to endure while in Hell. The milder climates they occupy while on the earthly plane are a vacation for the small creatures.

One of the bats closest to me starts to turn its head in my direction. I whip my head back into the concealed area behind the cave's curve, but I'm not fast enough. The bats beady black eyes lock on mine just as I pull out of view.

In the next moment, I hear a rustle of wings and air, followed by the sound of feet landing softly on the icy ground. The vampire peeks his head around the curve in the cave, his lips curved upward in an amused sneer. It isn't lost on me that he's purposely mocking my previous actions.

Understanding that I've clocked his insult, the vampire steps out from behind the wall and spreads his arms wide, giving us a small bow. This too is meant as an insult. The rustle of wings and displaced air grows louder in the concealed chamber, indicating that more of the bats are shapeshifting into their vampire forms.

"Angels, welcome to our home," the vampire lilts. "We are *so* happy you have graced us with your presence." His smile is predatory. He knows he's lethal, but he likes to play with his food before devouring it. And based on his emaciated form, he's highly motivated to turn this situation into a successful meal.

Three additional vampires step up behind the first, all with cocked heads and wicked grins. They're excited. Anticipatory dark energy fills the air, seeping out of their pores as though their bodies can't contain their delight at finding such tasty morsels have walked straight into their nest.

My stomach sours at the thought. How could I have been so oblivious to their presence? I should have been more alert, should have expected the cave wouldn't be empty. I keep failing the beings that depend on me, time and again. Maybe I don't deserve my position leading the Angelic Army any longer. Maybe I don't deserve Brie either.

I shake off my self-loathing. This isn't the time or place for these kinds of thoughts. Continuing down this line of thinking will only lead to more mistakes and put my comrades in further danger. I need to focus on the here and now. Later, I'll evaluate my place in Heaven and ruminate on the many mistakes I have made during my long existence. Right now, I need to focus on the battle that's about to spark off in front of me.

The vampire takes a deep breath, but not of air—of energy. Specifically, my energy. I feel it tug away from my being, slipping through the vampire's lips and sliding down his throat to settle within his chest, where it blackens. His smile grows wider. He's baiting me and we both know it. But still, it works.

My disgust at the thought of my energy corrupting within his being overtakes my rationality and I swing my sword at his neck. My movements are precise, honed from millennia of practice. The vampire jumps out of the way just in time, and the many vampires previously obscured from my vision by the curve in the cave jump into action. They dart forward and spread themselves amongst us, battling each of us five on one.

The vampires lack our training, but desperation fuels them. Clawed fingernails swipe at me, and razor-sharp teeth snap at my throat. They fight with a ferocity born of insatiable hunger. The intensity of it makes me uneasy. It also makes their actions hard to predict—more dangerous, more lethal.

I have no time to worry about my comrades as I parry and thrust against the vampires encircling me. One lunges, and I grab it by the throat, hurling it into the path of another vampire's gnashing teeth. The second vampire doesn't stop in time, sinking her fangs into the first vampire's shoulder.

Dark wisps of corrupted energy rise from the wound as the bitten vampire wails in pain. I don't give it so much as a thought as I block the claws slashing toward my face from the side. Another vampire barrels into me from behind, propelling me upward. My body slams into the icy ceiling with such force that shards of ice rain down as I ricochet off of it and crash to the ground in a heap.

My sword is gone, lost in the impact—a definite disadvantage, though this is why we train extensively in hand-to-hand combat as well. I push myself up just in time to avoid a kick to the gut. I catch the vampire's foot mid-air, twisting sharply until I hear the satisfying snap of ligaments.

She cries out, though I can't tell if it's from rage or pain. I don't dwell on it, ducking another vampire's kick aimed at my skull. When he misses, a third vampire swoops in, trying to pin me to the ground. I pull my knees to my chest and kick out with all my strength, striking his pelvis. His grip loosens in shock, and I follow up with an elbow to his temple, sending him sprawling.

Scrambling to my feet, I raise my guard, readying for the next attack. The vampires don't disappoint. Two of them fling themselves at me from opposite sides, moving in perfect coordination. I drop low, hoping they'll collide. But these two must team up often in fights; at the last moment, they clasp arms and use the momentum to swing around each other, landing gracefully—one in front of me, the other behind.

A kick from behind crumples my knees, but I use the fall to my advantage. Grabbing the vampire in front of me, I fling her over my falling body into the one behind me. I hear them collide just as my knees hit the floor. Immediately, another kick arcs toward me from the side. I roll to evade it, and my hand lands on my sword. Seizing it, I spring to my feet.

My breathing is labored, and my muscles scream in protest, but I manage to kick out behind me. The vampire attacking from the rear slams into the hard wall with a sickening crack. His neck snaps, and he collapses to the ground, unconscious. Though vampires can heal, it will take him time to recover. For now, he's out of the fight.

I spin and thrust my sword into the vampire charging toward me. I miss her heart, but the blade plunges deeply into her gut. I pull it out with a sickening squelch, readying for my next strike. But the vampire is still, her eyes wide as she stares down at the dark smoke rising from her wound. Dazed by the injury, her hesitation is a fatal mistake. I seize the opportunity, slicing my sword cleanly through her neck. Her head hits the ground with a dull thud, bouncing once before her body collapses lifelessly beside it.

Leaping over the body of the beheaded vampire, I reposition myself, gaining more space to move as a pair of vampires charge at me. One attacks from a low angle, the other from higher. As the higher vampire's arm wraps around my neck, I use her crouching partner for leverage, pushing off his back to flip over the female.

Her feet lift off the ground and her hold loosens. I change my trajectory, grabbing her throat in a poetic reversal of roles, and slamming her into her partner's back. They both crash to the floor, and I stab the edge of my blade clean through their necks.

Not wasting any time, I rise to my feet, swinging my elbow into the face of another vampire closing in on me. He staggers backward, dazed, and I use the opening to spin. The momentum slices my sword cleanly through his neck before he even registers the strike.

The remaining vampires pause, sensing the tide has turned in our favor. They hiss in frustration, and one by one, they shift back into their bat forms and flee toward the cave's entrance, their dark shapes vanishing into the shadows.

As the last bat disappears, I scan my team. They're battered, their energy visibly drained, but they're alive. Relief floods through me, and I bend forward, resting my hands on my knees as I struggle to catch my breath. That was one of the fiercest battles I've faced, and I can hardly believe we've all made it through relatively unscathed.

Gabriel staggers toward me, his face pale and drawn, exhaustion etched into every line. I straighten as he reaches me, and he pats my back a few times. "How are you?" he asks softly.

"I made it through. How about you?"

"The same," he replies, his voice thick with fatigue. His tone pulls at my chest, filling me with guilt. Gabriel is strong, but he's not a warrior. If this journey is taking such a toll on me, I can't imagine what it's doing to him.

A painful lump forms in the back of my throat. This is yet another example of my failure as a leader. I shouldn't have brought Gabriel on this journey. It was selfish of me to expect him to risk his life—and the life of his soulmate—to save mine. I've endangered all of these angels by asking them to come with me. I should have come alone.

I know having a group increases our chances of success, but the thought of losing any of them, of bearing the weight of their loss, is unbearable. If anything happens to them, I'll never forgive myself. Never.

Chapter 17

MICHAEL

"Let's scout the rest of the cave. Once we're sure it's clear, we can recover." My team moves to follow my instructions immediately, breaking off into pairs to check for any lingering threats in the ice cave. Raphael and Gabriel return first, giving a succinct "Clear" for their section. Kemuel and Haniel follow shortly, reporting that while the cave transitions into an ice tunnel further in, both the section they explored and the tunnel itself are clear. Ariella and Callista are the last to report back, confirming the same for their assigned area.

Finally allowing myself to relax, knowing we aren't in immediate danger, I sink back against the icy wall again. "Let's take this time to sleep. We'll guard in shifts. Kemuel and Raphael, you two are on first shift."

"Heard," Kemuel responds. Raphael echoes his statement, and I let my eyes drift shut, slipping into a light sleep.

It feels like only seconds have passed when a soft cry pierces my consciousness. I jolt awake, unsure if the sound was part of my turbulent dreams until I hear it again. My eyes scan the dim space, checking over my team and searching for any sign of danger.

Kemuel is already moving deeper into the cave to investigate the sound. I rise to my feet and join Raphael in his guard position. "Should we wake the others?" Raphael asks quietly.

"Let's wait until Kemuel returns. We all need as much rest as we can get."

Raphael dips his head in agreement, casting a protective glance at Gabriel's sleeping form. The soft rhythm of Kemuel's footsteps reaches my ears moments later, and my unease sharpens as I wait for him to round the bend.

"The sound seems to be coming from just outside the ice tunnel's exit," Kemuel reports, slightly out of breath. "I think it might be a soul in need of help. The blizzard has dissipated, but perhaps they were hurt during the storm."

I look at Raphael, wanting his opinion on how we should proceed.

"I think we should wake everyone and investigate together," he suggests.

"You two haven't slept yet," I counter. "And we don't know how long it will be before you'll have the opportunity to do so again. Are you sure you have the energy to keep going? I don't want either of you coming to harm because of fatigue."

"I'm fine to continue," Kemuel assures me. Raphael nods his agreement, but still I hesitate. It doesn't feel right.

I lower my gaze, weighing the pros and cons of moving forward versus staying put to let them rest. Ultimately, I decide to trust my team. They know their limits better than I do.

"Alright," I concede. "Let's wake the others."

With Raphael and Kemuel's help, the rest of the team is quickly roused, and we begin making our way through the dazzling white ice cave toward the shimmering ice tunnel. The soft sound that awakened me persists, growing louder with each step as we near the tunnel's exit.

The tunnel narrows, forcing us into a single-file line. Though the crystalline walls glitter with an otherworldly beauty, the tight space feels oppressive, and I fight the rising claustrophobia clawing at my mind. The light at the end of the tunnel is a welcome beacon of freedom, and my skin itches with the need to leave the confined space.

Finally, we emerge onto a broad ice shelf beyond the tunnel's mouth. I take in the open expanse, my guard still high but my tension easing slightly. Without the tunnel's visual obstructions, spotting potential threats will be much easier. Still, I scan the area warily, every sense on high alert.

A faint cry sounds again. It seems to be coming from a distance, beyond the side of the ice cave. As soon as everyone is out of the tunnel, I motion in the direction sound and signal for my team to follow. Another faint cry pierces the quiet and I swing around, jogging past the exterior wall of the ice tunnel. I round its edge just as Haniel yells, "Wait! It's throwing its voice!" but my momentum takes me around the bend before he even finishes the sentence, and I end up face to face with an ekek.

The bird-like humanoid towers over me. He must be at least nine feet tall. His webbed, papery wings extend behind him and his beak is open wide, awaiting his next meal. His arms reach out to me, his talons flexing, ready to capture me in his grasp. I quickly raise my sword in a defensive posture.

The ekek hisses, displeased that I have blocked his incursion, and backs up a step. Intelligence shines in his red eyes. I see them rise, gazing past me, and I know that my team is now at my back. The ekek hisses again, a calculating look puckering the skin between his eyebrows. He seems to decide the risk is worth the reward, because he opens his beak even wider and a thin, needle-like probe extends from the back of his throat.

I swing my sword wildly as the ekek reaches for me again. The sharp edge of my blade clashes with his wrist. Dark energy spews from the wound. His hand hangs limply, his talons unmoving, and he wails with even more rage. He leaps up, pumping his bat-like wings and swooping to and fro above us.

He dips and rises, trying to capture one of us from above with the talons of his feet. When he swoops toward Ariella, she releases a throwing star in his direction. Her aim is true: the throwing star embeds itself in the center of his skull and the ekek plummets to the icy ground.

The snap as he crashes into the thick ice is sickening, and I watch for a few minutes, waiting for him to rise and limp away. But he doesn't rise. His body lies motionless atop the ice in a heap. It's the only thing in sight, other than us, that isn't ice. He must have been truly desperate for a meal to attack us despite the numerical imbalance, and I can't help but pity the beast.

Swallowing past the lump forming in my throat, I ask my team, "Was anyone injured?" I get a few noes and a couple of head shakes in response.

"We're all fine," Kemuel reassures me.

I give him a small smile in thanks. He's known me for eons and must see the uncertainty in my actions.

"Why don't you take the lead for a bit," I instruct Kemuel. I could use the time to think, and for the moment, we only need to traverse the ice shelf. It's flat and clear—probably the safest place for us to venture across in all of Hell.

Kemuel smiles back at me gratefully and orders, "Let's move out."

I walk at the back of our procession, mostly lost in thought, until ice crystals start falling around us. I look up at the clear red sky and marvel at the diamond dust shimmering through it and scattering the sunlight. It's a breathtaking phenomenon, one most beings can only dream of.

The sparkle the shimmering dust creates is mesmerizing, and I watch as Callista and Ariella start spinning with their arms out, catching the small ice crystals on their tongues and laughing together. The mood of our group lightens as we continue walking along the ice shelf, relishing this moment. Our journey seems shorter, our goal less distant amid this once-in-a-lifetime experience.

Raphael slings his arm around Gabriel's shoulders, their heads bent together as they gaze dreamily at the diamond dust's beauty. And despite my soulmate's absence, even I can appreciate this wonder. The girls gasp as a halo of light forms in the rich red sky. The halo even has strips on the sides that resemble wings.

We're all distracted by the event, captivated by it. We can't help ourselves. But then, the halo flares, temporarily blinding me, and I hear a yell. In Kemuel's distraction, he walked right off the steep edge of the ice shelf.

Luckily, Kemuel has had his wings much longer than Callista, so unlike her response to falling, it's second nature for him to unfurl his wings and coast to a smooth landing atop the frozen lake at the bottom of the cliff. I let my shoulders sink with relief at his safe landing, taking a moment to let my heartbeat calm as well.

Kemuel waits for us on the frozen surface of the lake, and one by one, we each glide down to join him. I retake the lead, with Kemuel and Haniel bringing up the rear. We're almost to the gate. We've made it through another circle—through the most treacherous circles.

I increase my speed as the Gate for the fourth circle comes into view. I'm nearly giddy with excitement. I want to break into a run just so I can reach the Gate faster, but I hold myself back, walking purposefully toward it instead. I'm so focused on the Gate that I don't register the near-silent cracking sound under and behind me.

That is, I don't register it until the hushed sound gives way to a loud crack, and the ice under Kemuel's feet falls out from under him. I whip around to see Haniel whip out his arm, attempting to catch Kemuel. They clasp hands, and I see Haniel shift his weight to the side, preparing to pull Kemuel up. But just as he does, Kemuel's glove slips off his hand, and he plunges into the freezing water below.

Haniel topples onto his back from the sudden lack of resistance. I rush over, reaching out to grasp Kemuel's arm and pull him out of the water. Raphael does the same, but in the milliseconds it takes us to reach the hole, it has already iced over. Kemuel bangs on the ice from beneath the surface, trying to break through. Raphael and I do the same from above, the other angels joining in as well.

I can't use my sword to pierce the ice, fearing the tip would impale Kemuel, so I strike the ice with its pommel. I put all my strength behind each blow, but the newly formed layers of ice remain unbroken. They don't even crack.

Kemuel's hand drops away from the ice. He stops banging against it. Panic floods through me as I turn to Raphael and plead, "Can you heal him? Give him some air? We need more time!"

Raphael's voice is choked as he answers, "I can't save him if I can't reach him. You know I need physical contact to heal others."

No. No, this can't be happening! My heart pounds in my throat, and my vision blurs as Kemuel's hand disappears into the depths of the lake. He's gone. There's nothing we can do. A burst of light from beneath the surface confirms my worst fears, and I shout my grief and anger into the barren expanse, "NOOOOOO!"

I'm inconsolable. How did I let this happen? Why him? Why not me? I would have gladly given my life in place of his. My mind flashes back to Erelah guarding the Heavenly Gate when we departed—how her eyes lingered on Kemuel, her worry for her soulmate clear in her gaze. And now he's gone. I came here to bring my soulmate back from the depths of Hell, and now I'll be returning without hers. Her soulmate died trying to save mine.

How selfish am I? Why is Brie's life worth more than Kemuel's? It's not. No life is worth more than any other. But I've just sacrificed his to save hers, without even realizing I was doing it. What have I done?

Chapter 18

LUCIFER

I trace the wood grain pattern of my polished, dark mahogany desk with my left hand while I run the fingers of my right hand through Cerberus' soft fur. Two of his heads rest on my lap, battling for space, while the third looks up at my face with tragic puppy dog eyes. He really knows how to lay it on thick.

No matter his manipulations, I still love him with all my heart. Some days, I feel like Cerberus is all I have—the only being who truly loves me. How pathetic is that? I have my own kingdom, rule over millions, yet I'm loved by exactly one being in all the realms, and he can't even talk to me.

My eyes prickle with pain, but I will the moisture away. I will not show weakness, not even to Cerberus. Hell is full of corrupted souls, and if they sense even a hint of weakness from me, it would mean my end.

Sometimes, I wish for it. But knowing that millions depend on me, knowing that I am the only Hellish being capable of maintaining the balance between light and dark on the more vulnerable planes, I know my wish will remain just that—a wish. I could never abandon my duties like that. I care too much.

I pull the stopper from my crystal decanter and pour the amber whiskey into one of the matching monogrammed glasses. Cerberus huffs at me, displeased that I've stopped petting him. Realizing my attention is now elsewhere, he lumbers over to his memory foam dog bed, situated by the large windows, and makes himself comfortable.

I lift the glass to my lips, inhaling the comforting cinnamon and vanilla aroma before savoring the spicy caramel and honey notes. My eyes drift over to the broken glass face of my abandoned Patek Philippe Aquanaut watch. The watch had been modified to function as a communicator between Heaven and Hell, but Sabriel was the only one who cared enough to use it.

And now she hates me. I destroyed the watch in a fit of rage after she disappeared. I don't have many clear memories from that time, but I do remember smashing the watch with my antique bronze paperweight—and feeling devastated afterward, knowing I had just destroyed my only way to reach her should she return.

I run a hand over my face. I've loved Sabriel for as long as I've known her. But she was Michael's soulmate. Off limits. I respected that—I understood the sanctity of their bond—and I never revealed my feelings to her. Until now. Now, when she hates me. Now, when her only memories of me are bad ones. I'm such a fool. A lovesick fool.

I didn't even mean to say the words. I just couldn't hold them in any longer, and they slipped out of my mouth before I could stop them. I wish I could take them back. I wish I had never uttered a single sound.

But the worst part isn't her rejection. It's that everything she said was true. Everything she went through, the reason she doesn't remember anything good about me—it's all my fault.

Maybe I should release her, but I can't. I don't want her to hate me. I don't want her to suffer. But I *need* her light to lead Hell. Perhaps if I had brought her here sooner, the imbalance on the earthly plane would never have occurred in the first place.

Surrounded by the darkness, encompassed by it, my sanity slowly slipped away. Yes, I was derelict in my duties, but I wasn't purposely neglectful. I was simply incapable.

The darkness infected me. I was pure when I fell to Hell. I made mistakes, showed hubris, but my intentions were pure. My soul was still light.

But slowly, the longer I stayed here, the darker my soul became. There was no way to purge the darkness while on this plane, so it just kept growing. And with that growth came the deterioration of my sanity.

Sabriel's light is so pure, so powerful, that even in the short time she's been here, my sanity has begun to return. How can I let that go? How can I sit back and allow the millions of subjects under my leadership to suffer because I prioritize one angel over all of them? I can't.

It's true that Hell is meant to cause suffering for the corrupted souls, but their suffering is corrective. It serves a purpose. It's not malicious. Their punishments were designed with the intent that one day, their souls would be reformed enough to ascend to Heaven. How could I deny them that possibility?

If I allow Sabriel to leave, my mania will return. And with it, the neglect of the leadership I unintentionally abandoned years ago. I'm not keeping her here for selfish reasons. I am selfish—I know that—but in this instance, I'm being selfishly selfless. I'm doing this for my subjects, for the souls that wander Hell in anguish, needing hope that they can one day be redeemed.

I gaze over at Cerberus, sleeping in his bed. His eyelids twitch, and his tail wags. I smile, glad he's having happy dreams. If Cerberus can find happiness here in Hell, can't Sabriel? I'd do anything to make that happen. Anything.

A strong knock on the thick door of my office interrupts my thoughts.

"Enter."

Boagdan steps into the room, bowing deeply.

"Yes, Boagdan, what do you have to tell me?"

"Your Majesty, the Laestrygonians have sent word that a small squad of angels breached their territory during the past few days. They were unable to prevent the threat from advancing deeper into Hell and wanted to alert you to their presence."

"That was kind of them. We will reward them for their loyalty."

Boagdan nods, acknowledging the instruction.

"Were they able to identify any of the angels?" I ask. We ensure that all of Hell's inhabitants are trained to recognize the archangels on sight, for the protection of both my citizens and my brothers. I may hate the way they've treated me since my fall from grace, but they're still my brothers. I would never wish them harm—not even Michael, despite my jealousy.

"I didn't ask, Your Majesty, and their communication did not include those details. But I can follow up with them."

"Yes, please do. I would assume that Michael is leading the incursion, but I'd like confirmation. If any of the others are with him as well, it would be helpful to know—it will give us an idea of the strength of their force."

"I will write an official inquiry as soon as I leave, Your Majesty. Is there anything else you would like me to address before I handle that?"

"Yes, there's another matter I'd like to discuss with you. Sabriel mentioned that during her time on the earthly plane, there was a murder—someone dear to her—carried out in my name."

"Unacceptable," Boagdan hisses, enraged on my behalf.

My lips curve into a slight smile. "I agree. The perpetrator must be found and punished—a punishment that I will deliver personally. Find the being and bring it to me. Justice must be served, and a message must be sent: no one acts in my name but me."

"I will find the being, Your Majesty. You can count on me."

I nod, dismissing Boagdan to attend to his duties. He turns and strides toward the door but pauses just before reaching it. Turning back, he meets my eyes, a faint smile playing across his lips. "It's good to have you back, Your Majesty. We missed you. I know it's hard for you, keeping her here, but we can all see how necessary it is. You're doing the right thing."

I swallow thickly, touched by his words. "Thank you, Boagdan. I needed to hear that."

He dips his head once more and he slips out the door, closing it firmly behind him.

The moment I'm alone again, guilt floods me. My chest tightens, and my stomach churns uneasily. I take another gulp of whiskey, relishing the burn as it slides down my throat. *Am* I doing the right thing? If I am, why do cold tendrils of dread dance along my skin? Why does the heaviness of regret weigh down my every movement? Shouldn't I feel better about this?

I think...I think I might have made a mistake. Possibly many mistakes. But I don't know how to fix it in a way that saves both Sabriel and my subjects. How can I, when I too am in need of saving?

If I release Sabriel, who will save me?

Who will save Hell?

Chapter 19

BRIE

I place the open book at my feet and glance down at page 233 for what I hope will be the last time tonight. I've already memorized the page, but the glance has become compulsive. I pull two hairpins free from my hair and unbend the first one into a ninety-degree angle. Then, I pick the plastic off one end with my nail and bend the other end into a small handle. The second hairpin, I bend into a hook.

I slide the hooked pin into the lock of my quarters' door, lifting it as far as possible within the mechanism. Then, I slide the other pin under it and jiggle, waiting for the click. It doesn't come, so I jiggle some more. My gaze drifts to the book again, confirming that I've followed the steps correctly. I have. I resume my jiggling, and after what feels like hours, the awaited click pierces the silence of the sleeping castle.

It sounds as loud as a gunshot to my ears, though I know that's just my nerves. I turn the door handle slowly, exhaling quietly when the doors part. I remove my improvised lockpicks from the small keyhole and slip them into my pocket. I might need them later.

Next, I bend down and softly close the book. Carrying it over to the pile of books I've brought from the library, I slip it into the middle of the stack. A faint noise breaches the silence of my room, and I freeze, my gaze snapping to the door. It doesn't move. I wait several minutes, muscles tense, but no other noises follow.

I creep to the door as quietly as possible, pulling it open slowly. Peeking through the opening, I confirm that the hallway is clear. It is. Everyone should be fast asleep at this hour, but one can never be certain, and it doesn't hurt to be cautious.

I slip through the opening and tiptoe to the stairs. Climbing carefully, I stick to the left side of the stairs for the first four steps, lift my leg high to bypass the fifth, and hug the right for the remainder of the staircase to avoid the squeaking parts, until I reach the landing for the conservatory. The glass door opens easily at my pull. Only the doors to my quarters are locked, it seems.

Stepping into the greenhouse, I inhale deeply. The herby scents of the plants calm me, and I pause for a moment to relax before resuming my mission, tipping my head back to admire the luminous night sky through the glass ceiling. Hell is such an odd place—unexpected in its beauty and filled with contradictions. I could see myself growing to like it here, and that thought terrifies me.

Shaking off those musings, I stride past the burnt orange couch against the side wall, grabbing my gardening gloves, shears, and basket from the glass table as I go. I make my way to the far corner of the greenhouse, where the more dangerous plants are grown.

I haven't spent much time in this section of the room as I didn't want to arouse suspicion, but I've studied the greenhouse layout extensively. That, coupled with the knowledge I've gained from *Plants for Poisons, Potions, and Phytotherapy,* should be all I need.

I walk softly as I weave between the neat rows of plants, knowing that Lucifer sleeps in the room below. Finding the wild rosemary first, I cut a few sprigs from the back of the plant, where their absence is less likely to be noticed, and place them in my basket. I move further along the row, barely identifying the mountain laurel in the dim light. It's harder to conceal the missing portion of this shrub. I cut off a few clumps of the deceptively beautiful pink and white flowers, hoping it will just look as though the plant was recently pruned.

Next, I locate the pretty purple and red spider flowers. Their colors are hauntingly alluring in the dark of night, as though the lack of light makes them even more enchanting. I snip several stems and place them carefully into my basket before walking over to the large blinding tree. Pulling a small glass vial from my pocket, I cut into the bark at the rear of the tree. A milky white sap seeps from the wound, and I position my vial beneath the dripping sap. The vial fills slowly, and I wait patiently, knowing this will be one of the best weapons in my arsenal when I attempt to escape.

Corking the filled vial, I place it, too, into my basket and quietly creep back to the door, still wearing my gloves and holding the gardening shears. To my hyper-alert ears, the click of the door as it closes sounds as loud as a clash of cymbals, and I pause for several seconds before descending the tower's stairs.

I bypass the landing that leads to my quarters, continuing all the way down to the ground floor of the castle, through its long interior hallway, and into the kitchen. Dee usually escorts me to breakfast a few hours after sunrise. I'm guessing the kitchen staff starts preparing food an hour or two beforehand, so I'll need to finish my work before the sky begins to lighten.

I pull open the door to the walk-in pantry, still cautious about making noise, and step inside. Motion-activated lights flicker on, forcing me to quickly shield my eyes with my hand. The harsh light stings after skulking around in the darkness for so long.

Placing my basket on the floor in the middle of the pantry, I glance around at the multitude of shelves. This is my first time inside of it, and it's overwhelming. Jars and baskets of all shapes and sizes line the shelves, their colorful contents creating a rainbow of enticement.

The pantry is well-organized, and I quickly find the section housing herbs. Dragging my gloved finger along the shelf, I read the names on the jars. Some are herbs I'm familiar with, while others are new to me. It seems Hell uses a mixture of foods: some imported from the earthly plane, and some native to this realm.

Finding the jar labeled "rosemary," I take it to my basket and pull out a sprig to compare with the wild rosemary I collected in the greenhouse. The size and texture seem similar enough to my untrained eye, but the coloring of the two plants is noticeably different. I sigh and return to the shelves to search for green food coloring.

I nearly cheer when I find a bottle of green food coloring spray but catch myself just in time to suppress the sound building in my throat. Grabbing some baking paper from a lower shelf, I set myself up on the pantry floor. Carefully, I spray each sprig of wild rosemary, matching the colors of the two plants as closely as possible.

It's an arduous task requiring immense concentration, but also a necessary one. Once the sprigs are properly colored, I leave them to dry and turn my attention to the mountain laurel. Returning to the kitchen, I find a small bowl and fill it with water. I submerge the delicate flowers in the bowl and set it aside to soak.

My last bit of work is the most dangerous. I cut a small hole in the middle of a sheet of baking paper and slip one bunch of the spider flowers through it. Pulling a small jar out of my pocket, I position the fragile petals of the flowers within its confines and start to shake them. The baking paper acts as a barrier to keep me safe from any rogue drops of the nectar I'm shaking out—the nectar that is capable of causing death within minutes.

I don't want to kill Lucifer, and have no intention of doing so, but the beasts I might encounter on my way out of Hell are another matter. And though it is a last resort, if killing means the difference between captivity and freedom, I will do what I must to escape. I shake as much nectar as possible from the clumps of flowers and cap the jar.

I test the wild rosemary, satisfied that the coloring has dried quickly, and slip the sprigs of the edible variety back into their jar before returning it to its place on the shelf. The toxic version, I wrap carefully in a cloth. They'll be ready when I am.

Gathering up the remnants of the spider flowers, I head out of the pantry and deposit them into the trash, hiding them beneath the rubbish already in the bin. Now, all I need is to find a strainer, and I'll be nearly finished.

Grabbing a paper towel from the holder on the counter, I remove my gardening gloves and place them atop the towel to avoid contaminating the counter with their poison. Then, I begin rummaging through the kitchen, searching for the netted tool.

Cabinet after cabinet, drawer after drawer—I leave no space unchecked. My urgency builds. It *has* to be here somewhere. I can't imagine this massive kitchen doesn't have a strainer.

My teeth clench as my search continues to come up empty. I've opened every drawer, every cabinet. I scan the kitchen again, unwilling to give up just yet. As I turn around one last time before admitting defeat, I notice the gleaming utensils sitting in the drainboard. Could it be?

I approach, hopeful. A few pots, some silverware. Lifting one of the larger pots to see what lies beneath, my heart leaps—there it is, the strainer I've been searching for.

I grab it, not tempering my movements in my excitement. Its metal rim clangs against the pot as I slip it out of the drainboard. I freeze. And wait. Listening. But nothing happens. I exhale in relief and relax.

Returning to the pantry, I fish the mountain laurel out of the water where it's been soaking. Feeling lighter on my feet now that I'm nearly done for the night, I turn to dispose of the remains in the rubbish bin.

And almost trip over my own feet.

Because a figure fills the doorway.

I've been caught.

Chapter 20

BRIE

I don't move. I don't make excuses. I just stand, with my feet rooted to the ground, and stare at the figure in the doorway. For her part, Dee stares back at me, cataloging my features, my stance, and the supplies on the floor behind me.

I lick my lips, my mouth dry with apprehension. "Dee, hi. Did I wake you?"

She gives a noncommittal hum, her eyes still taking in the scene. "What are you doing in here?"

I glance past her toward the kitchen door, weighing my options. I could be honest and risk her exposing my plans to Lucifer. I could try to run past her and flee the castle now—not ideal, and I'm far from prepared, but it's still an option. How viable that option is, though, is another matter entirely. I could also lie, invent an excuse. But what would I even say?

Dee has been kind to me since I arrived. She's seemed to be on my side—a true friend. Shouldn't I treat her as such? If she really is a friend, I can trust her. She has to understand.

"Dee, I need to go home. I need to get back to one of the higher planes. I don't belong here. This isn't my home, and...the darkness, I think it's corrupting me. I don't know who I am anymore. I'm doing things I never would have even considered before coming to Hell. Being here is affecting me, and I'm scared. I'm terrified of who I'll become. Some days, I feel like a completely different person. A person I don't like. I can't stay here. I won't."

Dee gazes at the wilted mountain laurel in the strainer I'm holding, but her face remains unchanged, her expression unreadable. "So, you're planning to do what? Drug Lucifer and run?"

"Yes." There's nothing more to say. That's exactly what I'm planning to do, and I'm not going to lie about it. I just have to pray she won't betray me.

"I see," she says stiffly, and I wait, saying nothing more. "Well, I guess I understand why you want to leave. And you're right—you don't belong here. I can't say I'm happy about what you're planning, but I won't stand in your way. You're a sweet girl. You deserve to be free. What do you have so far?"

I breathe a sigh of relief and explain what I've prepared. Dumping the wet flower remains into the rubbish bin, I hide them once again beneath its prior contents and wash the strainer as thoroughly as possible. Dee watches everything in silence, neither objecting nor interfering.

I turn to her, wavering on how involved I can ask her to be. "I was hoping to find a few syringes. Two would be best. Do you know if the castle has any, and where they might be?"

Dee's eyes shift to the side, and I can see her debating whether she wants to help me or not. After a moment, she looks back, her shoulders slumping. "Yes, we have a few in the emergency medical kit. I'll get them for you." And with that, Dee sweeps out of the room.

While I wait, I pull several bottles of water from the pantry. Dee returns after a few minutes with two syringes in hand. I can't stop the smile that spreads across my face when she hands them to me.

"Thank you," I tell her, genuinely meaning it. I feel so lucky to have met someone in Hell who is on my side. I will never forget her help in this, and somehow, I will find a way to repay her for it.

I pop the cover off of the first needle and stick the tip into one of the water bottles, keeping the seal of the bottle intact so it won't be apparent it was messed with. I suck the clean water into the syringe until it is about half full. Then, I pop off the cover of the second needle and place that one into the poisoned water I prepared. I suck up about the same amount of contaminated water as I did fresh water. Locating the hole from the first needle, I slide the second needle through the small opening and depress the plunger.

I dump the extracted fresh water in the sink and repeat the process until all the bottles I pulled out have been befouled. I'm counting on the poison building up in Lucifer's body so that I have a few more days to prepare before it affects him. I've only chosen substances that will cause paralysis and unconsciousness, nothing that should kill him. The other two vials are for the guards.

"What else do you have in your plan?" Dee asks as I dump the rest of the contaminated water and thoroughly wash the bowl it was in. I tell her about the nectar from the spider flowers and the sap from the blinding tree, but when I finish, she frowns.

"That's it? That might get you out of the castle, but what will you do once you reach the ninth circle? You'll need to travel through all the circles to reach the astral plane, and you don't even plan to have a weapon with you."

Dee shakes her head. "Oh, dear, you're going to need a better plan than that. Let's return your gardening supplies to the conservatory, and then we'll talk. Dawn will break soon, and you'll want to be back in your room before then."

I nod, finishing my cleanup and retrieving my basket from the pantry along with my gloves from the counter.

As I turn away from the counter and head toward the door, Dee holds out a hand to stop me. "Best you grab a few knives while we're here."

I gape at her. Did she really just say that? Yes, yes, she did. Dazed, I make my way over to the drawer where I saw knives during my rummaging, pulling a few out. I wrap them in a dish towel and carefully place them inside my basket with my other supplies.

We walk up to the greenhouse in silence, and I return my supplies, keeping the knives and poisons with me. As soon as we enter my room and I hear the click of the door latching behind us, I whirl on Dee, brandishing the wrapped bundle of knives. "Knives? Really?" I hiss.

She shrugs. "You'll need weapons if you're going to make it through the circles alive."

I immediately deflate. She's right, and I'm foolish for not thinking of that sooner. I'm not exactly a criminal mastermind, but taking some knives from the kitchen should have been one of the first steps in my plan. The fact that I didn't think of it shows just how woefully unprepared I am.

I grimace at my own stupidity. "Dee, I think I need your help."

"Yes, you do," she replies, sounding resigned. "First, we need to hide the knives and poisons you're taking with you outside the castle. You should be able to get outside without a problem while the staff panic over Lucifer, but you might not have time to come up to your room to get them. They need to be someplace along your exit route so you can grab them on your way out."

"Maybe in one of the flowerpots?"

"Yes, we can bury them beneath the soil. Not too deep, though—you should be able to dig them out easily with only your hands. Once you make it into the ninth circle, we can meet up. I can take you through the Gate to my home in the eighth circle and give you more supplies, but from there, you'll be on your own."

My chest warms, and I throw my arms around Dee. "Thank you, Dee. Thank you so much." I step back quickly, giving her space after my outburst. "You're a good friend. I won't forget this."

Dee smiles at me fondly, but I catch a flicker of red in her eyes again. Is it my imagination? It's probably just a trick of the light. Dee squeezes my hand, jerking me out of my thoughts.

"You're welcome, dear. I'm happy to help." Her smile widens, becoming more toothy.

A shiver of unease passes through me, but I shake it off. I'm sure it's just nerves to be moving forward in my escape plans. Dee has been so helpful, and for the first time since I started planning, I feel like this could actually work. I might get out of here after all.

"Well," Dee says, "we have a lot to prepare in the coming nights, but for now, dawn is breaking. You should get a few hours' sleep before we ready you for the day. This will only work if Lucifer doesn't suspect anything out of the ordinary is going on."

"Of course, you're right. I can't show up to breakfast with huge bags under my eyes. He's too astute to miss something like that."

"That he is," Dee agrees. "Now that his mind is healing, he doesn't miss much."

"Do you think I'm doing the right thing?" I ask hesitantly, "I think my light that has been helping his lucidity. Is it a mistake to leave when I could continue helping him?"

"Could you continue helping him though? You said earlier that the darkness is affecting you. How long will it be before the darkness overtakes you? And what happens then? Then, you'll both be lost to the darkness. I understand why Lucifer brought you here, but if you're losing your light by staying here, there's no point in keeping you here. Lucifer cares about you too much to admit this to himself, but eventually, he'll understand that holding you here is pointless. Yes, he's regaining his reason in the short term, but in the long term..." she drifts off, but she's made her point.

Eventually, I won't have any light left to give him, and he'll return to the state he was in before I arrived. Permanently losing my light isn't worth temporarily restoring a portion of his. This captivity is only causing me harm.

But maybe I should wait a bit longer before slipping the poisoned water and the tainted rosemary into his meals. Maybe I should give him just a little more time.

Chapter 21

MICHAEL

Kemuel is dead. His soul will never return. I've lost friends in battle before, but this—this death is different. Senseless. If Lucifer hadn't laid his trap for Brie, we wouldn't have come to Hell in the first place. And Kemuel would still be alive.

I knew this journey would be perilous. I warned the others before we left, giving them the option to stay behind in Heaven. But all of these angels are loyal and selfless. They risked themselves for Brie, knowing they might not return. We all set out with that knowledge. But *knowing* we might not all return and *living* that reality are two very different things.

Now, it's real. He's gone. He'll never return. And when I go back, I'll have to tell Erelah that her soulmate is never coming home. That he sacrificed himself for Brie. I can't let that sacrifice be in vain.

In a daze, I turn away from the thick slab of ice concealing the location of Kemuel's demise and stumble my way toward the Gate. It's only steps away. Just a few more minutes, and Kemuel could have made it safely through. But he didn't. That's not what happened. He didn't reach safety.

I trip through the Gate, unaware if the others are following. My hands shake as I desperately try to strip off my cold-weather gear in the overwhelming heat I've crossed into. I fumble with the zipper of my thick jacket, finally managing to grasp it and jerk it down, sloughing off the coat and abandoning it on the hot sand.

My lips tremble, and I struggle to breathe in the scorching air of the fourth circle as I step out of the insulated cold-weather pants. Now wearing only the warm-weather layers I had on beneath the cold-weather gear, the heat is slightly more bearable. But the pain in my chest is not. That pain hasn't changed, and there's nothing I can shed to make it easier to endure. The pain of Kemuel's death will live within me forevermore.

Only now do I notice that the soles of my boots are sizzling and smoking against the scorching sand. I look up and see that the rest of my team did, indeed, follow me through the Gate. Vacant eyes and slack faces meet my gaze when I finally have enough presence of mind to take them in. Struggling against the weight pressing on my chest, I manage to choke out, "We need to move before our shoes melt."

No one responds. No sounds of acknowledgment or nods of acceptance. Just silence—silence, heat, heaviness, and pain.

I take the silence as agreement and start trudging forward, away from the Gate. I trust that the others will follow, though I lack the awareness to check. The heat presses down on my already weak limbs, but I keep moving. We need to find shade and shelter as quickly as possible if we want to survive. It's too late for Kemuel, but I still have the others to protect, and I'll be damned if I lose anyone else.

Sweat streams down my back as I plod through the loose sand of Greed's desert. I vaguely note the mummified corpses scattered across the open landscape as we pass them. There are so many, and as the sun blazes down on us, I fear we might end up among them.

My strength wanes in the unbearable heat. Each step is a gargantuan effort, and my forward motion is driven by sheer will alone. The air is suffocatingly thick, and my breaths come in heaving gasps. But still, I move forward.

The soles of my boots sizzle and smoke, wearing thinner and thinner as the scorching sand melts them away. Ahead, the steep, sunbaked slopes of rock promise relief. I can see the shadows they cast, offering a reprieve from the blistering glare of the sun. Though the rock above crumbles in waves, the danger of falling debris is eclipsed by my desperate need for shade.

I barely reach the shadowed area before collapsing face-first into the ground. Sand coats my eyelashes, and jagged rocks cut into my skin through the balaclava, but the brief rest provides a much-needed recharge. Rolling onto my back, I pull down the balaclava to free my mouth and take a few sips from my hydration pack.

"We need to dig a few inches into the sand, then we can set up one of the tents to rest until the heat diminishes."

My team moves sluggishly, but they follow the order. Each of us scoops sand to the side, forming a square roughly the size of our tent. Once the tent is erected, we set up our handheld misting fans inside to cool it further and crawl in.

It's clear we're all still in shock from Kemuel's loss. I don't know what to say or do. They're my team, and I'm supposed to lead them. But in this instance, there's nothing I can do or say to make things better. So, I stay silent.

I let my friends—my found family—stew in their thoughts while I do the same. I wish things had gone differently. There's so much I want to say to him, words I'll never get the chance to speak. Amidst the fond memories and longing for more time, there's the sharp sting of guilt. I was the reason he was here. I brought him on this mission. I should have done more—tried harder to protect him. I should have taken the rear instead of him.

So many *should haves.* Would any of them have made a difference?

I wipe my eyes quickly, swiping away the dampness before anyone notices. I fix my face into a mask of strength, even though I feel anything but. I can't show how I'm really feeling—can't show weakness. That's not my role here. My role is to lead, and to do that, I must be strong. I shove my feelings aside, compartmentalizing my remorse and boxing it away in my mind. But the doubts linger, whispering faintly: *Should you even be leading at all?*

Even with the fans, the interior of the tent is stuffy and oppressive. The heat is muted but still manages to seep in and smother us. Small stones plunk and clink against the tent's top as the rocks above slowly crumble into pebbles. My nostrils burn from the dryness as I struggle to draw each heavy breath, unable to fully relax in such conditions.

I take another gulp of water, savoring the brief relief as it soothes my parched mouth and throat. At the same time, I remind myself not to drink too much. Water is scarce in this circle, and I need to ration what little I have left.

I watch as the light dims ever so slowly and the air begins to cool. Nightfall is closing in, and soon, we'll need to move again.

Just as the thought crosses my mind, a raucous howl cuts through the light conversation of my comrades. I still, instantly recognizing that the animal responsible for the noise is far closer to our tent than I'd prefer. I don't fully grasp just how close until claws rip through the sturdy fabric of our shelter. My head snaps to the left, where four long slashes mar the tent's wall, and eerie yellow eyes peer through the openings.

Adrenaline surges through my body as my fight-or-flight response kicks in. "We need to get out of here. We'll be sitting ducks if we stay. Leave the tent—anything not on your person stays here. Go. Now."

I lead the team out, brandishing my sword in the direction of the threat. But in my distraction, I fail to notice that the monster tearing into the tent isn't a lone predator. Claws rake down my back, and I gasp at the searing pain. I swing around blindly, the agony clouding my senses, but my blade finds its mark regardless, ripping into the attacker. As my vision sharpens, I see the beast recoil.

Taking quick stock of the situation, I count five hyena-like creatures prowling around the tent. "Form a circle. Aim to kill," I order.

The team complies, moving cautiously, their weapons poised. We inch forward amidst the predators, swiping at any that lunge too close. The creatures snarl and howl in frustration, circling us with predatory intent. But eventually, they seem to decide we're not worth the effort and lope away, retreating into the shadows.

I inhale deeply, willing the adrenaline coursing through my veins to subside. My heartbeat thunders in my chest, but as the predators vanish into the distance, it begins to slow.

We were lucky they chose to retreat, but I know our luck won't hold for much longer. The sinking feeling in my stomach and the prickling at the nape of my neck tell me what I already fear: Greed is too treacherous to traverse unscathed.

Something will come for us. It's just a matter of time.

Chapter 22

MICHAEL

The air around us cools further as dusk gives way to darkness. Sand dunes loom on either side of us, shadowed smudges against the clear night sky. We trek through the loose sand. My boots sink downward with each step I take. Animals and monsters chitter, caw, and roar, and my head is on a swivel as I watch for any one of them to jump at us from the concealment the towering dunes provide.

We walk for what seems like hours. My feet ache and my mouth is parched. I ran out of water a while ago, but still, I walk. And walk. I pine for water. Wish for it. Beg for it.

The sand becomes harder and easier to walk on just as dizziness overtakes me. I stumble but manage to catch myself. A pulsing headache starts in my temple and I press my hand to the area. The pressure provides no relief. I need water or soon I will collapse.

The dunes diminish and the night sky lightens as we walk further. We haven't been attacked by the circle's inhabitants since we fled the tent, but I know I'm no longer in any shape to fend off an attack should one occur. I see a dark shape in the distance. I squint at it. It looks like it might be a depression in the thickly packed sand. Could we be fortunate enough to have found a water hole?

Other dark shapes rise in the distance, and I realize the terrain is changing. Quickening my pace, I feel the anticipation build. Dawn arrives, and the excitement in the air is palpable as we all stumble toward the depression ahead. My toes drag against the ground, and I worry I might fall, but the promise of water pushes me forward. It's all I can think about, consuming my thoughts, and the idea alone makes my tongue dart out to lick my cracked lips.

Ariella rushes past me, the first to reach the water hole. I watch her collapse to her knees at the edge of the depression. She looks out across the barren expanse before her, and then her head falls into her hands. A guttural, inhuman cry of frustration and anguish escapes her lips. No words, just raw despair that I can feel deep in my bones.

That's when I see it: the water hole is dry.

I drag my heavy legs forward, focusing on one step at a time as the hard-packed sand gives way to cracked dirt. This circle feels like the epitome of Hell, and the journey through it feels much longer than that of the others. I intend to crouch beside Ariella's sunken form, but my coordination is long gone. Instead, I crash down onto my knees, the impact jarring my bones and making my teeth clack together.

"We'll figure it out. We'll find water somewhere. I promise." I mean for the words to sound strong, but my mouth is so dry they come out as a scratchy whisper. Ariella turns her tear-streaked face toward me, her gaze running over my cracked and sunburned features. She grimaces but nods.

I gently grip her arm, and together we rise from the ground. "Let's keep going." The words feel like razor blades scraping against my throat, but I force my feet to propel me forward. I've lost all feeling in my legs; the searing pain in my throat and the desperate need for hydration drowning out all other sensations. I stumble over the lip of the playa, swaying side to side, but I press on.

On the far side of the basin, cacti dot the barren landscape, and a surge of hope lifts my spirits. My steps grow more purposeful as I push toward the nearest cactus. One moment I'm trudging forward, and in the next blink, I'm standing in front of it. Did I black out while walking? Or am I hallucinating?

Shaking off the doubt, I drop my pack and fumble with the side zipper, finally tearing it open to retrieve my spile. I clutch it like it's the most precious thing in all the planes. The cactus towers above me, its long, sharp spines a clear warning to stay away. But I'm desperate, and desperate beings do desperate things.

Ignoring the sharp spines, I shove the spile into the cactus. The spines pierce my hand and arm, but the dull pain is nothing compared to the sharp, unrelenting need of my dehydration.

The spile sinks into the cactus's thick, fleshy stem, and a slow trickle of water begins to flow out. Raphael lets out a jubilant "whoop," and my teammates crowd around me. Grabbing a water bladder from someone, I hold it beneath the spile as the glorious water drips into it.

The bladder swells as the water pools inside. I pull it away and hand it to Ariella first. She takes a long, greedy sip before passing it on. It trades hands several times, making its way through the group, before I return to refill it.

The relief I feel as I finally take my own sips is profound, almost overwhelming.

But then, out of the corner of my eye, I notice Ariella stumbling away from us. Her hand presses against her stomach, her eyes wide and glassy, before she doubles over and heaves. The water she just drank comes back up, dampening the dry soil and splashing against her boots. She heaves again, more water leaving her body and sinking into the ground at her feet. She tries to speak, but it just ends in more regurgitation.

My attention is pulled away from her by a gurgling sound to my left. I turn slowly, dread pooling in my stomach. Callie is on her knees, a circle of moistened soil in front of her. "Oh no," Gabriel rasps behind me, and then he's stumbling away too. My eyes widen and a pit opens up in my chest.

My own stomach begins to churn, and I pull away from the cactus, trying to gain distance from the others. I cough a few times, closing my eyes and focusing on my breathing. Raphael is the only one among us seemingly unaffected. His healing ability must be neutralizing the toxicity of the water. He rests a hand on Gabriel's back, green healing energy pouring out of him and flowing into my brother. Gabriel dry-heaves a few times but doesn't vomit like the others.

My stomach flips and rolls, but my own self-healing seems to be strong enough to counteract the water's toxicity. Regaining a small measure of composure, I try to think of anything I can do to help my comrades. The additional dehydration could become the final nail in their coffins, and I can't lose anyone else. But no matter how strong my drive to help them, I know there's nothing I can do.

Once Gabriel is well enough to stand, he waves Raphael off, and the healer moves on to Haniel. Raphael heals Haniel, Callista, and Ariella just enough to stop their retching, but their dazed eyes and jerky movements show that the additional dehydration has taken its toll. We pair up, each helping the weaker members of our group to keep moving.

We weave our way across the desert, skirting the sparse cacti rising from the sunbaked dirt. No one dares to tap another cactus—we've learned that lesson. Ruins appear as blurred shapes in the distance, the air before them shimmering and wobbling in the oppressive heat. The sun is high in the sky, and we desperately need shade and shelter. The ruins might provide us with both. They could be our salvation.

Ariella leans heavily against me as I press on. Her movements are sluggish, her weight dragging against my side. But the thought of resting in the ruins lifts my mood. I don't have water to give her, but rest will be good for her. Good for all of us.

My thoughts are interrupted by a commotion behind me. Callista is shouting incoherently, then suddenly breaks into a stumbling run toward the ruins. Gabriel catches her around the waist before she gets too far. I make sure Ariella is steady on her feet.

"Can you stand without my help? I need to check on Callista." She nods slowly.

"But the lake!" Callista babbles. "Don't you see it? There are animals drinking, and the sparkling water looks so clean. I have to reach it. Aren't you thirsty? Why are you stopping me?"

I follow her pointing finger, but there's nothing there—just the same barren dirt we've been trudging through for hours and the ruins looming in the distance. No lake. No animals.

"And the palm trees!" Callista continues. "I could easily nap under one of those big branches! Why are you keeping me from it?"

"Yes! I see it. Water!" Ariella suddenly shouts.

I turn, only to see that she's been moving away from us this whole time, walking in the direction Callista was pointing. "Ariella, come back. It's a mirage. It's not real," I tell her patiently.

"It is!" she insists.

Heavens above, why is she choosing *this* moment to be stubborn? Ariella has never disobeyed a command before—never. But the dehydration and desperation must be fueling her actions. I start toward her. She's weak; catching up to her shouldn't be hard.

And it isn't. But just as I'm about to reach her, a hyena rises up from the dirt between us, its sandy brown fur perfectly camouflaged. Within milliseconds, the hyena transforms into a thin man with sunken eyes and pronounced cheek bones. His black irises cause a chill to creep up my spine, and I hesitate. The ghoul smiles at my hesitation, and I know I've made yet another mistake.

Quick as lightning, the ghoul scoops Ariella into his arms. He takes off with her into the ruins. I give chase, but he's too fast. He disappears within the ruins in seconds, and I force myself to stop and wait for the rest of my team. If this turns into a battle, I can't go it alone. But with each second that passes, I know that my chances of rescuing Ariella alive are dwindling. The cold fingers of despair creep up my limbs as I wait. I can't lose another one. I just can't.

Chapter 23

MICHAEL

I inch forward, my body crouched alongside a crumbling yellow wall. I scan the area ahead and motion to the right with two fingers. In my periphery, I see Raphael and Gabriel move in the direction of my signal. I raise my hand, clenched in a fist, and peer cautiously around the corner in both directions. Clear. Flattening my hand, I jerk it forward and sprint to the dilapidated wall of the next building.

A cacophony of laughing barks echoes through the ruins, flooding my ears and momentarily disorienting me. The reverberation confuses my senses for a heartbeat before dissipating. I run to the end of the wall, my boots soundless atop the loose dirt. Haniel follows close on my heels, adrenaline briefly overpowering his dehydration. I glance over my shoulder to confirm that Callista is keeping up, then refocus and push forward.

Noticing a window carved into the crumbling wall ahead, I signal the team to halt. Holding up three fingers, I silently count down. When my fist closes on zero, I vault through the window, rolling across the floor and springing to my feet with my sword drawn.

Another burst of mocking laughter taunts me as I scan the empty room. I plaster myself to the right of the only door in the hollowed-out space, with Haniel mirroring me on the left. Peering cautiously around the opening, I see no danger. Spinning around the door frame, I scan the narrow hallway beyond.

The passage is empty, with doorways at both ends. Soundlessly, I motion for Haniel and Callista to check the one at their end, then stalk toward the opening at mine.

I pause to steady my breathing, trying to tame the surge of adrenaline coursing through me. Then, I swing into the decaying space.

The blood drains from my face, and my heart pounds in my chest. It only takes me a fraction of a second to take in the scene before I'm jumping into action, sprinting toward the nearest ghoul and swinging my sword through its thick neck. Its head rolls across the dirt floor before the other seven ghouls, still in their hyena forms, even realize I'm in the room.

"Seven!" I choke out the alert through my rising bile, slashing my sword at another ghoul.

Ariella's lifeless body lies on the dirty floor, covered in bite marks, savagely torn open, and drained of blood. Some of her organs are sprawled on the floor around her, distinctive in their red hue.

The ghoul in front of me wants to play. It transforms, morphing from its hyena form into a perfect replica of Ariella. It's horrifying. I know it's not truly her because her broken body lies motionless before me, but the sight drives me to the brink of insanity.

My blood burns, my pulse thunders, and my vision narrows. The only thing I see is the ghoul wearing Ariella's face.

I lunge, jab, and swipe, but she's skilled and experienced. She evades every strike, a mocking smile twisting the stolen features of her face. Then she opens her mouth, and the hyena's barking laughter erupts from it, fueling my fury.

But with my anger comes recklessness.

I swing harder, faster—desperate to land a blow—but my rage makes me sloppy, and she exploits every opening with infuriating ease.

I briefly register that the others have entered the room and are engaged in battles of their own, but the thought merely flits across my consciousness before disappearing into the void created by my rage. The ghoul slides around me, her fingernails extending to claws. She steps closer and swipes at me. I swing my sword down, but it's a touch too slow. Her claws swipe deeply into my side. In the same moment, though, my sword makes contact with her wrist, the momentum of the swing strong enough to sever her hand. The claws rake down my leg as the hand falls to the ground. The ghoul wails, a desperate howl that sounds eerily incongruous coming out of a human mouth.

She snarls at me and doubles her efforts, lashing out at me with pure brutality. I parry, deflect, and counter. Sweat drips down my forehead and into my eyes, temporarily blinding me. I swipe it away, but the momentary handicap was enough for her to land another blow. My left knee buckles when her claws tear into the back of it. I lose my balance and topple onto the monster.

We grapple on the ground. I throw an elbow into her nose, finding a modicum of satisfaction when I hear the loud crack it causes. I seize the advantage it brings, wrapping my arm around her neck, but she's not giving in easily. Her fangs sink into my arm, forcing me to relax my grip. She rolls out of it completely and gnashes her teeth at my face. She might have bitten my nose off had I not grabbed a knife from my boot and stabbed her in the heart.

The ghoul's face slackens and Ariella's features disappear as it transforms back into its hyena form in death. I pull my knife out of the monster's chest and jump to my feet, taking stock of my teammates and gauging where my help would best be directed. Callista is holding her own in a one-on-one match. Raphael and Gabriel are once again fighting back-to-back, holding their ground against three ghouls and appearing close to defeating one. Haniel, however, is locked in a two-on-one battle and is clearly at a disadvantage.

I sprint to Haniel's aid, quickly dispatching one of the ghouls from behind before it realizes I'm there. Haniel exhales a puff of relief as I join him against the remaining ghoul. I signal for him to swipe low, and he swings his leg out, kicking the ghoul off its feet. As it teeters backward, I swipe my sword upward, severing its head cleanly from its neck. We both watch as its body crumbles to the ground.

Haniel nods his thanks before dashing to assist Callista in her fight. I do the same for Gabriel and Raphael. They instinctively make room for me to join their dance of blades. The three of us move as one—swiping, jabbing, blocking. To an outsider, it might appear as though we share one mind. Our coordination is seamless, our movements perfectly synchronized.

With the balance shifted in our advantage, it doesn't take long to dispatch the remaining ghouls. When the last one falls, silence fills the room. No one speaks as we slowly converge around Ariella's mangled body.

A sob escapes Callista, but she quickly covers her mouth with her arm, muffling the sound. Tears streak down her dirt-covered cheeks as Haniel moves closer, gently wrapping an arm around her shoulders in a quiet offer of comfort. Likewise, Raphael and Gabriel cling to each other, their faces etched with grief. And me? I'm alone.

I swipe a dirtied hand through my hair, struggling to stymie my own tears. Taking a deep breath, I kneel beside Ariella's broken form. Kemuel found peace in his last moments—the flash of light told me that. But Ariella's death was too gruesome, too brutal. It's up to me to bring her the peace she was denied.

I let my angelic energy flow into my fingertips and draw the rune for tranquility on Ariella's cheek, the only piece of her intact enough to hold it. The thought alone makes me ill. The rune lingers on her skin for a moment before sinking into her being. It travels through her mutilated form, expanding until it encompasses her completely. Then, in a flash of brilliant light, her body disappears.

The air shimmers and sparkles in her absence, and the weight on my chest doesn't feel quite so heavy anymore. Knowing she's found peace doesn't erase the pain of her loss, lessen how much I'll miss her, or relieve my guilt. But it does offer me a sliver of solace.

I stand numbly, staring at the spot on the floor where Ariella's body once lay. Time stretches, my senses dulled and my strength depleted. This mission has taken too much from us already. But we have to press on, or all we've lost will have been for nothing.

Taking two steadying breaths, I tear my gaze from the floor and look around at the rest of my team. Each and every one of them looks shattered. But they are fighters—all of them, even Callista. I know they will compartmentalize their pain, as we all must, to see this mission through.

"Gear up," I say softly, "We leave in two."

Raphael and Haniel both nod, acknowledging my words. Callista looks up at me with empty, glassy eyes and then returns her gaze to the ground. My brother says nothing, does nothing. Gabriel doesn't acknowledge my statement in the slightest, and I'm not sure if he's lost in his thoughts, convening with the divine spirit, or simply questioning why he didn't receive premonitions that could have prevented these losses. Raphael and I will need to talk to him, but now's not the time. Later. Always later.

A dull roaring sound breaks our silence, and I run to the entrance of the decrepit building to see where it's coming from. An enormous dust cloud consumes the desert, rolling toward us. "We need to go, *now*!" I yell.

The others pour out of the doorway, and we all start running through the ruins, in the direction of the Gate. It's not far. The dust cloud gains on us, battering everything in its path. We reach the Gate and I wave the others through before me. As soon as Raphael is through, I take the three steps needed to cross. The storm engulfs me as I make that last step. It's brutal and suffocating, and just before my body crosses the threshold of the Gate, a single distressing thought worms its way into my mind: *Is this how Kemuel felt while he was drowning?*

Chapter 24

BRIE

"I have a surprise for you, Brie."

Lucifer's soft purr startles me. He's barely spoken to me since our blowout. Though he still requires my presence during meals, our interactions have been reduced to him staring at me with an expression full of pain and regret, while I try to ignore his stare and eat as quickly as possible so I can be excused from the table sooner.

My guilt has become a constant companion, hovering over me like a dark cloud and prickling under my skin. Poisoning Lucifer feels like it could be the greatest mistake of my existence, but it's too late to undo what I've set in motion. He now disappears whenever we aren't in the dining room. His previously ever-present figure has been conspicuously absent, and that only adds to my guilt, knowing it's because I've hurt him.

"Does this version of you enjoy surprises?" His soft question interrupts my rumination. I raise my eyes, meeting his penetrating gaze for the first time since our fight.

"It depends on the surprise," I answer, noting that he didn't call me Sabriel but instead acknowledged that I'm not the angel he remembers. The swirling unease in my stomach intensifies, and I can't tell if it's from guilt or some deeper appreciation—or perhaps a mixture of both.

Lucifer's deep chuckle envelops me like a plush blanket, bringing with it an uncomfortable comfort that only adds to my turmoil. The sensations riot within me, my visceral reaction to him clashing with the logic of my conscious mind. I realize too late that my lips have curved into a faint smile. Quickly, I force my face to go blank before he notices.

I will not fall for Lucifer. I love Michael. Michael is my soulmate.

I repeat the words to myself several times, turning them into a much-needed mantra, and trying to ground myself. But then a brush of warm air against the helix of my ear sends a shiver rolling down my spine.

"Where did you go?" Lucifer whispers, his breath stirring the wisps of hair on my temple.

I was so focused on repelling the sensations he causes within my body, I didn't even notice him rise from his chair—let alone circle the table.

His hands settle on my exposed shoulders, their warmth searing into my cool skin. I try to sit as still as possible, but fail terribly, as another shiver races up my spine as he leans closer, his nose brushing against the sensitive edge of my ear. His slow inhale resonates in my ears, and I close my eyes, straining to keep myself in check.

Lucifer's fingers gently squeeze my shoulders before he straightens and steps back. I exhale shakily before sucking in the cooler air of the room, desperate to rid myself of the lingering whiskey and campfire scent that clings to him. Rising to my feet, I ask, "So, what is this surprise?"

Lucifer beckons for me to follow him, leading me down the spiral staircase and into the throne room.

It's the first time I've entered the throne room since arriving in Hell, and the flashback descends on me like a hurricane. I see myself on the smooth stone floor, tears streaming down my face, the pain of my loss cracking a hole in the middle of my chest.

A firm grip on the back of my neck pulls me from the memory. Lucifer's face hovers inches from mine, his thumb gently tilting my chin up. His touch is gentle, his voice soft as he whispers, "Stay with me."

His breath brushes over my lips in a feather-light caress, anchoring me to the present. His green eyes bore into mine, seeming to delve into the deepest recesses of my soul. His face looms closer, the small distance between us closing ever so slowly.

I blink, severing the connection, and take a deliberate step back.

"I'm here. We can continue," I say, the words barely making it through my thick throat. Lucifer stares at me for a second more before turning away from me. My whole body sags, as though I were a puppet whose strings were cut. I didn't even realize how tense I was until that tension was released. What is happening to me?

While I'm trying to pull myself back together and combating a mini mental breakdown, Lucifer strides to his throne and presses a button on one of its arms. A few feet in front of the throne, a square portion of the floor splits in half, revealing a gaping hole with stairs leading downward. Lucifer glances at me, gauging my reaction, and I quickly close my mouth, embarrassed at my slack-jawed expression.

He motions for me to descend the stairs ahead of him, and I comply—until I see the rows of cells at the bottom. Panic floods me, and the hallway ahead blinks in and out of focus. Is this a punishment? Is Lucifer going to lock me up?

Spinning around, I prepare to flee, but he's already there. His arms reach out, hands settling on my arms, holding me in place.

My panic spikes into full-blown terror. Spots dance in my vision, and my body locks. I can't move, can't even blink. My breaths come in short, shallow gasps, pulling in too little air. Lucifer pulls me against him, pressing my body to his and rubbing a hand up and down my back in slow, soothing motions.

"Shhh, you're fine. You're okay. Nothing is going to hurt you. I'm here. Nothing will hurt you. I will always protect you. You're fine. You're okay."

How can he say that? He's about to lock me up, and he's telling me I'm fine? My panic spirals as the last remnants of rationality flee my mind. *This is it.* He must know about my plan—this is my punishment. My eyes begin to water, but before the tears can fall, another voice sounds from deeper within the space.

"Hello? Who's there?"

My body stops shaking, going deathly still. That voice—I know that voice. It taunts me in both my memories and my nightmares. It haunts me. I hear it saying, "Bri-ennnnna" with all of its smarmy confidence, followed by the emotionless words, "You're too late," and the deafening bang of a gunshot.

Every night it replays. Every night I relive Callie's death. And every morning, I wake up drowning in the regret of being unable to save her.

I tilt my head up at Lucifer, my mind racing. During our fight, I accused him of being responsible for Callie's death. Is this...? I study his face. Is this his way of apologizing to me?

His lush lips curve into a smile as he looks down at me with fondness. He gives a subtle nod and whispers, "Your gift."

A slow, shuddering breath escapes me as I step out of his comforting embrace. Turning, I walk down the dim hallway, dread pooling in my stomach. I follow the voice until I reach the cell that's occupied. The dungeon is dank and foul, with a dirt floor. Inside the cell stands Chad, his fingers holding the bars in a white-knuckled grip.

I feel Lucifer's presence behind me, close enough to sense but not touching.

Trepidation is written across Chad's face as his gaze flickers between me and Lucifer. There's no recognition in his eyes when he looks at me. I remind myself: *I look like Sabriel now, not Brienna.*

But Chad must realize who Lucifer is. His body shakes as he releases the bars and sinks to one knee, bowing his head. His voice quakes as he says, "My King, I am but your loyal servant. Everything I have done has been for you. Have you come to reward my loyalty?"

Lucifer's body crowds me from behind and one of his hands snakes over my stomach. The other pulls lightly on my French braid, tilting my head up toward his. He looks down at me with so much devotion, it makes my body tremble. "When you were Sabriel, you loved dealing out vengeance to those who deserved it. Tell me, my darling Brie, when this rat murdered your friend, did you vow to hunt him down? Did you tell him that you would enjoy exacting a price for his actions?"

"I did," I whisper, my eyes locked on Lucifer's. His responding smile is blinding, and for a moment, I forget myself. I allow my body to sink into his, enthralled.

"Brie? What...that's not...no." Chad's whining disbelief breaks the moment and I turn my gaze to him, narrowing my eyes.

"Hello, Chad. Remember me? Bri-ennnnna." I mimic the disgusting way he used to butcher my name. "I look a little different now, but it's me. And I sure as Hell remember you. Aren't you glad you ensured I would remember your name?"

His eyes widen as his gaze continues to ping-pong between Lucifer and me. "Your Majesty," Chad starts, but Lucifer cuts him off with a raised hand. Shadows escape his palm and wrap around Chad's mouth, silencing any further attempts at pacification. I watch Lucifer's dark energy with fascination. He doesn't use it much. But there's something so beguiling about it. Addicting. Like soft velvet whispering over sensitive skin, you can't help but relish in the feel of it—and want more.

The shadows continue to seep from Lucifer's palm. Some circle around Chad's wrists, others around his ankles, holding him in place. Pulling a key from his pocket, Lucifer unlocks Chad's cell and stalks inside.

Humming sounds from the stairs and I hear the snick of a door opening. I look in the direction of the noise just as Boagdan appears, wheeling a cart. The metal rattles as the wheels catch on small pebbles in the dirt floor.

Boagdan gives me a respectful smile and nod as he passes me, pushing the cart into Chad's cell before retreating back up the staircase. I eye the cart as Lucifer removes the towel covering it to reveal a plethora of metal implements. Scalpels, pincers, pliers, and spiked batons of various sizes lay in perfect order, waiting to be used.

I look up at Lucifer, who's watching my reaction intently. Then, I look at Chad, who is struggling against the darkness binding his limbs. I expect my stomach to roll, bile to creep up my throat. I expect to be repulsed and sickened by the prospect of Chad's torture. But I'm not. I'm hungry for it. I *want* to see him punished. I want him to pay for murdering my best friend. I feel the expression of resolve creeping across my face: the pinch of my lips, the narrowing of my eyes. I shift my gaze back to Lucifer, knowing there's no coming back from this, and nod. It's time for Chad to meet his retribution.

Chapter 25

BRIE

I watch dispassionately as Lucifer pulls the last of Chad's fingernails from his body. He jerks from the pain, but stopped fighting against the torture about an hour ago. Though his body sags in his bindings, his eyes are still alert, and he is feeling every ounce of pain Lucifer is dealing out.

I know I should be intervening, that if my soul were still filled with light, I wouldn't be feeling satisfaction as I watch Lucifer drive a screw through Chad's kneecap. But I don't intervene, and I do feel satisfaction as I watch Lucifer's artistry. It tells me that there is no longer any doubt as to whether the darkness pervading Hell has seeped into my soul during my time here. And I should care. I should be devastated by that realization. But I'm not. And *that's* what bothers me.

Chad passes out from the pain again. This is the fourth time he's lost consciousness since Lucifer started working on him. Lucifer wipes his hands on a towel and approaches me, his eyes wary. "I think that's enough for one day."

"I agree." I say, my voice startlingly emotionless.

"How are you feeling about all of this?" Lucifer asks me hesitantly.

I shake my head, then look him directly in the eye. "I feel that he's getting what he deserves."

Lucifer's hesitance fades away and he smiles softly at me. We exit the cell, Lucifer pushing the cart ahead of us and leaving it in the hallway, out of Chad's reach. He locks Chad's cell and slips the key back into his pocket. I lead the way out of the dungeon.

There's no wobble in my step or uncertainty in my mind as I leave Chad to suffer in pain. I don't look back or second-guess leaving him there to rot. I simply leave, not knowing how long Lucifer will keep him down there—and not caring.

"I think I'll spend some time in the library. Would you like to join me?" I offer, extending an olive branch.

Lucifer gifts me another of his blinding smiles. "I would love to. Just let me get cleaned up first. I don't want any remnants of that rat tainting your presence."

My heart flutters, and I chastise myself for it. *That should not be giving me the warm fuzzies.*

I make my way to Lucifer's private library and curl up in the reading nook that's quickly become my favorite spot in the castle. I don't bring a book with me; I just want to stare out the window and think for a bit.

Michael's voice echoes in my mind as I lean back into the nook's soft pillows: *"You always were one for righteous vengeance."* He said that to me during my first flying lesson, and it's stuck with me ever since.

I felt it when Chad murdered Callie and I threatened to hunt him down. My own words replay in my mind: *"I will kill you *slowly and painfully, and you will beg me to show you mercy, but I will not! You will beg for Hell when I get my hands on you!"*

I meant every word. I meant them with every fiber of my being. And my soul was light. Uncorrupted.

Is it possible that I'm just paranoid about the darkness influencing me, and what I'm feeling is the righteous vengeance my soul has craved all along? But it feels like Lucifer took it further than I would have. I don't know. I wish I did. Without my memories of the old Sabriel, I just don't know. Surely an angel wouldn't feel satisfaction at such brutality—would they?

Lucifer quietly enters the library and sinks into the brown leather armchair he typically occupies. He holds a glass of whiskey loosely in one hand, occasionally sipping the amber liquid. The rich scent wafts over to me, reminding me of him. It comforts me, and I relax further into the pillows.

I'm questioning everything right now. I know I'm darker now than I was, but I can't tell if it's truly me or the darkness influencing me. Does it even matter? Either way, my soul is darker. The question is: *How dark?*

Can I be redeemed, or am I too far gone? Would I even want to be redeemed? What I'm doing now feels...right. Maybe this is who I was always meant to be.

I told Lucifer I don't belong here, but I don't know if I belong in Heaven either. Maybe it wouldn't be so bad if I stayed.

My gaze drifts back to Lucifer. He's holding Gabriel García Márquez's *One Hundred Years of Solitude* loosely in one hand, lazily sipping his whiskey as he reads. Warmth blooms in my chest at the sight, but my mind is quick to remind me that I belong to another.

I sigh and look away from Lucifer, directing my attention inward. I focus on my angelic energy, feeling how it flows throughout my body and pools in my chest. There's a little string of energy that seems to extend outside of my body. I didn't feel it or notice it until I came to Hell, but since I did, it's seemed to be getting looser and looser. As if whatever it connects to was initially far away, pulling it taut, but has since been getting closer, allowing the string to slacken.

I know in my heart that Michael is on the other end of it, and as it gets looser and looser, I know that it means Michael is coming for me. Knowing that he's coming for me should give me joy and relief, but instead, it fills me with dread. I dread what he will find when he arrives—*who* he will find when he arrives. Because I'm not the same Brie who sacrificed herself to seal the last Hell Gate. And I'm certainly not the same Sabriel he fell in love with.

I glance at Lucifer again. Lucifer knows I'm not the same Sabriel, and everything he's done today has shown me he accepts that. He accepts who I am now. Would it really be so bad to stay with someone who respects you enough to show you that kind of acceptance? Surely not. Maybe I could tell Dee that we should cancel the escape plan. Lucifer would never need to know about it.

I watch him take another sip of his whiskey, focusing in on the hand that holds the glass. There's not a single piece of evidence indicating that he was torturing Chad just minutes ago. Why doesn't that bother me?

I sigh, more loudly than intended, and Lucifer looks up. "What's wrong?" he asks, closing his book and placing his glass on the table beside him, giving me his entire attention.

"Do you think I'm turning dark?"

His eyes flash, and his lips curve downward. "You haven't had any flares of pain in a while, so your soul has consumed enough darkness to metabolize it. But you're still my light, Brie. You haven't fallen yet, if that's what you're asking."

Fallen. I haven't even thought about it in those terms—I still forget my soul is angelic. I still feel human.

"I can tell something's bothering you. Is that what you're worried about? Being like me?" The sadness in Lucifer's tone shocks me. He's showing so much vulnerability right now, and all I want to do is comfort him. I want to hold him in my arms and kiss his pain away.

My eyes widen as I wrap my arms tightly around myself to keep from doing something stupid. I have a soulmate—one I love. Why am I having these thoughts?

"I like who you are," I whisper to Lucifer. His eyes smolder at my words. "I think there's something I need to do. Can I have the key to Chad's cell?"

Lucifer stands, pulling the key from his pocket. I meet him in the center of the room, my fingertips brushing lightly against his palm as I take the key. Without a word, I make my way to the throne room, finding the button that opens the door to the dungeon. Lucifer follows silently, his acceptance of my actions unspoken but deeply appreciated.

When we reach Chad's cell, he's awake and moaning on the floor. I grab a dagger from the torture cart and unlock the cell. My feet are silent as I approach the crumpled man, too far gone in his pain to notice me. I kick him forcefully, throwing him onto his back. Tears leak from his tightly shut eyes, and the stench of urine fills the air.

"Please, no more. Please, please. No more," Chad begs.

I crouch beside the sniveling man, careful not to touch his trembling form. "I told you that you would beg," I whisper, and his eyes snap open, wide with terror. "Do you regret your actions now?" I ask softly.

"Yes! Yes," he whimpers.

"Good. Then justice has been served."

I plunge the dagger into his chest. His body disintegrates into wisps of darkness, and the dagger clatters to the ground. Picking it up, I study its intricate detailing, marveling at its beauty.

And feeling no regret whatsoever.

Chapter 26

MICHAEL

Rain falls in sheets around me as I step out of the gate into Wrath, the fifth circle of Hell. I open my mouth, close my eyes, and tilt my head toward the cloudy sky, gulping down mouthfuls of the warm liquid as large raindrops beat down on my face. Water. Glorious water. I've never been so happy for rain before. After our long trek through the desert, this is exactly what we need.

Thunder booms above us as we bask in the blessed rainfall, minutes slipping by unnoticed. The forest is dark, and the raindrops slide off the leaves above, meeting our open mouths. My body hungers for more as I finally close my lips and glance around. It was foolish to let my guard down, but the lure of water after such intense thirst was too powerful to resist.

My lapse in judgment proves costly. When I finally scan our surroundings, my vision is swamped by a deluge—a muddy torrent rushing toward us. The flash flood surges forward, a chaotic wave dragging tree branches, rocks, and dead plant matter along with it. If the wave didn't hold such a distinctive form, I might not even recognize it as water with so much debris atop the surface.

A natural path has formed among the trees, leading away from the gate and providing the flood with an easy route to travel. We need to get off the worn forest floor to stay safe. "Angels, head into the thicket as fast as you can! Get as far from the footpath as possible. Go. Now!"

Desperation and alarm are thick in my voice, spurring my team into action. Once I'm certain they've heeded my order, I lunge into the dense undergrowth. Vines snag my limbs, and fronds scratch my skin as I fight my way through. To my right, I glimpse Raphael and Gabriel dodging tree trunks and leaping over roots, the floodwater creeping closer with every step.

The wave hits suddenly, slamming into my legs with a force that knocks me off balance. I stumble and fall into the rushing water. Sticks scratch at my skin, and the undertow pulls hard, threatening to drag me away. Desperately, I grab onto a tree trunk, wrapping my arms around its smooth bark. My legs are swept by the water's force, but I hold tight, clinging with every ounce of strength I've honed over the many years of my existence.

I press my forehead against the unyielding tree, silently praying that we can make it through this circle without any more losses. I still haven't processed Ariella's death, and I won't be able to while we're immersed in danger such as this, but I know it's affecting me regardless. I focus on my breathing as I wait out the flood—one breath in, one breath out, one breath in, one breath out.

It does little to calm me. I'm hyperaware of the rain as it pelts my skin, and the pull on my legs as the flood claws at me. As the roar of the water begins to quiet, my emotions surge in its wake. Tears slip from my eyes, mingling with the rain streaking down my face. It's a rare moment of privacy to let my weakness show, hidden by the storm.

When the drag of the water lessens, I relax my grip on the tree and test my footing in the waist-high muddy pool. The undertow swirls faintly, but it's no longer strong enough to pull me away. I wade in the direction I last saw Raphael and Gabriel, forcing myself to tuck my emotions back into mental box where they belong and replacing them with the iron determination I need to keep moving.

I find Raphael and Gabriel just as Callista and Haniel come into view. My team appears unharmed, easing the constant worry gnawing at the back of my mind. Together, we slog through the murky water, heading toward the upward slope of a hill.

I can't wait to escape this water. Not only are we wading through debris, but I have no idea what may be lurking in the water's depths and that makes me very uneasy.

My feet are soaked inside my boots, water sloshing with every step. I'm thankful my pack is waterproof, and I have a dry change of clothes inside, but I didn't pack a second pair of boots. Unless I find a way to dry them, I'll have to endure wet boots and the blisters they'll inevitably cause. They'd heal quickly with my angelic energy, but it's still a discomfort I'd rather avoid.

As the water continues to recede, we begin the upward climb toward the summit of the nearest hill. The foliage on the slope is as dense as it was in the valley below. With the added weight of water sloshing in my boots, each step feels heavier and more cumbersome. I carefully pick my way over fallen tree trunks and around sprawling bushes, evaluating every placement of my feet amidst the sea of blackened wood and red leaves.

Belatedly, I realize that the understory is thickening as we ascend. Vines, ferns, and palms crowd my path, further obscuring visibility. The brush directly ahead is barely discernible, and branches slap against my body as I push forward. Leaves ruffle underfoot, and I hone in on the steady hum of insects and the crackling sounds we create with our steps.

I push yet another branch out of my way. Sweat drips into my eyes, and I swipe it away with my free arm. But in my distraction, my grip on the branch loosens. It slips out of my fingers, snapping back and smacking me in the face. The force sends me staggering backward, tripping over a tree root and landing hard on my backside.

Blowing out a sharp breath, I vent my frustration. I sit on the forest floor for a moment, needing just one minute to collect myself before I move on.

Fixing my gaze forward, I let determination fuel me again. I will get up. I will continue. I will not let Kemuel's and Ariella's deaths be in vain. I will reach Brie and bring her back to the heavenly plane. This is my purpose, and I will achieve it. Failure is not an option.

Pushing myself off the forest floor, I shove the offending branch aside and plod onward. I nearly stumble again when the forest abruptly opens onto a patch of cleared land. Leaves still carpet the damp soil, but the trees and underbrush have been burnt away, forming a three-foot-wide path that winds up the hill.

Relief and fear surge through me in equal measure. Half of me is grateful for the easier climb ahead, no longer hindered by the rainforest's obstacles. The other half is consumed by apprehension, because standing a few paces ahead is a tribe of souls, their spears pointed directly at me.

"Michael, why did you stop?" Raphael's voice carries a note of complaint as he bumps into me from behind. I realize my team can't yet see through the dense brush bordering the path. Sure enough, another bump followed by a soft "Ow, my nose!" signals Gabriel has collided with Raphael the same way Raphael collided with me.

"We have company," I intone, stepping to the side to give my team room to enter the clearing.

"You should have alerted us sooner," Raphael grumbles, his uncharacteristic tone of irritation concerning me. Our sunny, carefree healer seems worn down by this journey, his spirit fraying under the strain. But just as I can't spare the time to process our losses, I can't dwell on Raphael's state right now either. That worry will have to wait as well.

When Callie stumbles out of the thick vegetation, the soul at the front of the tribe raises a single brow, silently scrutinizing us. Her gaze shifts among us, taking in our group dynamics. I remain silent, hoping my teammates will do the same. This tribe has the upper hand at the moment, with upwards of twenty members compared to our five. We could fight them if necessary, but avoiding a battle is far preferable. We're all weary and don't want to start a conflict that can be avoided.

At last, the woman finishes her assessment and speaks. "You have a female with you. Girl, tell me: are you captive? Do these men hold you against your will?"

"No," Callista replies assertively. "We are actually trying to rescue another female from captivity."

"Oh?" This piques the interest of the leader of the tribe. "Hmmm." She taps a finger against the shaft of her spear before lowering it. Her stance is still tense, and the warrior in me knows that she could still spring into battle effortlessly, but her action serves to signal that the tribe will not attack us unprovoked.

I step forward cautiously, hands raised in a supplicatory gesture. "My name is Michael, and this is my team. We are just passing through and mean you no harm."

The woman's intelligent eyes rove over my weapons, but she nods. "I am Chanda. My tribe will not hinder your progress, but you must be aware we are not the only beings here. Many of the other tribes take pleasure in attacking anything and everything they encounter. And don't even get me started on the dragons."

Chapter 27

MICHAEL

"Dragons?" Callista squeaks.

Chanda makes a low hum of acknowledgment as her dark eyes brighten in amusement. "Come," she says. "You can rest at our camp."

"That's very gracious of you," I respond, thankful for the chance to rest and dry out my boots.

The tribe's camp comes into view as we near the top of the hill. Like the path, the foliage at the summit has been burnt and chopped away, leaving a wide circle of level ground. More tribe members move about the camp, occupied with various tasks. Most pause to greet their returning hunters, but their excitement quickly shifts to confusion and wariness when they notice us following behind.

"We met some travelers during our return. I have welcomed them into our camp as guests. Do not worry, my friends. They will not do us harm," Chanda announces.

Despite her reassurance, the unease among the tribe lingers. Chanda's confident demeanor wavers briefly as though she's grappling with something internally. She closes her eyes, takes a deep breath, and declares, "We must meditate."

My eyes widen in surprise as every tribe member immediately abandons their work and gathers in the camp's center. Sitting cross-legged, they begin to hum low in their throats, summoning tranquility. These souls are far more self-aware than most. They recognize the sin that plagues their nature and fight against it rather than succumbing. They seek salvation—a task very few corrupted souls undertake.

As I watch them meditate, I can't help but admire their determination. Living in the rainforest is a grueling challenge, yet they've embraced it fully. Their skin, ranging in tones from bronze to espresso, shimmers in the heavy humidity, but they seem unbothered, focusing instead on calming the rage that condemned them to this circle of Hell.

The men are bare-chested, with loincloths woven from leaves providing some modesty. The women also don loincloths, with the addition of matching bandeaus. Their attire exemplifies their intelligence and resourcefulness, utilizing the resources available to them rather than relying on trade, and allowing them to better blend into their surroundings should they encounter predators. We got lucky in finding this tribe.

When the humming fades, the tribe members open their eyes, their expressions calmer. They resume their tasks with an air of serenity, while my team and I linger awkwardly at the camp's edge. Wood cabins with leaf-covered roofs dot the perimeter.

Will Chanda offer us a cabin for the night? We could use the rest. I haven't seen such substantial accommodations since this journey began, and the thought of a bed almost makes me groan aloud. I really hope they have beds.

Chanda's sharp eyes meet mine, and it feels as though she can read my thoughts. "A few of my tribe members have agreed to share a cabin tonight so one will be available for you. The cabin only has two beds, so some of your group will need to sleep on the floor, but at least you'll have shelter from the elements. I'm sorry I can't offer more."

"That is more than enough. Thank you, Chanda. Your generosity will not be forgotten."

As we settle into the idea of rest, a thought strikes me: perhaps, when we leave, we can grant these souls an angelic pardon, allowing them to ascend with us. From what I've seen so far, they may have earned such grace.

The cabin is small but cozy, with a single room furnished with two beds and a chest at the foot of each. The air inside is thick with the scent of wood, which feels homely and comforting. It will be a tight fit with three of us on the floor, but it's far better than anything I'd dared hope for.

Finally, I pull off my soggy boots with an audible sigh of relief. I set them near the door to dry and stretch out on the wooden floor, already feeling the weight of exhaustion pulling me toward sleep.

It's hard to believe we stumbled upon such safe lodging. Perhaps the divine spirit truly is smiling upon us.

A high-pitched scream awakens me. For a moment, I'm confused. Where am I? I look around the darkened room. The earthy wood smell and the shapes of the two beds remind me that I'm in a cabin in Wrath. Shouts of alarm and panicked screams filter into my consciousness and I bolt upright, rushing to get my feet into my partially dry boots.

Behind me, Raphael and Haniel groggily regain awareness, rousing the others. I pull open the thick wooden cabin door, peering out into what can only be described as pure chaos. Tribe members are screaming and shouting, running in every direction. Several cabins are ablaze, engulfed in bright yellow flames that blaze almost blindingly against the darkness. Overhead, dragons spew fire indiscriminately from their massive maws.

The large beasts descend on the camp like vultures on a carcass, swarming their target and picking it clean. Souls flee the mayhem, only to be picked off mid-stride. The fires spread rapidly, cabin after cabin igniting as though the wood were soaked in accelerant.

I've witnessed countless tragedies in my time, but I've never seen a situation as dire as this. There seems to be no escape. And as my team stands behind me, waiting for my command, I have no idea how to lead them to safety.

The weight of responsibility is crushing as I weigh my options, knowing we must act quickly. Staying in the cabin will leave us like fish in a barrel—easy targets. Stealth is our only chance at survival.

My heart aches for the souls who so generously shared their camp with us. There may not be a single survivor after this massacre. While every instinct urges me to help them, I know that doing so will doom my team. The dragons are too numerous, and we are too few.

The ground trembles as the dragons land, swarming their prey in layers. The cabins continue to burn, their wooden beams cracking loudly, adding their own mournful tones to the symphony of death and despair. Smoke rises in thick plumes, darkening an already oppressive night.

I slink out of the cabin, clinging to its frame to remain hidden from the monstrous creatures. Raphael's energy brushes against mine, signaling that he is following my lead. I round the corner, scanning the camp for possible escape routes.

A dark shimmer amidst the trees behind the cabin draws my attention. Squinting, I try to discern what I'm seeing, but the shapes remain unclear. I glance back toward the center of the camp. The dragons are still occupied, but their interest will wane soon—there aren't many souls left to consume.

Crouching, I edge toward the trees, desperate to identify the shimmer. The darkness is unrelenting, and as I peer upward, I realize with a jolt that it's growing even darker.

Horror dawns as I tilt my head back. Above me, diving with claws outstretched, is a massive ruby-red dragon.

The creature is terrifyingly beautiful. Its scales glow from within, a mesmerizing cascade of light and color. The dragon opens its mouth, and I glimpse embers glowing deep in its throat. Panic propels me forward, sprinting toward the shimmer in the trees.

A hysterical laugh bubbles from my chest when I realize the shimmer is a waterfall. Without hesitation, I leap into the rushing water just as the dragon releases its fire. The water heats around me, but I'm already careening down the falls. My only hope is that my teammates are able to follow.

The water batters me relentlessly, tossing my body side to side as I plummet. I break through the surface briefly, gasping for air, only to be dragged under again. My limbs flail as the current hurls me downward until, finally, the flow slows enough for me to swim upward.

I breach the surface once more, pulling deep breaths into my burning lungs. Doggy paddling until I regain my bearings, I swim to shore.

The mist from the waterfall clouds my vision as I drag myself onto solid ground. Looking up, I see the glow of flames still consuming the camp above the falls. My chest is tight, my breathing labored as I scrutinize every inch of the plunge, searching for any sign of my teammates.

But I see nothing other than the curtain of water.

The night has gone eerily silent. The cries and screams have subsided, the crackling of the fires too far away to be heard. The rush of water and my gasping breaths are the only sounds that fill the air. And still, I wait. Where are they?

Chapter 28

MICHAEL

The panic I experience as I await my teammates has become a familiar feeling as of late, the perilous nature of Hell preventing any sense of security. The darkness that permeates this plane whispers enticements into our souls like a siren's song, but as a group we are stronger. Alone, we are fallible. And as I wait for the familiar heads of my fellow angels to emerge amidst the rolling rapids, that taunting fear of solitude creeps in. What if they didn't make it?

Seconds feel like minutes, and minutes feel like hours as I wait with bated breath. Searching. Hoping. Dreading. My eyes scan the water again and again, until finally, movement at the lip of the waterfall catches my attention. I watch helplessly as a figure takes a running leap off the cliff, narrowly missing a torrent of dragon fire before vanishing into the plunge.

Overhead, the luminescent dragon roars in frustration. It circles the waterfall, seeking its prey, before turning back toward the camp and disappearing from view. The sight brings a sliver of relief—at least one of my comrades has survived the massacre.

I refocus my gaze lower, waiting for the figure to surface in the punchbowl at the base of the waterfall. My heart stutters as the agonizing seconds stretch on. Then, heads begin to emerge in the calmer waters—heads, plural. My relief is palpable when I see each of them emerge, and it takes my brain a minute to process the fact that all four of my teammates have made it. They're here. Safe.

We follow the streambank away from the waterfall, slogging through shallow waters to its opposite shore. I glance back at the wreckage of the camp, now distant enough that my survival instincts can ease slightly. "Let's pause here and forage," I suggest.

Supplies have dwindled dangerously low, with packs abandoned during hasty escapes and delays in our journey. We have a few nutrition bars left, but it's better to save them for critical moments. Especially since rainforests, even those in Hell, are abundant with edible resources.

I weave through the trees, plucking fruit from branches and berries from bushes. The brief reprieve from danger feels like a balm to my spirit, and I savor it. Too much of this journey has been plagued by tragedy. It lingers in the back of my mind constantly, even when my mind is focused on survival. The longing for my missing soulmate gnaws at me, a phantom ache that colors everything I do.

Popping a tart berry into my mouth, I savor its burst of flavor, a welcome change from the dry nutrition bars that have been our main source of sustenance lately. When I return to the stream, Callista is already there, holding a shirt filled with mushrooms. They resemble portobellos, though with thinner stems.

"Good work," I say.

I don't know Callista well—only through Brie's stories and our shared experiences on this mission. The others I've known for eons, and they feel like extensions of myself. Callista, though, unsettles me in a way I can't quite pinpoint. I've noticed Gabriel watching her strangely as well, though he hasn't vocalized any concerns. It makes me wonder if he knows something about her that I don't.

"Thanks!" Callista's chipper response pulls me from my thoughts. We've all been muted since Brie was taken, but Callista's constant optimism hasn't wavered, even as she mourns. "I love mushrooms. I was so excited when I found these. This is going to be the best meal of our journey!"

I nod, unsure how to respond to her relentless enthusiasm. Is it exhausting to be so upbeat all the time? I'm steady. Stoic. I wouldn't say that I'm grumpy, just...consistent. Battles demand bursts of energy, but that's different from maintaining a constant high. Even Raphael, with his exuberance, has moments of contemplation and seriousness. Callista, though, seems to embody boundless energy in every fiber of her being.

Shaking off my musings, I grab another berry to eat. The freshness is a small but welcome comfort. Nearby, Raphael crams an entire handful of berries into his mouth at once, juice dribbling down his chin.

"You're giving gluttony a run for its money, I see," I remark dryly.

Raphael smirks, his grin cheeky despite the mess on his face. "Jealous, Michael? Envy would be thrilled to add you to its roster."

Gabriel scoffs, "My brother is far too wrathful for envy to be his main vice."

"I am justifiably vengeful. There's a difference, little brother."

"Is there?" Haniel cuts in. "Does your justifiable vengeance make you feel wrathful?"

"Occasionally."

I can't hold in my laughter, and neither can the others. The moment lightens our dark moods, however briefly. Callista smiles faintly, standing just on the edge of our group. I feel a pang of sadness for her. It must be lonely to feel excluded from the banter built on millennia of friendship.

I take one of the mushrooms she collected, a small gesture that I hope will help her feel included and valued. It's not much, but it's something. The mushroom is firm but tender, with an earthy flavor. I'm not particularly fond of mushrooms, but if this can help her feel included, I'll eat it.

"These mushrooms were a great find, Callie," Haniel compliments, intuitively catching onto the intention behind my action.

Callista's smile brightens, more genuine now, bolstered by Haniel's praise. It should be another nice moment, but a pang of yearning sullies it for me. Brie is always on my mind, but now, watching Callista interact with Haniel, my longing for her feels unbearable. I miss her so much. I dread what she might be enduring—what Lucifer might be putting her through.

Part of me blames myself for her sacrifice. Maybe if I had told her I loved her, or if I had given her the ring sooner, she would have stayed, and we could have found another way. But I didn't, and she didn't. Regret swarms my mind as my fingers trace the outline of the ring I've kept zipped away in my inner pocket. There's no going back. All we can do is move forward.

Like a dark shadow blotting out the sun, my mood turns grim. Sitting here is unproductive. We've eaten enough. It's time to move out. I stand, ready to gather my pack and give the directive, but suddenly, the world spins around me. I sway, my vision warping. No. No, no, no. This can't be happening!

I stagger toward a tree. Time becomes fragmented, passing in flashes. The tree seemed far away, but in the blink of an eye, I'm stumbling into it. How did it get so close? Did it move, or did I? A high-pitched giggle cuts through the air.

I lean against the tree, one hand steadying myself as I turn toward the group. The world tilts, and I lose my balance.

Another high-pitched giggle. Suddenly, I'm on the ground. When did that happen? Raphael stares at his hand, repeatedly moving it toward his face and pulling it away again. Did he injure himself?

Lights twinkle in my field of vision, like fireflies on a summer night. Brie loved twinkling lights. She strung fairy lights all over our garden back home. Home. Brie. I miss them both.

I swipe at the lights, trying to will them away. They only bring nostalgia, and I don't want to pine over what I've lost. The lights don't retreat. They keep twinkling, taunting me. "Go away," I mutter. They don't listen. Stubborn little things.

"I think..." Callista gasps between giggles, "I think I'm tripping." Her giggles turn into hysterical laughter as she rolls onto her back, kicking her legs in the air. Haniel reaches out and starts playing with a strand of her short, pink-streaked, light brown hair. I think he's braiding it. I've seen Brie do something similar before.

"Michael." A whisper, soft and fleeting, carried on the wind. Real or imagined? "Michael, I miss you." The voice is feminine, melodic—it sounds like Brie. But Brie isn't here. She's with Lucifer. *She's with Lucifer!* I have to get to her!

I teeter to my feet and stumble toward the group. "We need to go! We need to save Brie!" Overwhelming panic consumes me. We need to reach her! We need to save her!

"Raphael! Raf! We need to save Brie!"

Raphael pauses, his hand mid-motion, and turns toward me, his eyes unfocused. A huge grin spreads across his face. "Brie? Brie is great. She's the bestest friend ever," he says dreamily, then turns to Gabriel, repeatedly poking my catatonic brother's cheek.

The panic that plagues me continues to consume my being as I turn my gaze back toward the rainforest's mass of trees. And that's when I see her. My whole world lights up with her presence. Brie, my Brie, is walking through the trees toward me, a serene smile on her beautiful face. She's here. She's safe. But...how did she know where to find us?

"Brie!" I call, my joy suffusing my voice. She pauses, her eyes locked on my face. I start toward her, but falter when her serene smile transforms into a look of shock. She looks downward and I follow her gaze with my own. A patch of red blossoms across her white sundress, steadily growing in size, framing the metal tip of a lance puncturing the center of her chest.

Time stands still as I stare, horrified, as blood oozes from the puncture wound. "No," I whisper. "No." This time it's louder. A demon rises out of the ground behind Brie's frozen form. His hand holds the shaft of the lance and he smiles behind his mask of shattered black glass as he twists the long wooden pole.

Brie's mouth forms an "oh" and her hands slowly lift toward the wound. The demon throws his head back and cackles, his bleached skin stretching beneath his brown leather breastplate. When his head rights itself, the black horns atop his head have grown to twice their original size.

Blood flows through Brie's fingers as she presses her hands against the wound. More and more escapes her fingers, until rivers of the thick red liquid are pouring down her dress in streams, turning the brilliant material a dark ruby color. It shimmers in the low light, reminding me of the dragon I fled.

I try to run to Brie, but my feet are stuck in the moist soil. What trickery is this? I pull my legs with all the power I can muster, but they don't move an inch in any direction. I look down at my boots. Why won't they move? Helplessly, I look back up to Brie. The second I meet her soulful hazel eyes, she bursts apart, shattering right before my eyes as the demon, too, disappears in a cloud of smoke.

Chapter 29

BRIE

I stare up at the shiny black ceiling above my bed, once again held captive by my thoughts. The castle still feels like a cage, despite its elegance. I haven't been allowed outside since the disastrous trip to the ninth circle. It was such an enjoyable day—until it wasn't.

A soft knock sounds at the door, followed by a now-familiar grumbling. I smile. "Good morning, Dee." I don't need to look to know it's her.

Dee's presence has become comforting, a stark contrast to the unease I once felt around her.

"Good morning, dear. How are you feeling today? You had quite the day yesterday."

That's one way to put it. I would agree that murdering a soul could be considered "quite the day", though I think it might be a bit of an understatement. A flash of the moment I plunged the dagger into Chad's chest surfaces in my mind. It soothes me.

Rationally, I know the memory should disturb me, but instead, it fills me with a perverse pleasure. He deserved to die, and I'm glad it was by my hand. I did the realm a favor by ending his pathetic existence.

Another smile curves my lips, this one meaner. Malevolent. Vicious. Dee watches me warily as I tear myself away from my thoughts. Her wariness feels unwelcome. Can I still trust her?

Letting a thread of my angelic power seep into her, I attempt to read her emotions. I need to be sure she's still an ally. My empathic energy slithers into her mind, and my gaze locks on her tainted soul. "Dee, are you still onboard with my escape plans?"

Dee jerks, her expression going slack. "I am onboard with your escape plans," she says robotically. I can't sense her emotions, but I can feel my energy twisting within her.

"Dee, I can trust you, can't I?"

"Brie can trust Dee." Her voice is flat, unnatural. I've never heard her sound like this before—almost possessed. My energy twists and turns within her, grasping at her emotions and twisting them into something unrecognizable.

Realization dawns, and I gasp, pulling my energy back abruptly. Dee's eyes clear, and her face shifts into a moue of confusion. "What happened? I think I zoned out for a minute there."

"I...um... Are you feeling okay?"

"I am now. How odd." Dee turns away, abandoning the conversation to rummage through the closet.

Seizing the moment, I look inward, focusing on the well of angelic power radiating from the center of my chest. I see the strands of light green that signify healing, deep violet for visions, pale lavender for reading emotions and the truth of a soul, and a muted white, bordering on gray, that should be a pure, snowy shade. I also see, weaving around the strands of each color, tentacles of depthless black.

The black magic strangles the other strands, corrupting their hues as it grows stronger. Terror grips me, stealing my breath. I stagger to the wall, placing a hand against it to steady myself. Dee hums blissfully from the closet, completely unaware of my silent breakdown.

I gasp for air, the weight on my chest only growing heavier. My magic. My soul. They're corrupted. I'm falling. I'm transforming into a fallen angel. And once the transformation is complete, there will be no redemption. I'll be barred from Heaven, even if I make it back.

My magic has twisted into something dark. Instead of reading Dee's emotions, I manipulated them, bending her will to mine. How long the effects will last, I don't know, but this power is dangerous—and as I fall farther, its allure will only grow stronger.

Now is the time. I need to run. "Dee," my voice seems to come from far away, like my consciousness and my body are in two different places. "It's time. Hide the poison in Lucifer's breakfast. Do it today."

Dee turns to me, and for a moment, time stands still. A shadow passes behind her eyes. "Are you certain?"

"Yes. It needs to be today."

"You're rushing it. The plan isn't fully prepared. You're risking a lot, and it will be sloppy. In a few days' time, we could have everything ready. You'd be more prepared."

"I don't have a few days. I'm turning dark. It has to be today," I press, desperation heavy in my words.

"If you insist," she acquiesces.

"I do." My words are solid and assured, but inside, terror and anxiety have taken residence. This is it. I'll only get one chance, and if this escape fails, I can't even imagine the response that will await me when Lucifer finds out. I *must* get this right.

Dee helps me dress and bustles out of the room with the poisons in a bundle in her arms. She'll need to slip them into Lucifer's meal somewhere between the kitchen and the dining room, so the kitchen staff can't implicate her or reveal our deception. But I trust her. She's proven to me that I can.

My body trembles and my pulse races as I descend the stairs to Lucifer's private dining room. I can't even feel my legs as they move down the steps. *I'm doing the right thing*, I tell myself, but I can't quite make myself believe it.

"You're jumpy today. Is everything okay?" Lucifer's smooth, deep voice penetrates my drifting mind.

"I'm fine," I reply, though we both know I'm not. My twitchiness at every small sound reveals the truth.

"I hope you're not upset about the scum." Genuine concern shines in Lucifer's eyes, and my throat tightens with guilt. He's worried about me, and yet I'm about to poison him into paralysis so I can flee. *What has happened to me? I really have become dark, haven't I?*

"He got what he deserved," I reply, meeting Lucifer's gaze for the first time this morning. My conviction burns brightly, chasing away the terror and fear. It fortifies me, leaving only resolve. I *can* do this.

I take my seat across from him just as Dee pushes the cherrywood serving cart into the room. She carefully shuts the door behind her before Cerberus can follow, a precaution I appreciate. Lucifer has a habit of sneaking scraps to his beloved dog, and I had been explicit with Dee that I didn't want Cerberus ingesting any of the poisoned food.

Oblivious to the danger we're protecting him from, Cerberus howls in displeasure and scratches at the door. Lucifer turns to Dee, perplexed. "Will you open the door for Cerby, please?"

"Your Majesty," Dee hedges, her tone apologetic but firm, "I'm sorry to be the bearer of bad news, but at Cerberus's last health check-up, the doctor said he was—and I quote—'roly poly' and could stand to lose a few pounds. I'm starting him on a diet today. For his own health and well-being, of course."

Lucifer's mouth drops open as he stares at Dee. I cover my own mouth to stifle the laugh threatening to burst out. Dee's placid confidence is disarming, and Lucifer's baffled expression—eyebrows scrunched, mouthing the words *roly poly*—is almost enough to make me abandon the plan. Almost. But then Dee glances at me, a fleeting look that reminds me what's at stake.

"We only want what's best for Cerberus, Your Majesty," Dee prods gently.

That seems to jar Lucifer back to his senses. "Of course, yes. If the doctor feels that Cerberus needs a diet, who am I to argue?"

Dee bows her head respectfully, then begins pulling platters from the cart and serving us. My eyes catch on the flecks of rosemary in Lucifer's eggs, and a pang of doubt surges within me. When Dee uncaps his bottled water, nausea rolls over me. *I can't believe we're actually doing this.*

The first symptoms of the wild rosemary's toxicity should appear within a few hours. Paralysis and coma from the mountain laurel will likely set in around six hours after ingestion. If I can slip out of the castle amidst the confusion and panic caused by his initial symptoms, I should gain about half a day's head start before a search party is organized. I'll need to remain cautious, but I shouldn't be actively pursued until after nightfall.

Lucifer takes his first bite of egg and sips his water. My stomach churns. When he notices me watching, he smiles gently. "Aren't you hungry?"

My insides twist at the question. "I don't have much of an appetite today, I'm afraid."

"I'm sorry to hear that. Is it the darkness? Are you in too much pain from metabolizing it? I can have Dee bring you a pain reliever."

"No," I blurt, slightly too high-pitched, "my stomach is just a little unsettled. That's all. I'm sure it will pass." Truthfully, I haven't felt the pain of metabolizing darkness in days. That should have been my first clue that I was turning dark. Once enough darkness saturates your soul, the pain vanishes. It hadn't even occurred to me until now.

"I do hope you feel better soon," Lucifer says, his voice laced with genuine care. "Don't hesitate to tell me or Dee if you need anything, alright?"

His concern twists the knife in my heart. I want to sweep the plate off the table, yell at him to stop eating, and wrench the fork from his hand. I want to freeze time, pull the dominoes off the board, and undo the chain of events I've set into motion.

But I also don't.

So I stay quiet, watching him consume the tainted food, my voice barely above a whisper when I finally reply, "Of course."

Chapter 30

MICHAEL

Time passes in flashes. I'm pulling at my legs. I fall as I try to reach the place where Brie disappeared. Now on my knees, my lower legs sink deeper into the mud. Raphael is frantically telling me to stop moving.

The haze in my head dissipates slowly. Looking around, I note Raphael sitting patiently a few feet away, holding a large stick, his eyes clear and focused. Gabriel lies motionless by the stream, his eyes closed and breathing steady. Callista skips around the trees at the forest's edge, giggling and singing to herself, while Haniel stumbles after her in a clumsy game of tag.

"Were we drugged?" I ask Raphael, though I already know the answer. I need the confirmation anyway.

"Yes," Raphael replies. "Turns out the mushrooms were psychedelic. My healing ability brought me out of it about half an hour ago. I think the others will be affected for a few more hours."

"Makes sense," I reply, catching his inference: they don't have the healing abilities Raphael and I do; it'll take them longer to recover. "Why are you sitting there holding a stick?"

"Because you're stuck in quicksand."

"I'm—" I look down at my legs, sunk shin-deep in mud, and try to shuffle out. "Oh. I am, indeed, stuck in quicksand." I chuckle, but there's no humor in it—just bitterness.

"Grab on," Raphael instructs, extending the stick toward me. I take hold and begin rocking gently back and forth to loosen the mud's suction. When I feel it release with a soft pop, Raphael pulls me free.

We head toward Gabriel's still form, Raphael probing the ground with his stick as we go. I can't believe I got stuck in quicksand *while* hallucinating. The memory of Brie bursting into fragments of darkness flashes through my mind, sending a shiver up my spine. That image will haunt me for a long time.

"Do you think he's stuck in a prophetic vision?" I ask, gesturing to my brother.

"Likely. I suspect the mushrooms will have affected him more strongly because of his predisposition to visions. Whether it's prophetic or hallucinatory, though, I can't say. He hasn't spoken at all."

"His visions usually last seconds. If this is one, it's been hours. The potential damage to his mind worries me."

"Me too," Raphael says, frowning as he studies Gabriel's slack face. "But pulling him out of it could cause more harm. We'll have to wait for him to come out of it naturally. If there are any ill effects, hopefully I will be able to heal them."

"Hopefully," I echo. I glance around, uneasy. "It's strange we haven't been attacked more. We've been too lucky, and it makes me nervous. I can't imagine Lucifer doesn't know we're here, so why hasn't he sent more demons after us?"

"I've been wondering the same. And I can't attribute the minimal number of attacks to luck. It's clear to me that Lucifer isn't hindering our progress through Hell, but I can't fathom why."

"Do you think he's leading us into a trap? Maybe he wants us to reach the castle so he can ambush us there?"

"It's possible. I haven't spoken to him in centuries, so I can't gauge his thinking anymore. Millennia ago, I never would've imagined he'd hold Brie captive. He's not the angel we once knew."

"No, he's not." I pause, guilt threading through me. "And I feel like I'm partly responsible for that. I should have done more to help him. Maybe if I hadn't rebuffed his attempts to contact me, none of this would have happened."

"You couldn't have known, Michael. And this isn't your fault. If you hadn't cut off contact with him, you'd be down here ruling Hell beside him. You would have fallen. Setting boundaries was necessary for your own well-being. We've been over this—you can't always put everyone before yourself. It ends up doing more harm than good for everyone involved."

"I know. I know it was necessary, but that doesn't alleviate my guilt."

Raphael doesn't respond. What more could he say? We've had this conversation thousands of times. In the end, what's done is done. No matter how I try to rationalize my actions, the guilt lingers. It always does. I've tried to change how I feel, but I can't.

Gabriel's eyes snap open, and he jerks upright with a gasp. Raphael wraps his arms tightly around Gabriel's shoulders, murmuring reassurances. Gabriel's chest heaves as his gaze darts around the small shore, taking in his surroundings.

When his eyes land on me, his posture softens.

"Are you okay?" I ask.

"I'm fine," he replies, his voice steady but weary. "It was an intense vision. It felt endless, but I'm okay."

"Can you tell us what you saw?" I ask carefully. Gabriel is bound by the divine spirit, limited in how much he can divulge about his visions. Usually, if he's permitted to share, he volunteers the information. When he shakes his head, frustration races through me like an electric charge. I know it's not his choice to withhold what he's seen, but I hate being left in the dark, especially knowing how traumatic his visions often are.

"I'm sorry," I offer, knowing he feels just as conflicted about the restrictions as we do.

Haniel and Callista come down from their psychedelic highs not long after. Both of them seem unaffected beyond lingering amusement from their pleasant trips. At least we don't need to worry about their mental states as we move deeper into the rainforest, leaving the stream and its treacherous quicksand behind.

We once again weave through the dense foliage, wearier since our intoxication. Thankfully, it's not long before the vegetation starts to thin. Visibility extends as the plant life diminishes, helping me to feel more secure. I know there are more tribes of souls wandering around this rainforest, along with various demons and monsters, and an ambush is the last thing we need.

We begin to see wisps of darkness floating past us and twining around tree trunks. The gate is near. As it comes into sight, I roll my eyes toward the sky, lamenting the hurdles of this expedition.

Refocusing on the present, I come to a halt a good distance away from the monster guarding the gate.

Cacus lazily drags his antique timber club in circles along the ground in front of him. Its distressed indents from years of use capture fragments of mud with each pass. He's the picture of nonchalance as his lips turn up slightly. "Archangel Michael," he greets, dipping his head in respect. "It's been a long time."

"It has," I agree. "How have you been, Cacus?"

"Oh, you know. Keeping busy down here." He spits a wad of fire into the dirt, a damp leaf floating nearby directly in its path, igniting before it lands on the blackened ground.

I look at the heads he has nailed to the wooden doorframe he erected around the gate and work hard to keep the revulsion from my face. "I can see that," I manage. Cacus grins at me, proud of his decorations. His teeth are sharp points within his giant mouth, blackened with grime and ash.

"My team and I would like passage to Pride. Will you allow it?"

The fire-breathing giant looks thoughtful for a moment. Giants are usually characterized as dim-witted, but Cacus is anything but. He's one of the most intelligent beings I've ever met. I can see the sparkle in his eye when he decides how he can use this situation to his advantage. But I also see the scowl that follows that sparkle, telling me that he decided not to implement the decision.

"Lucifer has ordered me not to hinder your progress. He won't be pleased if I do anything other than allowing your passage."

Lucifer did what now? My brain stutters for a moment. Why would he do such a thing? While it is possible he's leading us into a trap, I doubt he'd want to make it easy for us. So why is he protecting us?

"How kind of him..."

Cacus lets out a booming laugh that shakes the towering trees around us. He knows what I'm hinting at. Lucifer is known among his subjects to be many things, but kind is not one of them. Cruel, powerful, ruthless—certainly; but kind—no. "Yes, how very kind of him. I wonder what tricks our dark king has up his sleeves. Sadly, I'm not privy to such information."

"Pity," I say. "It was a pleasure to see you again Cacus. I hope the next time is under similarly pleasant conditions."

"For me as well, Michael. I know you're an Archangel, but I actually like you."

His words drive a smile to my face and a warmth to my chest. It's about the greatest compliment a being could receive from the giant, and while I find parts of him intolerable, it pleases me that he likes me enough to say it. I know his words aren't empty ones.

Cacus picks up his weathered club, smacking it against his large hand a few times before stepping to the side of his wooden doorframe. I motion for Haniel to pass through first. Callista follows him. Cacus focuses his beady black eyes on me intently as soon as she's through, putting a meaty hand out to stop Raphael from following her through.

"There's something you should know. You need to be prepared for what you might find. There are rumors among the traders that your soulmate is turning dark. They say one of the castle staff has seen the change in her aura."

A tingling erupts in the center of my chest and my stomach hardens as worry and disbelief war within me. Brie's strong. She won't have gone dark. She can't have. But...if she does, what does that mean for us?

Chapter 31

BRIE

I'm in the greenhouse when the commotion starts. For the past hour, I've been trying to boost the health of some of the more neglected plants, only for them to die before my eyes. Dark tendrils weave through the green healing energy, turning it deadly. Now, instead of healing the plants and helping them flourish, my power sucks what little energy they have out of them. They end up as husks, depleted of everything that gave them life.

My hope that the reversal of my power was a fluke didn't truly vanish until after the fifth plant I killed. I can still feel its faint whine of sorrow reverberating in my soul. By then, it was undeniable: it wasn't a fluke. I have gone dark, just as I feared.

I didn't see it happening at first. It began so subtly—little white lies here and there. Harmless, I told myself. Nothing too extreme. Nothing that should've escalated to this point. But it did. I see that now.

Those little white lies became treacherous and subversive. Then, my actions followed suit. The darkness spread, and when I delivered the killing blow to Chad, I was already infected by the darkness—my treachery and deceit gone too far. And now, now I'm clinging to a desperate hope, a Hail Mary attempt to preserve what little light remains, even as it dims more each day.

The shouts and hurried footfalls echoing on the hardwood tell me my plan has begun. Resolved, I leave the withered plants behind and descend the spiral staircase. On the floor below, Lucifer's quarters are in disarray—the doors wide open, staff racing frantically about the room. I catch a glimpse of his inert form on the bed before continuing downward.

A pang of remorse twists in my chest as I move as silently as I can through the castle. I slip furtively into the drawing room but pause, stiffening at the sound of voices in the entrance hall. *Please don't come in here, please don't come in here.* Pressing myself into a dark corner of the room, I listen as Boagdan hastily updates a doctor on Lucifer's condition. The voices fade as they pass into the throne room, heading toward the castle's heart.

When silence finally returns, I rush to the large windows lining the drawing room wall. Unlocking the first, I heave the lower frame upward. My breaths come quick and shallow from both fear and exertion as I push against the screen. How do you pop this dang thing out?! Dee was right; I wasn't as prepared for this escape as I should've been.

I push on the screen's corners with all my might, but it refuses to budge. Frustrated, I alternate between pulling and pushing until, miraculously, one corner pops loose. A feeling of invigoration suffuses my body. *I can do this.* I work on the top corner of the same side, this one yielding more easily, allowing me to finally pull the screen free. Sliding it down the stone wall outside, I then turn and stick my legs through the open window.

My feet land in one of the large planters lining the castle's exterior, crushing the flowers and struggling to find purchase among the bushes. *Great,* I think, rolling my eyes. *I've killed more plants today than I did in my entire lifetime on Earth.* With my footing somewhat secure, I pull my upper body through the window, tumbling off the planter's side in the process. *Graceful, Brie. Real graceful.* It's fine though—I would've ended up crouching here anyway.

The narrow space between the planters offers little cover, my knees and shoulders poking out as I dig into the soil to retrieve the satchel buried within. Dirt flies in every direction, coating my fingers, but the rough texture of buried fabric sends a jolt of triumph through me. Pulling the satchel free, I reach inside and retrieve the vial of blinding sap. The milky white liquid glimmers within, ready to be used.

I edge out of the gap between the planters and creep alongside them to the edge of the thick obsidian wall. Peering around the corner, I count fifteen sphinx guards standing in a group at the entrance to the hellfire moat's bridge. They're talking to each other casually, not appearing alert or on edge, but even so, I won't be able to sneak past them unnoticed. Even if my abilities were working normally, I can't gamble that the sphinx guards wouldn't sense my presence even if I were glamoured. I need a distraction.

The grounds surrounding Lucifer's castle are primarily open, but there is one gnarled, ancient-looking tree that caught my eye every time I gazed out the windows. Its massive height and thick foliage would routinely draw me in, and I spent hours admiring it. For this reason, I also know that the tree contains a pair of beautiful black-feathered birds with bright red wings and razor-sharp beaks. I'm willing to bet that these gorgeous avian creatures will be territorial about their newly completed nest.

I launch myself out of my hiding spot and sprint to the tree's large trunk, tucking my body behind it. No shouts or war cries sound from the sphinxes, so I know I traversed the gap unseen. I pull the rough canvas bag onto my back, hooking its straps around my shoulders, and pocket the small vial of blinding sap. Grabbing the lowest branch of the tree with both hands, I pull myself up onto it. The rough bark cuts into my palms, but I ignore the bite of pain it causes and repeat the process.

I climb higher and higher until I'm perched several branches above the small nest being guarded by the birds. Uncapping the vial of blinding sap, I let a few drops fall on either side of the branch I'm perched on. Then, I leap over to the next branch and release a few more drops. I doubt the guards will encircle the tree when they arrive, so I focus the sap on only two branches.

I move over a few branches, watching the sap slowly slide down the bark, and pluck leaves off the tree as I go. When the sap is just about ready to drip off the tree, I throw the leaves at the nest and jump down to the ground, hiding once more behind the tree's massive trunk. As I hoped, the birds are not happy with the disturbance. Squawking and trilling at the top of their lungs, they immediately attract the attention of every guard in the vicinity.

The guards rush over, panicked by the birds' loud distress calls. They gather beneath the nest, looking upward to locate the source of the commotion. My timing is perfect. As their heads tilt back, beads of the blinding sap drip from the branches above, hitting several of them directly. The birds, already agitated, dive-bomb the guards, and they don't see the little beads of liquid until it's too late.

Within seconds, half the guards are temporarily blinded by the sap. Several others develop blisters on their faces, and the remaining guards are so preoccupied with helping their comrades that they are oblivious to their surroundings. I suppress the cheer bubbling inside me and sprint to the bridge as quickly as my legs will allow.

At the other end of the bridge, two guards have left their posts and are standing together between the high structures. They spin around at the sound of my rapid footsteps, but I don't break stride. Uncapping the vial of sap, I splash the remaining liquid into their faces. They shriek as their vision darkens, fumbling and rubbing their faces with their front paws, only to blister those as well. Their anger is palpable as they turn their focus toward apprehending their attacker, but they're too late. I've already left them behind, and they're too disabled to follow.

This time, as I venture into the ninth circle of Hell, I cut to my left. The central market's stalls might offer good cover, but they are also crowded with too many beings—too many chances for someone to alert a guard to my presence. Instead, I head toward the city I've seen so often from the windows of the castle, and the high-rises that populate it.

The towering buildings, with their gleaming windows, call to me like a beacon. It will surely be easy to get lost among the hustle and bustle characteristic of all cities. There must be narrow alleyways I can find, and dumpsters I can hide behind. Cities are easy places to disappear in, and I'm banking on the assumption that those in Hell are no different.

Pulling the hood of my black cloak over my head, I keep my gaze fixed downward, focusing on my feet as I pass guard tower after guard tower. I'm glad that I changed into dark trousers and a matching blouse after breakfast this morning. The more casual clothing mirrors what I saw most locals wearing in the market, and I hope it will help me blend in.

So far, none of the guards I've passed have looked at me suspiciously, but I also know that they haven't yet been alerted to my escape. Their movements are too casual, their stances too relaxed. At the moment, time is my friend, but the second Hell's guards get that alarm, the risk that I will be recognized increases exponentially. I have to get as far into the city as I can while the guards are still ignorant to my absence. And I'm under no illusion that this ignorance will last long.

Chapter 32

BRIE

Well, I was wrong. When I thought it would be easy to disappear within the city area of Treachery, I didn't account for all of the street cameras. Or the patrolling drones. I noticed that Hell had some items similar to Earthly items, but these are the first technological items that I've seen on this plane. Of all the things Lucifer could have chosen to import from Earth, of course he would choose surveillance equipment. Because, why not? This is just my luck.

I duck into an alleyway behind a boisterous eatery to avoid the spotlight of yet another passing metal contraption. The patrons inside glance briefly in my direction before the lively fiddler in the center of the room recaptures their attention. One detail I hadn't fully accounted for before heading into the city: all the buildings are made entirely of glass.

I mean, I knew they had glass, because I've noticed the reflection of the sun upon the glass during the day, but I didn't realize that *every single building* within this circle is constructed entirely of transparent material. Even the bathrooms—and that's an image I'll never be able to scrub from my mind.

Noting the red lights circling the lens of a camera mounted in the far corner of the alley, I quickly tilt my head away to avoid being caught on film. Slinking behind the building, I continue weaving my way farther from the castle. The kitchen staff are bustling at the back of the eatery, too frantic to notice me as I slip past.

Ahead, a spotlight cuts back and forth across the ground, signaling the approach of another drone. I hurry toward a dumpster and crouch behind it, keeping my head low. I'm pretty sure the dumpsters are the only objects in this circle that aren't transparent.

It makes sense in a convoluted way. Treachery contains the souls most likely to betray or commit treason against the crown, so of course, their every move is surveilled to prevent such acts. Unfortunately for me, it also makes escaping Lucifer's clutches that much harder.

The drone whirs past my hiding spot, and the spotlight dims as it recedes into the distance. I stand quickly, eager to escape the rank stench of rotten eggs and sour waste. The passage ahead leads to a dead end, forcing me to climb the wall to continue forward. While backtracking might be easier, it could also attract unwanted attention.

I know the exact moment that news of my escape reaches the guards. It's impossible to miss: a blaring siren rings out, echoed through the speakers of every mounted street camera. Well, that answers the question of whether the cameras have microphones. If they have speakers, I can assume they're equipped with mics as well.

"Residents of Treachery: A code yellow is in effect. Return to your homes immediately. A curfew will begin in ten minutes. Any soul remaining on the streets after curfew will be disposed of."

The warning rings in my ears. *Disposed of?* What does that mean? Whatever it entails, I'm certain I don't want to find out firsthand. The passage I'm jogging through quickly fills with panicked souls as the announcement repeats. Surprisingly, the chaos actually makes it easier for me to blend in because I'm no longer the only one running.

Souls push and shove in every direction. A small female with wavy white hair stumbles and falls within the frantic crowd. Those around her don't so much as pause, trampling her without hesitation. I shove my way through the crowd until I reach her, jabbing with my elbows and hands to prevent further trampling of the petite soul. She shakily rises to her feet and moves back into the throng without the slightest acknowledgment.

The horde thins as I near the outskirts of the city, most souls having already reached their homes. Now, only a few stragglers remain on the streets, though the number of guards patrolling has increased. I keep my head down and my hood up, my steps quick and purposeful, trying to give the illusion that I, too, am rushing home to one of the towering high-rises.

I weave my way past another of the buildings, and spot tall stalks of wheat in the farmland beyond. Those stalks are my salvation. I glance around, noting that the streets have now emptied, and sprint toward the wheat field. The faster I leave these vacant streets, the safer I'll be.

Panting hard, I push my speed. My breath comes out in a rush when I cross from the cobblestone thoroughfare onto soft soil. The wheat stalks gently brush my skin as I walk diagonally through the rows of plants. They are a few feet shorter than myself, so I keep my knees bent as I prowl through them, choosing stealth over speed.

A few guard towers are situated throughout the farmland, and I give each one as wide a berth as possible. With the sky darkening, I have a better chance of remaining unseen in my dark clothing. This escape may have been a little rushed, but so far, everything has gone to plan.

The wheat field transitions into a corn field. The stalks of corn are much taller than the wheat, a welcome change that allows me to stand upright. My body screams in protest, muscles aching from maintaining such an unnatural position for so long. I take a few seconds to stretch, easing the tension, before continuing to move through the tall plants.

The cover provided by the corn field ends abruptly as a shallow stream cuts through the farmland, glittering faintly in the darkness. I remove my shoes and roll up my trousers before stepping into the chilly water. Rocks litter the streambed, their jagged edges cutting into my feet. I wince as one particularly sharp stone digs into my sole.

Once I reach the opposite shore, I duck back into the shelter of the crops to inspect my foot. A jagged gash mars the bottom of my sole. My first instinct is to activate my healing energy, but I pause, the memory of the greenhouse plants flashing vividly in my mind. My healing energy didn't restore them—it drained them, siphoning their nutrients and leaving them as withered husks. Best not to take such a risk at the moment.

After slipping my shoes back on, I don't walk far before encountering another body of water. This time, it's a river—deeper and wider than the stream. There's no way around it. If I want to reach the gate, I have to cross. A bridge a few paces to my right spans the expanse of the water, but walking across it would be like wearing a flashing sign that announces *"HERE I AM."* So, into the river I go. I sidle up to the edge of the bridge, using its dark shadow as additional cover, and wade into the water.

I'm nearly halfway across when the unmistakable whirr of a drone fills the air. My heart sinks as I look downriver, searching for the source of the noise, and see it following the path of the river. Its spotlight sweeps back and forth, focused solely on the water. Shiznits. I'm too far from the shore to reach land in time, which leaves me with only one option: I'm going under.

Taking a deep breath, I hold the air in my lungs, cheeks puffed, and submerge. The water covers my head as I pull myself deeper. Tilting my face upward, I watch the spotlight's beam slicing through the water's surface. Every muscle in my body tenses as the light passes over me. It doesn't pause or waver, and I begin to think I'm safe. But just as I'm about to rise for air, the drone spins around and its spotlight swings back toward me.

I scramble back down into the depths of the water. My air is running out and my lungs are screaming at me to take another breath. The drone circles above, still searching. I pull myself deeper still, until I can barely see the light of the spotlight. My need to pull in air becomes more insistent. I don't know how much longer I can last. I need air, and I need it now.

I push myself up to the surface. Right when my head breaks the water, the drone turns away from me and continues on its way. That was way too close. I gulp down air as though it's the finest wine in existence. My lungs burn as they recover from the lack of oxygen, and my gasps are loud in the silence left in the drone's wake.

Once my pulse steadies and my breathing evens out, I swim toward the shore. Hauling myself out of the water is a monumental effort; my wet clothes weigh me down, and my muscles are fatigued from both the swimming and the oxygen deprivation. Still, I made it to the other side, and for that, I am thankful.

The gate is concealed from my view by a dense patch of bean bushes, but I know it isn't far now. Pushing into the thick, leafy greenery, elation swells in my chest. I'm close—so close—to the spot where Dee told me to meet her. My foot throbs painfully, but compared to what could have gone wrong, I'm relatively unscathed. That alone feels like a small victory.

Lost in my jubilation, I don't realize that the bushes ahead of me are swaying in the windless night until it's too late. My foot catches on an indentation in the ground, my ankle twists, and I fall forward onto my hands and knees. I look back toward my injured ankle, but my attention is immediately captured by the sight beyond it.

My foot leans on the edge of the largest burrow entrance I've ever encountered. I whip my head back around, understanding suddenly dawning. A few paces in front of me, creeping silently through the bean bushes, is the burrow's occupant. Its eyes glow through the foliage and I can just barely make out its body as it readies itself to pounce.

Chapter 33

BRIE

I read about manticores in the bestiary, but reading about them and seeing one in person are two totally different things. The beast's face is like a mix between a human and a lion, with flattened features and massive fangs. Its spiky brown hair flows seamlessly into a mane of the same color. Its jaw is also rimmed with a beard of thick fur. Its powerful body is that of a lion, but its tail has spines like a porcupine and a stinger at the end.

The beast is massive and terrifying. And smart. When he realizes I've seen him, he purrs, "Hello, angelic one." His voice is magical, luring me into a disarming sense of security. All the while, the beast creeps closer to me.

I need time to strategize against this formidable foe, so I decide to play his game. "Hello, manticore," I reply, my words soft but lacking the seductive quality his voice carried. He chuckles at my response, clearly relishing the prelude. His mouth spreads into a grin, revealing three rows of razor-sharp teeth.

While I'm momentarily distracted by his fangs, the manticore lowers his shoulders and launches at me with astonishing speed. I barely duck under his leap and narrowly avoid the spine that flies from his tail immediately afterward. Spinning quickly, I draw one of the kitchen knives and the vial of spider flower nectar from within my cloak. He charges at me again, and this time I meet him head-on. My knife pierces his neck—not deep enough to strike anything vital, but sufficient to keep his powerful jaws a hair's breadth away from my jugular.

The manticore pulls back, and my knife slides free, its tip dripping with black, shadowy ichor. I use the blade to deflect another spine hurtling toward me. His tail lashes out, the stinger arcing toward me, but I leap aside just in time. The truth is clear: he's stronger than I am. It's only a matter of time before exhaustion overtakes me and he gains the upper hand. Still, I will fight with everything I have, even when I'm certain my demise is inevitable.

The manticore lets out a trumpet-like roar, his patience clearly fraying. I take some satisfaction in his frustration and successfully manage to dodge a volley of spines. As he pounces again, I drop to the ground, my knife grazing his underside. The cut is shallow: it won't cause serious harm, but it's enough to annoy him further.

Distant voices mix with the manticore's heavy breaths. His head snaps toward the sound, and he growls when he spots an approaching squad of sphinxes. Intelligent enough to recognize the greater threat, the manticore snarls and flees, his powerful form retreating into the darkness. The guards, oblivious to my presence, pursue the manticore. Their heavy steps thunder past me as I lie motionless on the ground, not a single one sparing a glance downward.

I send a silent prayer of gratitude up to the divine spirit for the fortunate intervention. Had the guards not arrived, I doubt I would have survived the encounter. The area falls quiet as the guards and the manticore vanish into the distance, leaving me time to gather myself.

Securing the knife and vial back within my cloak for easy access, I rise from the ground and prepare to continue my journey toward the Gate when inspiration strikes, and I drop back to the ground, searching for the manticore's discharged spines. I learned in my reading that they contain a potent venom—a weapon that could prove invaluable.

I find a handful of the spines and carefully place them into one of the reinforced pockets sewn into my cloak. I can only hope the fabric holds and prevents any accidental punctures; stabbing myself with manticore venom would be an ironic end to my escape.

With my arsenal now bolstered, I resume my trek toward the Gate. Dee assured me she would handle the two guards stationed there and meet me on the other side. I pray she succeeded and isn't rotting in Lucifer's dungeon for having helped me.

The towering black-marble structures flanking the gate to the eighth circle come into view. I squint upward, scanning the tops of the guard towers. No figures are immediately visible, but the darkness makes it hard to be certain. I hold back, caution overriding eagerness. I've come too far to let impatience undo me now. I need to be absolutely sure before making my approach.

The crops in this area of the farmland are lower, so I have to hunch my back and bend my knees to slink through them unseen. I creep closer, trying not to ruffle the plants as I go. When I've just about reached the towers, I confirm that the guards aren't at their stations.

I'm not sure what Dee did to draw the guards away, but whatever it was, it worked. The guards are nowhere to be seen. For a moment, I wonder if they joined the group chasing the manticore, though it wouldn't make much sense for them to abandon their posts for that. Honestly, it doesn't matter what drew them away. All that matters is that I've reached the Gate and can finally cross into the eighth circle.

I approach the Gate hesitantly, hardly daring to believe I've made it this far. Souls typically need permission to travel outside their assigned circle after arrival, but Dee was adamant that those rules wouldn't apply to me since I technically don't have an assigned circle. Her confidence reassured me, but skepticism lingers in the back of my mind. The only other alternative would have been asking Lucifer himself for permission—a conversation that was never going to happen for obvious reasons. So, here goes nothing.

The Gate looms before me, an inky mass of swirling darkness. I bite my lip, shake out my limbs, and step forward into the writhing shadows.

"You made it!" Dee's cheery voice greets me as I step out of the Gate and regain my bearings. It's my first glimpse of the eighth circle of Hell, and let's just say, it's not what I expected. The Gate is nestled at the edge of a sprawling forest. At first glance, the trees look lush and healthy, with thick bark, strong branches, and vibrant leaves. But when I focus, I can see beyond the glamour of Deception. In reality, the trees are withered and bare, their branches thin and broken, their bark peeling and lifeless.

The stark contrast between the forest's illusion and its true state is jarring. A cold wind swirls through the trees, and the sound of branches snapping echoes through the eerie silence. Dee seems utterly unbothered, smiling brightly as she begins leading me through the woods.

"Is your house far?" I ask quietly, focusing on my footing. Walking through a forest is always precarious, but traversing an unfamiliar one in the dark of night feels downright treacherous. I've barely taken a few steps and have already nearly tripped over exposed roots twice.

"It's not too far," Dee replies, her voice casual. "But it is on the edge of the circle. I value my privacy."

"I can understand that," I say. "I can't wait to see where you live! I feel like I know you so well, and yet I also know little about you."

Dee laughs softly, a low sound that feels almost too quiet for the space. "You'll learn more about me sooner rather than later," she says. Something about her tone feels ominous, but I push the thought aside. This is Dee—she's the one person I've met here that I feel like I can count on to have my back—so I know my ears are misinterpreting her inflection.

As we emerge from the forest, dawn begins to break. A small village sits at the edge of the woods, its run-down houses bordered by patches of dirt yards. Souls are already starting their day, some pulling weeds while others hang laundry on clothes lines.

The moment they notice us, their tasks cease. Every soul we pass stops what they're doing to stare at us, their wary gazes tracking our movements as though they expect an attack at any moment. Their distrust puzzles me, but I don't dwell on it. I know nothing about the social dynamics of Deception, and if the illusions in the forest are any indication, suspicion is probably justified here.

Beyond the village lies a river. Like the forest, its appearance and reality are two very different things. The river glistens like a jewel, its clear water effervescent, burbling softly toward a large lake. A gleaming silver bridge arches gracefully above it, a masterpiece of architectural brilliance, inviting travelers to cross safely. But as I've already learned, nothing in Deception is ever as it seems.

In reality, that's all an illusion. The riverbed is there, but the water dried up long ago, if it ever existed. The riverbed is bone dry, as is the large lakebed the river connects to. And that gleaming bridge spanning the river is actually a decrepit wooden death-trap. Anyone who tried to use the bridge to cross the river would surely fall through a hole on one of the many rotting planks.

Instead of heading toward the bridge, Dee leads me down into the riverbed to cross. I slip and slide on the steep slope of the riverbed, but manage to get down without twisting my ankle again. I have to use a few rocks embedded into the opposite slope to heave myself up the other side, but I make it through. On the opposite riverbank lies another village, and I'm convinced one of these houses will be hers, but she leads me through this village too and into another forest.

The trees here are even more mangled and gnarled than in the forest near the Gate. Darkness seems to engulf them, and though it is now daytime, little light penetrates through the bare branches that comprise the forest's canopy. The amount of darkness here unsettles me. This place feels evil—more evil than any place I encountered in the ninth circle or the castle. The small hairs on my arm stand on end. My muscles tense, ready to propel me away from here. I take a few steps backward. I don't like it here. This isn't right.

But just as I'm about to sprint back toward the village, Dee turns around and points through the trees. "That's my house," she says proudly with a large smile on her face. I peer in the direction of her finger and chills rack my body. *This* is where she lives?

MICHAEL

Knowing Lucifer has ordered our safe passage brings me little solace given Cacus' parting words. *Your soulmate is turning dark.* I shake my head and try to pull in a breath, but the air is too thin and my lungs are left wanting. My chest constricts and I gasp for air again, unsure if the difficulty breathing is from the low oxygen level within the sixth circle or my panic attack. Because I'm definitely having a panic attack right now.

Gabriel's face appears inches from mine. His baby blue eyes penetrate my soul, his divine wisdom causing flecks of silver to grow within the blue. My little brother is so much like me, but also so incredibly different. He's strong in a different way than I am, and I lean on that strength now.

"Breathe with me," he says, pulling in a long slow breath, holding it for several seconds, and then blowing it out just as slowly. I mimic his actions. A sharpness I didn't even notice disappears from my chest and my heart rate slows.

I grab onto Gabriel's bicep and continue to follow his breathing pattern. The point of contact brings me more comfort than I can put into words. Slowly, I return to myself. The air is still thin, and I still struggle to pull in a full breath, but I'm certain these lasting difficulties are due solely to the environment.

I squeeze Gabriel's arm as a gesture of appreciation, then release my grip. He takes a single step away from me and nearly disappears into the darkness of our surroundings. Despite the small glow emanating from all of our wings, it's nearly pitch black. Haniel ignites a small orb of brilliant white angel light within his palm, illuminating our small group. And even with his angelic light shining brightly, the ring of light doesn't spread much further.

Pride, also sometimes called Vanity, is bathed in darkness. Always. Surrounded by a ring of mountains, the souls within this circle never see daylight again once they arrive. And although we are currently atop one of those mountains, the angle of the mountains relative to Hell's suns guarantees that the light from Hell's suns is blocked, even here.

We pick our way down the mountain. My lungs burn from the acidity in the air. I can feel my self-healing engaging to heal the acid burns within my lungs before they blister. Raphael is going to have his work cut out for him with how often he'll need to heal the others while we're here. I don't envy him.

At the bottom of the mountain lies a bog. The brown color of the bog water reminds me of excrement, and I grimace. I really don't want to wade into it, but I know we need to. The only way to avoid it would be to climb up and down the mountains all the way to the gate, but that would take us much longer. If Brie really is falling to the darkness, we don't have the time for that. And even if she isn't falling, we don't know what Lucifer is doing to her. We need to reach her as quickly as possible.

That reaffirmation of my reason for undertaking this whole journey buoys me. I take my first step into the bog. The cold water surrounds my foot, lapping up my shin. I shiver in revulsion.

I slog forward through the disgusting liquid. It feels like I'm walking through a slimy film. The water is heavy, like a thick custard. And the smell is pungent with undertones of saltwater brine, decaying plant material, and wet dog.

My nose wrinkles of its own accord. I can hear Callista behind me, squealing "Ew, ew, ew, ew, ew!" every few seconds. My jaw ticks. I agree with her sentiment, but does she really need to be so vocal about it?

The irritation catches me off guard. I'm not usually so sensitive about the small things, and the fact that I am now worries me. It's common for the energy of our souls to sense things before we consciously realize them. I fear that's what's happening now—that my soul knows something I haven't yet realized.

I straighten my posture and raise my head. If that's the case, there's nothing I can do about it right now. My focus must remain on the task at hand: rescuing Brie. That's what matters.

The longer I'm in the water, the more the submerged portions of my legs burn. Each step becomes increasingly painful, and I grimace as the acid gnaws at my skin. Reaching the ladder that leads to the only village in Pride feels like a small victory. But raising my leg out of the water to reach the first rung is excruciating. If my powerful self-healing abilities are struggling against this level of pain, I can only imagine the torment for those without such gifts.

I climb the ladder quickly so the rest of my team isn't stuck waiting in the acidic water for longer than necessary. At the top, a small wooden platform edged with rope fills the short distance between the ladder and the open door to the welcome center. The first time I visited Pride, I laughed out loud at the concept of a welcome center in Hell, but I've since learned that the inhabitants of Pride take their hospitality very seriously.

All the buildings in Pride are elevated above the water on stilts, connected by rickety wooden rope bridges. Constructed entirely of wood, the structures resemble small houses, typically accommodating only one or two souls per building. My group gathers on the tiny platform, packed together like sardines despite there being only five of us.

Five. A pang of devastation hits me straight in the gut. I can't hold back the sorrow that engulfs me as I'm reminded of the comrades we've lost. This mission has left permanent scars on all of us. We'll need to work through the traumas as soon as we're back on a higher plane. For now, I need to focus on the present.

"Are you all coming in or what? You can stand outside all day if you want, but I wouldn't recommend it."

The deep, scratchy voice jolts me from my thoughts, and I realize I've been staring at the polished wooden sign with black lettering nailed above the door that reads *Pride Welcome Center*. Blinking, I look toward the source of the voice and find a grotesque soul standing in the doorway.

Every part of him is disfigured, to the point where it's almost painful to look at him. His face appears as though it's endured repeated third-degree burns, likely from the acid rain. His hands are missing fingers, and the ones that remain are twisted and deformed. Beneath his oversized clothing, his body looks emaciated, sickly.

Despite his painful appearance, the soul exudes a jovial energy, smiling broadly and beckoning us inside with an air of superiority and exaggerated grandeur. "Well, now that you're all inside, hello! Welcome to Pride, the sixth and best circle of Hell. My name is Fikhar, and I run the welcome center here—as you can see." He chuckles. "What brings you to our wonderful village today?"

Raphael steps forward, brushing past me to take the lead. He's better with social interactions than I am, so I'm happy to stand back and let him handle this. "We're just passing through, but would appreciate accommodations for the night, if you have the space," he says smoothly.

"Ah, I see." Fikhar taps a knobby finger against his chin, feigning deep contemplation. His performance grates on me. I clench my fists, struggling to suppress a growl. I don't have the time or patience for these petty games. Sensing my frustration, Gabriel steps up beside me and bumps my shoulder lightly, grounding me.

Raphael must also sense my growing irritation because he doesn't wait out Fikhar's theatrics. Instead, he adds with an eager tone, "I would also love to see, first-hand, the great feats of engineering you and your neighbors have accomplished."

I stare at the back of Raphael's head to stop myself from rolling my eyes. *Great feats of engineering?* The bridges are barely functional, swaying precariously in the slightest breeze.

Nevertheless, Fikhar preens at the compliment. "How could I ever deny such a request from a connoisseur such as yourself? You clearly have an eye for quality, my friend. We do have a guest cabin available on the far side of the village, but only the one, so you'll all have to lodge together. Pride is in high demand, you know."

"Yes, of course. I can't imagine it would be any other way," Raphael replies smoothly, flattering the man.

"Let me get you one of our brochures. It has a map of the village." Fikhar walks the three steps it takes to reach a brochure display. It's reminiscent of the kind you see in hotels on the earthly plane, with brochures advertising nearby attractions. This display, however—a floor stand with seven levels of pockets wide enough to hold five types of brochures per level—is filled with the same brochure in every single slot.

Fikhar pulls a brochure from the top pocket, revealing an identical one beneath it. Apparently, each slot is packed with multiple copies of the same glossy tri-fold. He brings it to Raphael, opening it with a flourish to reveal the interior map, and pulls a pen from his pocket.

"We are here," Fikhar declares, circling the building labeled *WELCOME CENTER* in big, bold letters. "This is the dining hall," he says, circling another building as though the label isn't self-explanatory. "And here..." he circles the building marked *GUEST ACCOMMODATIONS* "...is where you will be staying. Any questions? I'd escort you, but I can't leave the welcome center unoccupied."

"Of course not! Your role here is very important," Raphael responds without missing a beat.

"I'm so glad you understand. I'll see you during the evening meal, once the night shift relieves me of my post."

"Looking forward to it. Thank you for your help," Raphael calls out as we begin filing out of the welcome center. Fikhar waves exuberantly, his face beaming with self-satisfaction.

Chapter 35

MICHAEL

My knuckles whiten from the tight grip I'm maintaining on the rope railings of the wooden bridge. It sways back and forth with every small movement I make, and I'm convinced one of the planks is going to fall off as soon as I step on it.

"Come on, Michael," Gabriel groans. "Isn't acting in the face of fear supposed to be one of your virtues?"

Sometimes I hate how reasonable my brother can be. Yes, it's supposed to be one of my virtues, but that doesn't mean I never hesitate. I still experience fear just like everyone else does—and I'm allowed to take a minute or two to compose myself before I surmount it.

"Why don't we just fly?" Callista asks. "Actually, why didn't we fly over the bog as well?"

It's a fair question. "The acidity would do irreparable harm to our wings," Raphael explains as I take another step forward on the swaying bridge. "And because our wings are direct representations of our souls, damage to our wings causes damage to our souls. That's not something I can heal."

"Oh," Callista frowns. "I kind of understand, but not really," she admits.

"You'll understand it better when you get into your Introduction to Angelic Energy physics class. It's a hard concept for new angels to grasp, and they explain it much better than I do," Raphael tells her kindly.

While they talk, I manage to cross the flimsy bridge without it collapsing. I know I'm being a little dramatic, but I'm heavier and bulkier than the others, so I feel like my fears are justified. Plus, the souls in Pride would be proud of their work even if it were shoddy and sub-par, so I can't fully trust any of their construction.

I join the others on the platform in front of our lodgings. Like the welcome center, this cabin also has a large sign above the door announcing its purpose. We open the door to reveal a modest cabin. Made completely of wood, it gives off a rustic feel but is tidy and clean. The smell of lemon polish lingers in the air as I step inside.

The entrance leads into a shared common area with two bedrooms and one bathroom adjoining it. Only the inner circles of Hell have plumbing. As the sixth circle is considered one of the middle circles of Hell, the bathroom is essentially a washbasin and a pit latrine. Still, it's better than what we've had so far.

I check out the bedrooms through their open doors. I'm actually impressed when I see decent mattresses on the beds. The souls in this circle must have traded a lot for those. "Ok, Callista, you get one bed. Haniel, you can take the other. Raphael, Gabriel, and I will sleep on the floor. Let's get some rest while we can."

There's no argument. Everyone cozies up on whatever surface I've assigned them. It's been too long, and we've been through too much since we last had some decent rest. As soon as my head hits my pack, I'm out.

Chatter and boasting fill the dining hall as the souls around us compete for our attention, each trying to one-up the story before. "And then," a soul named Durmad pauses for dramatic effect, "I rushed him right as he fired the gun. The bullet hit me straight in the chest, and I didn't even flinch."

"That's because you were dead on impact," Jashwi says, her voice droll. "Being killed by a bullet doesn't mean you accomplished anything to be proud of."

"Because being a model is *so* exciting," Durmad rolls his eyes. "All you did was stand around in front of weird dudes with cameras."

"At least I was pretty," Jashwi says, examining her nails with exaggerated nonchalance. She has the attitude of disinterest down to a tee.

My gaze volleys between the two as they bicker. I can't decide if they're friends, enemies, or frenemies. They're definitely competitors. Suddenly, the room shakes violently, and everyone freezes. Conversations are cut off abruptly, leaving the room in tense silence.

"What's going on?" Callista whispers, but the souls around us quickly shush her.

The room shakes again, and I peer out of the open window next to our table. The odor hits me before I see him—a stench like rotten feet on steroids engulfs the room in seconds. My food threatens to come back up, and I pull my gaiter up over my nose to buffer the smell, thankful I left it on. I glance at the others. They aren't as fortunate, holding napkins to their noses.

Callista is readying to draw her sword, but I place my hand on her arm, shaking my head. She gets the message. The room shakes more violently as the mapinguari comes into view. The giant, primate-like creature towers above the village's buildings, even on their stilts. Thick, mud-colored hair covers the tough hide beneath, which I know from experience is nearly impenetrable.

Mapinguari are almost impossible to defeat. It's painful to do nothing, knowing the fate they bring to those who have wronged the flora and fauna they protect, but it's smarter to let them exact their justice and be on their way. They won't pursue anyone other than their target unless provoked.

The monster reaches the dining hall and peers through the doorway with his single eye. It roams around the hall, stopping on a young soul sitting in the corner by himself, terror written all over his face. He must be a new arrival. The mapinguari pulls back and sticks one meaty finger through the window nearest to his target, wiggling it around. The wooden window frame splinters under his strength.

The soul jumps up and runs away from the mapinguari, who frowns and pulls his finger out of the window. He's about to reach his hand into the open doorway of the dining hall when several souls from various areas of the hall jump to their feet and swarm the fleeing newbie. These souls clearly don't want to see more of their dining hall destroyed, nor do they want to become the mapinguari's next targets.

The souls apprehend the newbie and drag him toward the door. He screams and struggles, fighting them the entire way, but his resistance is futile. They shove him from behind, and he stumbles the last few steps on his own. The mapinguari plucks him up like an hors d'oeuvre.

The soul is frantic now, kicking, screaming, and spitting, but the mapinguari is unphased by his tantrum. The monster steps back, giving us all a full view of the massive second mouth in the middle of his stomach. The grotesque mouth opens wide, and the mapinguari tears off the soul's arm, dropping it into the gaping maw. The other arm follows, then both legs, until finally, the mapinguari devours the rest of the soul entirely.

The mapinguari's single eye roams over us once more before he turns and lumbers away from the village, the dining hall trembling with every heavy step. The souls around us release an audible sigh of relief as the monster disappears from view. "There's always one," Jashwi says flippantly, as the room begins to buzz with life again.

"What do you mean?" Callista asks.

Jashwi taps her nails on the table in a steady rhythm. "Souls in this circle receive one of four fates. The best and most difficult to achieve is to repent, learn from your mistakes, and heal your soul of its corruption. It's almost unheard of, but it is possible."

Not to be outdone, Durmad picks up the thread. "Fate number two: don't repent, don't reform, just stay as you are and chill here. That's what we're doing." He winks at Callista, earning a sharp glare in return.

Jashwi smacks Durmad upside the head and continues, "The third option is what you just witnessed. It mostly happens to newcomers. They harm one of the native plants or animals, and the mapinguari take vengeance."

"Okay, doesn't that cover all the options?" Callista asks, directing her question toward Jashwi.

Durmad answers instead, still rubbing the back of his head where Jashwi hit him. She must have quite the arm. "Not quite. There's one more. You get worse. Some souls sink deeper into their sins while they're here. If that happens, you turn into a monster. When darkness infects humans, they gain certain abilities or characteristics. But down here, when darkness infects us, there's no stopping point. It can overload the soul and literally transform you. We've all been affected by the darkness"—he gestures to his face, marred with deformities—"and if our souls become completely black, we become *that thing*." He points toward the door.

Callista's mouth pops open, and it takes her three tries before she finally finds her words again. "Are you saying... Do you mean to tell me...you could turn into *that?*" she says, mimicking Durmad's gesture toward the door.

"Sure can," Jashwi replies dryly. "Fun times, right?"

I can't blame her for her sarcasm. If I were in her place, I'm sure sarcasm would be one of my main coping methods as well.

"Well, damn," Callista mutters, her gaze bouncing around the room.

"You said it, girl," Jashwi laughs, and brings her wooden mug up in the universal sign for cheers before downing the liquid within.

Chapter 36

BRIE

Dee grabs my arm, enthusiastically tugging me through the barren trees toward her home. It looks like a stereotypical haunted house. And unlike most things in this circle, there's no glamour concealing its disastrous state.

Dee's grip on my arm is punishing, but I don't complain as I follow her mindlessly. She's just excited to be home, I tell myself. Maybe it's been a long time since she was last here—that could explain some of the neglect. Though honestly, neglect doesn't quite cover it.

The house is three stories, a noticeable difference from the small, one-story shacks in the nearby villages. It's built from a mix of dark stone and graying wood, but both materials appear worn and brittle. The windows are either empty holes or so caked with grime that there's no hope of seeing through them. Leafless, thorny vines snake over the railings and climb the walls, adding to the structure's decrepit aura. Stone and wood alike flake away in patches, giving the entire house the appearance of something long abandoned.

Dee hauls me up the rotting front steps, of which huge chunks are missing. A nest of vipers hisses menacingly at me through the gaping hole in the middle of the third step when I land on it, and I quickly move up the remaining four steps before they decide to strike rather than just hiss. Dee, for her part, doesn't seem to notice any of it—or at the very least, doesn't react to any of it.

Her nails dig into my arm as we pass through the opening where a front door should be. The frame is warped, the wood no longer straight and pulling away from the walls. The pain in my arm sharpens, and when I glance down, I'm startled to see Dee's long, pointed black fingernails cutting into my skin. Were they always like this? I could have sworn her nails were blunt just this morning.

"Dee, you're hurting me. Can you loosen your grip a bit?" I ask, my voice shaky.

Her response is as sweet as usual, her tone saccharine and familiar. "Of course, dear. I must have gotten too excited." She doesn't look at me, simply leading me into a room to the right of the entryway. "Why don't you put your bag down while I ready a place for you to rest."

Dee doesn't wait for a reply before disappearing through a door at the back of the room. The door, hanging precariously on its hinges, slams against the wall a few times as she moves through it. I set my bag on the dusty floor, noticing the thick cobwebs clustered in every corner. Maybe this wasn't such a good idea. I can't shake the feeling that something is off with Dee, and the macabre setting isn't helping me feel more secure.

My unease deepens, churning in my gut. I open my mouth to call out to Dee, intending to tell her that I've changed my mind and will head for the Gate to the seventh circle instead. But before I can get the words out, something slams into the back of my head. Pain blossoms in an instant. I raise my hand reflexively to check the wound, but my arm only gets halfway up before my vision blurs and everything goes black.

When I come to, my head throbs with a vengeance. My thoughts are fuzzy, and the pain in the back of my skull is the only clarity I have. Did something fall on me?

I open my eyes, but my vision is still blurred around the edges. I try to lift my hand to my head, but something pulls at my wrist, keeping it in place.

I look down. Blink. Blink again. Then look further down. My head swims before I can see down to my ankles, and I pause, closing my eyes and breathing through my nose until the dizziness passes.

I train my gaze down again, trying for the second time to see my ankles. This attempt is successful, and my stomach plummets. I close my eyes again. This can't be happening.

I open my eyes and check again. The rope is still there. Both my wrists and ankles are tied to a chair I have no recollection of sitting in. This really is happening, isn't it?

"Good, you're awake. I was getting so tired of waiting." Dee's voice seems to reverberate in my ears as she walks into my line of sight.

"Why?" It's the only word I can muster. I understand my situation. I understand her betrayal—the phantom pain in my chest makes that truth crystal clear. What I don't understand is *why*.

"Because sweet, little Sabriel, you are Lucifer's weakness. And besting Lucifer is the ultimate prize."

"So you're doing this for bragging rights? Or did he do something to you personally?"

"Does it matter?" Dee raises an eyebrow, her tone dripping with disdain. She knows I'm trying to extract as much information as possible, and she's determined to give me only what she chooses. "Tick tock," she sings mockingly, "your prince should be here any minute now. Oh, and by the way, I told him all about your little plan. I didn't even bother putting the poisons in his food—I just told him you asked me to. He faked the whole illness so you'd think you had a chance of escaping. He wanted to crush that hope in a permanent way. He thought I was loyal to him. Little did he realize I was betraying you both. He'll figure it out soon enough, though."

"He knew? Everything?" I stutter, mortification choking my voice.

"Everything," Dee confirms with a cruel smile. She's enjoying this—taking pleasure in my pain, in the realization that I never had any chance of escaping. The way she stoked my hopes, only to ensure my failure would hit harder, was perfectly calculated.

The pain of her betrayal, the totality of my failure, the brutality of her cruelty—it's tangible. I can feel it thick in the air, taste its bitterness on my tongue. And what little hope I had left drains out of me. I shatter. I completely shatter. I thought I knew what it meant to be broken, but I was wrong. This, what I'm feeling now—this is broken. Irreparably so. I will never be whole again.

Pain blooms behind my eyes as tears threaten, but I bite down on the inside of my cheek, determined not to cry in front of her. I will not give her that satisfaction.

"Dee, I'm..." Lucifer's words trail off as he steps into the doorway and takes in the scene. His gaze lands on the knife Dee now holds to my throat.

"It's a trap! Don't come in!" I shout, panic lacing my voice.

Dee just laughs. "Oh, sweetheart," she says with syrupy mockery, "the trap was sprung the second you left the castle. You're not the smartest angel in existence, are you?"

Lucifer stands frozen in the doorway, his body taut with tension. His eyes flick between Dee, me, and the blade at my neck. Out of the corner of my eye, I notice my bag still lying near the wall where I left it. Dee must have brought the chair into the room after knocking me out. It makes sense—moving a chair in would have been much easier than moving me elsewhere. If I could just reach my bag, I might stand a fighting chance of getting out of this alive.

"Dee, what are you doing?" Lucifer's voice is cautious, though I detect the faintest note of disbelief. He didn't expect her to double-cross him.

"I'm giving in to my nature, Lucifer," Dee spits. "The darkness formed me, gave me my true self. And you think you can force me into civility? You think being king makes you more powerful than the darkness that revived me? You are sorely mistaken. I will not be caged any longer, and I will have my revenge for you ever daring to try."

Dee's form begins to shift and elongate, her appearance warping in real time. Her hair lightens and grows longer, her wrinkles smooth away, and her short, portly figure transforms into a tall, willowy frame. The kind grandmother I once knew is replaced by a young-looking, wraith-like being—a terrifying beauty with long, silver hair, blood-red eyes, and a white dress smeared with crimson. Her skin is deathly pale, so different from the vibrant flush of the older woman she pretended to be.

I gasp in shock. Dee cackles, delighting in my horror. But Lucifer seizes the distraction, launching himself across the room to pull the knife away from my throat. The two grapple violently, each vying for dominance, while I remain bound to this wretched chair.

I wriggle and strain against the ropes, trying to gain even the slightest leverage. The struggle seems futile until I feel the familiar brush of fabric against my arms. Dee didn't bother to remove my cloak. I'm really not the smartest of angels if it took me this long to realize something so obvious.

I bend my torso forward, brushing my cloak against my hands and pulling the material until I'm able to reach the inner pocket containing the kitchen knife. I bet Dee didn't have this in mind when she urged me to take the knives. I grip the handle as well as I can, given the awkward angle, and jerk my torso upward. The cloak fabric tears, and the knife comes free of the pocket. I quickly get to work sawing the blade against the thick rope holding me in place.

It takes time, but Lucifer is consuming every ounce of Dee's attention so she doesn't notice when the first binding falls away from my wrist. Once I've freed one arm, freeing the rest of myself is much easier. I manage to release all of the bindings with only small cuts in exchange.

I look over at the pair fighting several feet away. I could run. I could head for the gate, never look back, and leave both Dee and Lucifer to their fates, whichever way those fates may fall. Or I could stay and help Lucifer defeat the being that betrayed us both.

This may be my only chance at freedom. But this may also be my only chance to ensure that a more devious monster doesn't take Lucifer's place on the throne. I know what a being of pure light would choose, but I'm not that being anymore. And whatever choice I make right now will seal my fate. Do I keep what little light I have left and sacrifice my freedom, or do I sacrifice my light and keep my freedom? The choice is impossible. And yet, it's a choice I have to make. Right now.

Chapter 37

CALLIE

My mind reels with the information Jashwi relayed. It never occurred to me that the monsters were anything other than monsters. I guess I just assumed that they were products of evolution, like the different animals on Earth. But now—to know that the monsters we've been battling in each of Hell's circles used to be souls. I shudder.

Michael stands and declares, "We should be on our way." The others follow his lead without hesitation or question. I'm the last to rise, the sense of not truly belonging to their close-knit group weighing heavily on me. Their dynamic, forged over eons of shared battles and companionship, only underscores my feeling of being an outsider.

Logically, I know they share a deep bond because of their history together, but it still makes me question whether the divine spirit made a mistake in sending me to Heaven. Maybe it's not just this group I don't fit in with—maybe I don't belong with the angels at all.

Michael leads us out of the dining hall. Since he insisted we bring all our supplies with us earlier, there's no need to return to the guest house. A ladder extends from the platform outside the dining hall down to the bog below, and Michael descends without hesitation.

I grimace at the prospect of enduring more acid burns. Raphael had to give me three rounds of healing before my legs were fully recovered from our previous experience wading through the bog. He was utterly drained by the time he finished healing our entire group.

Haniel bumps my shoulder lightly. I glance up at him, and his dimples are on full display as he leans in and whispers, "This part of the bog isn't as acidic as the other part. You don't need to worry about the acid burns." Not for the first time, I wonder if he can read my mind. He insists that's not one of his angelic powers, but I'm not convinced.

Before I can thank him, Haniel steps onto the first rung of the ladder, descending with practiced ease. I make a mental note to express my gratitude later. His steady, supportive presence throughout this expedition has been a lifeline for me. I'm not sure I would have made it this far without having several epic breakdowns if not for him. And, well, I might be developing a bit of a crush on him—but that's definitely not something I plan on advertising.

I cringe as my foot breaches the slimy, syrupy bog water. I swam often in my human life, but this bog is unlike any water I've ever encountered. Its consistency is repulsive. Still, I keep my thoughts to myself, not wanting to complain or seem weak.

Haniel usually positions himself beside or behind me when we walk. I know he does it to ensure I'm not vulnerable at the rear of the group. His thoughtfulness brings a fresh wave of appreciation, but it also saddens me, emphasizing the absence of Kemuel and Ariella. I still can't believe they are gone. It doesn't seem real. But every time I glance to my side and Ariella isn't there, I'm reminded that it is—a reality I can't escape.

As long as Brie is okay when we reach her, everything we've endured will have been worth it. I'm not saying I would trade Kemuel's or Ariella's lives for Brie's—I would never want that—but if we've lost them and Brie isn't okay, their deaths will have been in vain. The thought is unbearable. That would be a reality I could never recover from.

Haniel walks beside me as we slog toward the mountains. Just as I begin to think this part of the bog isn't so bad, I notice shapes floating in the water ahead. Wait, not just any shapes. My stomach lurches when I realize what they are—bodies. There are bodies floating in the bog. And we're about to wade through them.

A wave of lightheadedness hits me. I reach out to steady myself, my hand gripping Haniel's shoulder. My stomach roils, and I heave, but I force myself not to vomit. Wading through a maze of preserved bodies is bad enough; I refuse to add my own vomit to the mix.

Haniel rubs small circles on my back, his touch soothing me enough to recompose myself. I manage to keep up with the rest of the group without drawing attention to my struggle. I roll my eyes at myself, annoyed. My sensibilities aren't delicate—I'm just not as hardened as they are. It's no surprise, considering their ages and experiences far outstrip my own.

We're about halfway to the mountains, wading through hundreds of floating corpses, when Michael suddenly stumbles. Raphael and Gabriel grab hold of him before he can topple into the water. It looks like they're supporting his full weight as he bends forward, clutching his chest.

Haniel and I rush forward, scanning for danger. Was he bitten by something venomous? I don't see anything threatening nearby, but maybe it's lurking beneath the murky brown water?

"Brie," Michael groans, and every particle of my being freezes. A shiver races down my spine, my hands begin to tremble, and my head shakes side to side without my consent.

Brie. The agonized way he moaned her name replays in my thoughts. I close the distance between us and grab Michael's shoulder. "Brie what? What happened?" I try to shake him, but his weight is too much, and my attempts don't jar him at all.

"Callie," Raphael barks. "Stop! Give him a minute."

I've never heard Raphael sound so commanding, and his tone pulls me out of my panic. Ashamed, I look down and step back. Michael remains collapsed in Raphael's and Gabriel's arms, though now he's rubbing the center of his chest instead of clutching it.

"Michael, tell us what happened so we can help you," Gabriel says soothingly.

"You can't help," Michael grits out, his eyes glassy. "My thread to Brie just lost most of its light. Our soulmate bond is weakening."

Gabriel sucks in a shocked breath while Raphael whispers, "How is that possible?"

Michael groans again before straightening, his resolve driving him to push forward toward the Gate with redoubled urgency. He moves so fast that I have to jog to keep up, the disgusting bog water splashing around me as I drag my legs through it. But I don't slow. Brie is in trouble.

Several minutes pass before Michael finally answers Raphael's question. "There are two possibilities: either she's mortally wounded, or she's lost all hope. Neither scenario bodes well for her—or for us."

Raphael and Gabriel exchange a grim look, but no one says anything. There's nothing to say. Nothing has changed. We still need to get to Brie as quickly as possible, just as we did before. What we'll find once we reach her, we'll face it then. For now, we press on.

I never thought I would be relieved to climb a mountain, but my first step out of the bog water and onto the steep incline is exactly that—a relief. "Wait!" Michael calls from farther up the mountainside. "Grab one of the bodies."

"What?" I heard him, but I'm certain I heard him incorrectly. I thought he said—

"Grab one of the bodies that are floating in the bog," he repeats.

"I'll need your help," Haniel says softly.

I have no desire to touch a corpse, but I can't let Haniel down. He's been my rock throughout this ordeal, offering support and encouragement when I needed it most. If this is the one time he's asking for my help, I won't refuse, no matter how much the task repulses me. So, despite my absolute revulsion, I follow him back into the bog.

"Do you want the arms or the legs?" he asks with a wince, knowing full well I want neither.

"I'll take the legs," I reply, dreading the task. I don't want to touch the corpse's feet, but I want to be near the face even less. I grab the body's bare ankles, struggling to keep a firm grip as they continually slip in my grasp.

Haniel clutches corpse's arms, walking backward to tow it along. Together, we drag the body back to the mountain and start climbing toward where the others are waiting. Our pace is slow, the weight of the body and the awkwardness of the climb making progress difficult.

"We'll need to trade off," Haniel warns the others. "The body isn't heavy, exactly, but climbing a mountain with it is awkward. Callie and I will both need a break."

I love that he's so considerate of me. Michael, on the other hand, glares at me like I've somehow disappointed him. Sometimes, I really don't know what Brie sees in him.

"Put the body down, Callista," Michael orders brusquely, as though I'd been complaining about carrying the thing. Still, I do as he says without comment, knowing he's stressed and that a snarky retort won't help the situation.

As soon as I put the corpse's feet on the ground, Michael prowls over. He orders Haniel to release the corpse as well, and then slings the body over his shoulder as though it weighs nothing and stalks up the mountain. Well, okay then. I hold in my gag as I watch the slick bog water seeping into his black shirt.

It feels like the climb up the mountain takes ages, but the Gate finally comes into view. I'm exhausted from the climb, but the urge to get to Brie propels me onward. The Gate is guarded by four majestic white horses. They are huge and gorgeous, the most beautiful horses I've ever seen.

Michael doesn't slow his approach when they bare their teeth at him. He simply throws the corpse he's been carrying to the right of the Gate. The mares converge around it, tearing into it savagely. They don't acknowledge any of us when Michael leads us past them and through the Gate, too busy eating the flesh off the bog body with satisfied slurps and whinnies of pleasure.

Chapter 38

BRIE

Dee's long black claws dig into Lucifer's bicep. He lets out a roar of pain as she pulls the muscle out of his arm. Black wisps of shadow and ichor drip from Dee's hand. Then, she pushes the severed body part into Lucifer's face. Literally.

Lucifer shakes his head and tries to back away from Dee, but her other hand has a death grip on his shoulder. He roars again, but I see the resignation in his green eyes. He thinks he's going to lose this fight.

I take one step toward the empty doorway when Dee rakes her claws down Lucifer's face. Shiznits, he really will lose this fight if I don't jump in to help him. Could I live with myself if Dee becomes the queen of Hell? I'll either be trapped down here or dead regardless, so I might as well make sure the kinder of the two beings holds onto his throne.

Dee is a formidable opponent. I don't want to get too close to her, but I need to intervene somehow. I brush my hands down my cloak in agitation, and the rigid lines of the manticore spines

I gathered pull my attention. I carefully remove one of the spines from my pocket, pull back my arm, and pray that I don't hit Lucifer by mistake.

I never really liked playing darts, but Callie and I would occasionally dabble in it when we went to bars. Thanks to eight years of softball, my hand-eye coordination is on point. I send the spine flying, and it sails toward the grappling pair. Lucifer sees it coming despite the gore dripping into his eyes, and drops at the exact moment the spine punctures the back of Dee's neck and lodges itself there.

Dee freezes, then slowly turns from Lucifer to face me. The slow spin is one of the creepiest things I've ever seen, and I know that my eyes have widened in response. A shiver rolls through my body, though I'm not cold. It's solely from fear.

She kicks backward without looking, knocking Lucifer right in the face. A crunch fills the room, and I know she's broken his nose. Dee tilts her head in an animalistic way, before allowing a smirk to twist her lips. Then, she bends her knees and launches at me.

I fumble within the pockets of my cloak, searching for the little vial I know is somewhere inside. I find it the moment she reaches me, spinning out of her reach as I pop the cap off. Then, I throw the spider flower nectar in her face. She bares her sharp teeth at me, and I see one, two drops of the nectar drip into her open mouth.

As she reaches out for me again, I dance to the side, grabbing her arm and pushing it up and away from my body. Dee whips her other arm toward my face; I grab that one too. We wrestle, each trying desperately to gain the upper hand. Lucifer comes up behind her, banding an arm around her throat. Dee thrashes, and more of the nectar drips into her mouth with the movement.

Then, she goes still once again. But this time, it's permanent. The nectar has done its job. Dee's eyes roll back in her head and her body slackens. Lucifer, being Lucifer, doesn't trust her stillness to signify certain death, and snaps her neck with a forceful twist of her head for good measure. Then, he slits her throat, to be extra certain. As soon as he pulls his dagger away from her neck, her body bursts into wisps of darkness and disappears into the air.

Lucifer is bent over and panting, but he still manages to pierce me with his gaze. His eyes, a vibrant green, promise retribution for trying to run, and the shadows roiling behind them reveal the sharp sting of betrayal. A sting that infuses my own being as well.

"You can't be trusted. I see that now."

We were escorted back to the castle by a platoon of guards not long after Dee's demise, and Lucifer immediately hustled me into his office. He's been pacing the length of it ever since, while I sit in one of the upholstered mahogany chairs in front of his desk, watching him stride back and forth.

"I thought if I just gave you some freedom, you'd come around to the idea of keeping me company here. Obviously, I was wrong," he continues. I already feel like garbage, but he knows exactly what buttons to push to make me feel worse. Each word hits me like a weapon, cutting into my soul and increasing my level of pain.

"I was trying to protect you. I wanted you to be safe and happy here. Hell isn't a kind place, but I did my best to shield you from that part of it."

And the knife twists. The main problem is that I know everything he says is true. He really *was* trying to protect me, in his own way. He wasn't willing to let me go, but he didn't want me to be miserable. He was trying to give me the best of a bad situation. It doesn't absolve him of his sins—he *did* kidnap me and hold me captive, after all—but it does make me feel that much more guilty for betraying his trust.

"There's only one solution that I can think of. If you can't be trusted to keep yourself out of danger when you're on your own, then I can't let you be on your own. And after Dee's deception, I can't trust anyone else to look after you either. It will have to be me."

"What do you mean by that?" It's the first time I've spoken since leaving Dee's house, and his face crumples at the sound of my voice.

He closes his eyes, inhaling a slow breath before resuming his pacing. He still won't look at me when he answers. "I mean that you and I are about to become attached at the hip. Where you go, I go. If you are in your quarters, so am I. If you are in the greenhouse, so am I. If you are dressing for the day, I am on the other side of the door, listening to your every movement. I will be watching you every second of every day to ensure you don't act dangerously again. If you aren't capable of protecting yourself, I will do it for you."

I gape at him. "You can't be serious."

"I am deadly serious. Not a second will pass without me by your side."

"I'd like to remind you that *you're* the one who hired Dee," I grit out, acid dripping from every word.

"Yes," Lucifer admits. "An error in judgement on my part. And although all of my remaining staff will undergo interrogation to discern the extent of their loyalty, should anyone else in the castle become a threat to you, I will be there to nullify it. I will not have you in the position I found you in ever again."

Finally, for the first time since we entered this room, Lucifer pins his eyes on me. His gaze is frigid, his lips pinched, and the distance between us feels like it could span an entire galaxy. I've really hurt him.

The truth of that thought sends me spiraling even further. I still don't really know what angel Sabriel was like, but as Brienna the human, I made many mistakes and did a lot of things I ended up regretting. But I've never experienced as much shame as I do now. And I'm not sure I ever will again.

The grief is choking me, sealing off my connection to one of the few things that give me life. I feel empty. It's as though Dee's betrayal and Lucifer's disapproval have stolen what little spark I had left in me after being trapped here. And now I'm just an empty shell of the woman I was—a weak impersonation with no ambition, no drive, and no hope.

I'm here. I'll always be here. I've accepted that now. It was silly to think I could escape. That will never happen. And even if I *did* manage to get out, I'd be sent right back here. I don't belong in Heaven anymore. I don't belong with Michael anymore. I don't even deserve to be on the earthly plane.

I've fallen into the darkness, and my light is hanging on by a thread. Hell is now where I belong. And Hell is where I'll stay.

Here, in Lucifer's castle. My gilded cage.

Chapter 39

MICHAEL

The pain in my chest is excruciating. But the implication of what that pain means is even worse. I check in on my link to Brie once more. I've been monitoring it obsessively since the initial shock of it dimming. It hasn't changed.

I try to keep my focus on our mission despite the throbbing pain. The best thing to do right now is to reach Brie as quickly as possible. If she's hurt, Raphael can heal her. If not, our arrival should restore her hope enough for the link to strengthen.

Surveying our surroundings, I'm not surprised to see everything around us cast in shades of gray. The sun sits just above the horizon, but the sunset in Envy doesn't provide the beautiful colors most would expect. That type of beauty is withheld from the seventh circle as one of the more subtle methods of punishing the souls here.

Still, after experiencing the prolonged darkness of Pride, I have to squint to allow my eyes to adjust to the low light. The gate deposits us into Envy's only market. Most of the stalls have closed for the night—not that they have many goods left to sell anyway. They don't have large inventories to begin with.

Large billboards positioned around the market advertise enticing goods that I know the stall owners can't acquire. They cast long shadows across the small square as we navigate toward the market's exit. There's a small inn near the edge of the market where I stayed the last time I was in Hell. It's been several millennia since I was here, but I'm certain the inn is still standing.

"Oh my goodness," Callista gasps from the rear of our small group. I immediately look for danger but don't detect anything amiss. Turning toward Brie's loyal friend, I prepare to follow her gaze, but I quickly realize her gasp wasn't in reaction to a threat.

Callista is staring at one of the food stalls, her eyes wide, a hand clasped over her mouth, and her face tinged green. She quickly looks away, but some sights can't be unseen, and I hear her gag moments later. Haniel begins rubbing circles on her back and whispers, "Aren't you glad we ate dinner in Pride?"

Callista's gagging transforms into a little laugh. "So glad," she responds. The stall owner, however, is unamused by Haniel's comment. Perhaps his whisper wasn't as quiet as he intended.

The soul scowls at our group, muttering to himself about privileged outsiders as he picks up a large tub of partially mashed but still writhing worms from beneath a sign depicting a thick, juicy hamburger. I quickly avert my own gaze, not wanting to be the next one to gag at the sight. I think we've insulted the poor soul enough already.

We follow the main path away from the market. The dirt underfoot is hard, littered with sharp pebbles I can feel even through the soles of my boots. Large trees line the sides of the path, and the exposed light bulbs hanging from them provide enough illumination to guide us.

At the first curve in the downhill slope, I follow a turn-off that should lead to the inn. The dilapidated building comes into view as soon as we clear the curve. The sight of it almost seems to reduce the weight of despair and regret I've been carrying. Almost, but not quite.

I knock gently on the thin wooden door, careful not to break through it like I did the last time I was here. Milton wasn't very happy about that. The sound of shuffling feet on the other side of the door tells me my knock was heard, and soon after, the door swings open to reveal a frowning Milton.

"You again," he sniffs. "I guess some business is better than no business."

"It's nice to see you too, Milton. How have you been?" I ask.

"I could be better," he replies, and I think that's the best response I could have hoped for from him. I've never seen Milton happy. He kind of reminds me of Eeyore, perpetually trudging around with a rain cloud above his head.

"Well, I think your day is about to get a lot better, because we need lodging for the night," I tell him, gesturing toward the rest of my group.

"Great, more cleaning," Milton sighs. "Follow me."

I stifle a chuckle as I enter the inn and follow Milton up the rickety staircase. I'm still in an inexpressible amount of pain, but I welcome the distraction that Milton's sour attitude provides. No matter what comes his way, he always finds the negative in it. It's inspired.

Entering the beige-colored upstairs hallway, Milton waves toward the open doors. "Pick whichever rooms you like. You're the only guests here."

"Thank you, Milton. We'll see you bright and early," I reply.

Milton grumbles at that, "Bright and early, pshhh. More like at the butt crack of dawn with drabby grey overcast skies." Then, he turns and heads back down the rickety wooden staircase to the ground floor, where his own room is.

"Goodnight!" Raphael calls after him, but Milton doesn't acknowledge the statement.

I head toward the open door closest to the staircase, wanting to be the first line of defense between my friends and danger should something happen. The room is dark and small, but I can just make out the outline of a single bed. I take a step toward it, then look down at my chest and pause. Turning back toward the hallway, I say, "Raf, a word please."

Raphael lopes over to me and I motion him into the small room, closing the door behind him. Igniting a ball of angelic light in my palm, I allow the pain to show on my face. "There's nothing you can do, right? I just wanted to make sure."

Raphael knows me well enough to see my nervousness in asking him for help. I don't even know why I'm hesitant to seek his aid in this situation. Perhaps because I know there's nothing he can do, and I don't want that confirmed.

His face falls as he says, "I'm sorry, Michael. Soulmate bonds are outside of my purview. Only the divine spirit can intercede in such matters. Have faith, though. You and Brie are both strong-willed, and whatever happened to dim your bond, the two of you will find a way to fix it."

"What if it breaks?" I ask him. "What if she's too far gone?"

"Then you'll bring her back. Anything broken can be rebuilt. You are her rock, and you will fortify whatever foundation of your bond is left until she can find the strength to start rebuilding it. And once she finds that strength again, the two of you will rebuild that bond together—just as you did the first time. Don't forget that your bond didn't immediately shine as soon as you met. The connection was there, but you had to work to strengthen it into what it became."

"You're right. I know you're right. I'm just...scared," I admit.

"Of course you are. Who wouldn't be, in your situation?" Raphael reassures me. "But you have to remember that courage is at the core of who you are. It's okay to be scared, as long as you take action regardless of that fear. That's what courage is, and that's who you are. Don't let the fear consume you. Once we find Brie, you'll find however much courage you need to bring her back to us—both physically and emotionally."

I find myself rubbing my chest again, and consciously stop the action. "Thanks, Raf. I appreciate your support through all of this."

"I'm sorry I can't do more," he responds, nodding to my hand that is once again drifting toward the most painful spot in my chest.

I look away from him, close my eyes, and fight against the tears that want to spill out. I've never felt as helpless as I do in this moment. I don't know how to handle it, though I do know that I'm not handling it well.

I steel myself and look back at Raphael, mask in place. He nods to me, his own eyes gleaming with unshed tears. His inability to help me causes him just as much pain as I feel.

"We'll get her back," Raphael says to me. But his words lack conviction. The bond dimming changes things, and neither of us is as confident as we were when we started this rescue mission. But we have to keep going. For Brie's sake. For Ariella. For Kemuel. For all the angels in Heaven who admire her or are inspired by her.

Raphael slips out of the room and I climb into the bed, fully clothed and with my boots still on. One of the main rules of the Angelic Army is to never sleep without your boots on while engaged in a mission. You never know what will come upon you in the middle of the night. And with that less than comforting thought, I let myself fall into a restless oblivion.

Chapter 40

MICHAEL

A loud bang interrupts my sleep, and I'm out of bed before my brain can even process what the sound is. Bang, bang, bang. "Knocking," I mutter to myself, shaking my head at my own skittishness.

I start down the stairs just as Milton opens the door and spits, "Yeah, yeah. We're coming," before slamming the door in the centaurs' faces.

"All souls of the seventh circle are required to attend the daily gifting ceremony," one of the centaurs yells through the closed door. "You have five minutes to join your escort before we knock the door down and drag you out."

Milton rolls his eyes. "Same story, different day. I think they were given a script to follow. Is everyone here?"

I glance at the group converging on the stairs behind me. "Yes, we're all here. Does everyone have everything you came in with? We won't be coming back." My team members nod as they yawn and rub sleep from their eyes, and I turn back to Milton. "Lead the way."

With a huff, Milton reopens the door and steps out of the inn. Our escort consists of two centaurs, both with wild hair and bulging muscles. Their humanoid torsos are bare, showcasing every detail of their toned physiques. As an angel for whom physical fitness is a necessity, I can appreciate the work required to maintain such sculpted forms. It also tells me they know how to use the heavy wooden clubs they carry.

The centaurs trot alongside our group as Milton leads us back to the main path and down the hill to a clearing. At the far edge stands a wooden stage. The clearing is filling with souls, each accompanied by at least one centaur guard. Once ensuring their assigned soul enters the clearing, the guards line its perimeter, keeping watch over the crowd.

"Why isn't anyone sitting?" Callista whispers, eyeing the three rows of chairs positioned in front of the stage.

"The seats are reserved for the souls from the eighth circle. We're not allowed to use them," Milton grumbles.

"What would happen if you tried to sit there?" Callista asks.

"You see the clubs the centaurs hold?" Milton responds. Callista nods. "They're not for show." She blanches and grimaces. The souls nearby, emboldened by her reaction, begin complaining more loudly about their circumstances.

As the hours pass and the sun rises higher in the sky, the souls' anger grows. Just as it's about to reach a boiling point, the souls from Deception file into the clearing and take their seats. Their harpy escorts line the front of the stage, and I can't help but notice one particularly mean-looking harpy becoming hyper-focused on me. When she spots me in the crowd, she leans over to another harpy and whispers something, prompting her companion to search for and fixate on me as well.

My gaze is pulled away from the harpies and up toward the stage as one of the largest centaurs trots onto it, positioning himself in front of the microphone. His chocolate-brown hair is messed, and his beard unkempt, but he holds himself with a confidence most could only dream of. "Good morning," he greets, his deep voice gruff as the speakers amplify it throughout the clearing. "As you all know, another day has dawned, which means we must commence another of our daily gifting ceremonies. These ceremonies highlight the best of Hell and their achievements toward reformation."

I scoff internally. This ceremony has nothing to do with reformation and everything to do with torture. It's yet another way of punishing the souls from both circles—a creative and subtle method of punishment, but punishment all the same.

The centaur on stage begins listing the various categories in which souls can excel and announces the winners of each. Gift after gift goes to the souls from Deception. The souls standing around us mutter bitter comments about how the souls of Envy never win anything yet are still forced to attend the ceremony each day—and forced to arrive hours earlier than the souls from Deception.

With each winner announced, the complaints grow louder and angrier. The murmur of dissatisfaction builds into an uproar, and before the ceremony concludes, the souls of Envy are shouting their displeasure.

"Quiet down, quiet down," the centaur at the mic booms, but the souls pay no heed. In an instant, the mob of souls from Envy escalates from verbal attacks to physical ones.

A soul toward the front launches himself at one of the souls from Deception, grabbing her by the hair and pulling her out of her chair. The chair topples backward in his wake as he drags the soul into the mass of the growing mob. And with that inciting action, mayhem ensues.

The souls from Deception leap over their chairs, pursuing the soul from Envy that took their neighbor. The two groups converge in an explosion of hate, anger, and resentment. Fists are flying, feet are kicking. It's complete chaos.

The centaurs wade into the fray, swinging their clubs in an effort to restore order. But there are many more souls than centaurs and they are quickly overrun. The souls attack the centaurs just as savagely as they attack each other, and the clearing turns into one huge brawl.

We're right in the middle of it.

I try to fight my way over to where I last saw that first soul that was pulled out of her chair. A fist flies toward my face; I dodge it and swing my arm in a hook, nailing the soul that swung at me right in the temple. His eyes roll back in his head and he crumbles to the ground, but another soul is already taking his place. I don't even know if the souls attacking me are from the seventh circle or the eighth. It's utter mayhem.

I push through the crowd, punching when necessary. A sharp pain flares to life on my calf, and I look down to see a soul with his arms around my leg and his teeth embedded in my pants. Did this imbecile just bite me? I pull my leg straight up out of his grip, detaching his teeth from my flesh, before stomping down on his hand. He cries out in pain and I glare at him as I inspect the newly formed hole in my pants.

"This is getting us nowhere!" Raphael shouts from behind me. "It's just wasting our time and energy. Let's get out of this mess. It's not our problem."

Raphael unfurls his wings, knocking over several souls in the process, and takes to the sky. I follow, as do the others. We fly into formation and turn toward the gate, ready to leave Envy, but are blocked by a line of harpies.

The harpy I noticed earlier hovers in the center of the line. Like all harpies, she's savagely beautiful with long, glossy black hair and big black eyes. The latter are pinned on my face. Her corset molds to her body like a second skin, but her sharp talons betray the danger that is an inextricable part of her nature.

"Where do you think you're going?" the harpy purrs, seduction dripping from every syllable. "Your group took some of ours. Did you not think that we communicate with our sisters in Sloth? We know what you did, and we demand vengeance for those you took from us. Lucifer may have a soft spot for you, but neither his orders nor your angelic status will protect you here. It is time you pay for your crimes."

"Your sisters attacked us unprovoked. We defended ourselves. That is no crime," I tell her, but she is unmoved by my words and charges at me with her talons extended.

We are drastically outnumbered by the harpies, by at least six to one. And while we have all shown that we are competent at defending ourselves, I don't like these odds. The harpies rush after their leader, swarming our small group.

I brandish my sword, imbuing it with my angelic light and sweeping it toward the harpies storming me. They circle me in droves. I swipe at the harpies pushing in on my right, only to feel claws raking down my left side. Spinning to push back the harpies on my left, talons dig into my back. I knock my elbow backward, trying to dislodge the talons, but then sharp teeth embed into my thigh. I kick the harpy with my other foot, and she pulls a chunk out of my thigh when my foot makes contact with her face.

There are too many. I don't know how my friends are faring, but I do know at least twenty of the harpies are targeting me. I'm happy that my friends won't be battling as many as I am, but I also know I'm overrun. Still, I swipe and jab, kick and knee. I fight like a beast, doing anything I can to push the harpies away from me. I manage to swipe my sword through the neck of one, and she vanishes in a burst of feathers and shadows, but that only enrages the others, and they redouble their efforts.

My energy drains rapidly as they take chunks out of my body, but I'm still fighting. I will never stop fighting. For myself. For Brie. For my friends and comrades. For everything that is right and just in the universe. I will never stop fighting.

I jab my sword at the harpy lunging toward my face, pushing her back. But just then, I feel tension at the end of both of my wings. I whip my head to the side just in time to see the leader of the swarm rip my wing out of my back. The pain is agonizing, even worse than the violent pain I felt when my connection to Brie dimmed. And then the pain doubles as my other wing is ripped out. And the harpies cackle with glee as my wingless body falls from the sky.

Chapter 41

BRIE

"Lucifer, you can't stand in here while I pee. I understand that I broke your trust, but this is where I draw the line. You can stand on the other side of the door and wait for me to finish."

Lucifer huffs, but allows me to close the door with him on the other side of it. I wouldn't be surprised if he's pressing his ear against it. True to his word, Lucifer hasn't let me out of his sight since we returned to the castle, and while I do understand his hovering, watching me in the bathroom is a bit excessive.

I splash cold water on my face and look at myself in the mirror as the water drips back into the sink. I'm still not used to seeing the brown hair that drapes over my shoulders. Letting my wings unfurl from my back, I note how they've changed since I arrived in Hell. The pure white feathers have become a dark gray, and the maya blue that swirls through them has deepened into a Prussian blue. The gold strip down the center of each feather has transformed into a burnt orange. At least the silver tracing the edge of each feather is still relatively the same.

I look deep into my own eyes, not recognizing who I've become. What would Michael think if he saw me now? I guess I'll never know.

Pulling the black towel off its hook, I dry my face and straighten up. I'm tired, and not just from this day. I'm tired of trying just to fail. I'm tired of missing everyone I left behind. I'm tired of fighting to survive. I'm just...tired.

I open the door and pass Lucifer, climbing straight into my bed. "I'm going to sleep," I inform him, not waiting for a response as I turn my back on him and curl into myself. Lucifer sighs as though he has the weight of a world on his shoulders, and well, I guess he does. Nevertheless, I ignore the sound, leaving my eyes open just long enough to see him settling onto the couch in the sitting room. And then I leave all my worries behind as I drift into sleep.

Warm lips kiss across my collar bone and up my neck, coaxing me awake. The feeling is delicious, and I arch into the soft caresses. Strong hands rove over my body, making me melt underneath them. "Look at me," a whispered voice commands, and I slowly open my eyes, getting lost in deep earthy green irises. I run my hands through his soft auburn locks as his lips meet mine in a soul-wrenching kiss. Our mouths lock as our tongues battle for supremacy, but he cheats like the fallen angel he is, wrapping my hair around his fist and pulling my head into the angle he likes best. His lips trail back down to my neck and he sucks deeply atop my pulse point.

I gasp and my eyes fly open. Wait, when did I close them? The pressure lighting up my body has disappeared, and I glance around rapidly. I'm alone in my bed. Lucifer's arm hangs off the couch in the sitting room. A dream. It was just a dream.

A wave of pain hits me like a tsunami, and I feel like someone has cut part of my chest out of my body. I look down, expecting to see a gaping wound, but my body looks normal and whole. Then, I feel something inside me snap, and I look into myself just in time to see the string that connects me to Michael wither and die.

A cavernous emptiness fills the spot that little string took up. I check, and check again. It can't be gone. It just can't. Did my dream do this? Is this the consequence of dreaming about Lucifer in the way I did. I wasn't unfaithful. I can't control my dreams. Please don't let our connection really be gone. But when I check again, it is.

A keening cry leaves my lips and Lucifer bolts upright on the couch, rushing over to me. "Who attacked you? Where are you hurt?" he asks in a panic, frantically looking all over my body for an injury. I don't answer. I can't. I simply let out another sound of anguish.

Lucifer climbs onto the bed and hugs me to him, rocking me as though I'm a small child. "Brie, tell me what happened. Talk to me," he whispers soothingly, but it just reminds me of my dream and I start hyperventilating. "Shhh," he coos, pressing my head into his chest.

I don't know how long we stay like that. It could be minutes, it could be hours. Time has no meaning in my agony. Eventually, I quiet and regain enough awareness to know that there's something I need to check. I need final confirmation that what I suspect is true.

I push Lucifer away gently and climb out of the bed on unsteady legs. I hold my chest as I stagger over to the bathroom. I don't bother closing the door. Placing both hands on the black-marble countertop, I look at myself in the mirror and let my wings unfurl.

Lucifer gasps. "No!" The exclamation is soft, but I can still hear it. I turn my eyes away from the mirror and meet his horror-filled gaze. "My link to Michael was the only thing keeping me from turning fully dark. That connection has just broken," I explain. I turn back to the mirror and examine my midnight black wings in its reflection. "I've officially fallen."

Chapter 42

CALLIE

I thrust my sword into the harpy's chest and she disappears into a cloud of darkness and feathers. The next one lunges forward, trying to gut me with her sharp claws, but I'm already spinning and swinging my sword downward. It slices through her wrist, severing her hand from her body, and she screeches. It's a terrible sound, filled with pain and rage, but I have no empathy for her. If she wanted to keep her hand, she shouldn't have attacked me.

I glance past her to see how my fellow fighters are faring. Raphael and Gabriel are working as a team, trying to take down four harpies. Haniel is battling only one. My eyes widen when they drift over to where Michael is.

I can't actually see him through the gigantic crowd of harpies surrounding him, but I can catch glimpses of his sword, alight with angelic light, swinging every which way. There must be at least twenty of the sinister creatures circled around him. It looks like a mosh pit and I honestly don't know how he's survived this long against so many.

I need to dispatch this last harpy quickly so I can help Michael. Now that I've seen the situation he's in, it's clear that he was the target, the two harpies that came for me just providing a distraction. I thrust my sword at the red-headed beauty currently trying to decapitate me with her long talons, pushing her back once more. But my eyes are still trained on the large mob.

The harpy gets in a hit while I'm distracted. It's just a graze. I retaliate by slamming my palm into her nose. The loud crunch that accompanies my strike makes me smile, and when she automatically raises her hands up to her nose, I rip the sword through her unprotected midsection. She doesn't even realize that I've dealt her a killing blow before she bursts into smoke and feathers.

I smile and ready myself to dive into the fray surrounding Michael. But when the smoke clears, I realize I'm too late. My smile drops and I can feel a rictus of alarm spreading across my face. I see, but I don't fully process. One of the harpies is holding a large wing primarily composed of sapphire feathers, with waves of yellow and gold feathers. As I focus my gaze on her, trying to process the scene, she hefts the wing above her head in triumph.

Little streams of light drip from the side that should be attached to a body and the wing is quickly dropped when the light burns into the harpy upon contact. Then, another wing is moving through the air, also in absence of the body it should be attached to. And Michael plummets toward the ground, wingless.

His body careens toward the dirt clearing beneath us at a breakneck speed. I pull my wings in tight to my body and speed after him, but I already know I won't make it in time. His body slams into the hard ground with so much force, a crater forms beneath him.

My panic and disbelief are overwhelming, and I blink rapidly to make sure this isn't all in my imagination. But he's really there. Collapsed on the ground. Unmoving.

A gust of wind brushes past me and I look to the side, realizing that many of the harpies are now speeding toward Michael's inert form. To ensure he's perished or to finish him off, I don't know. But I do know that if he's somehow survived his injuries and that fall, I can't let them reach him.

I curl into a ball as I freefall toward the ground, making my body as small as possible so I can reach the ground faster. I allow myself to slow only for the landing, and when my feet touch the ground, I'm relieved to see that a squadron of the centaurs are galloping over with their clubs raised, ready to engage the harpies. The vengeful she-beasts may have disregarded Lucifer's orders, but the centaurs have not.

They form a circle around Michael, swinging their heavy clubs at the harpies. The harpies return their hostilities with claws and talons. I fight my way to the crater. Raphael is already hovering over Michael's prone form. His green healing energy streams from his palm, but Michael's body doesn't accept it. The energy swirls over him, surrounding his body like a cloud, but doesn't seep in.

Raphael's face is drawn. He looks exhausted, but he keeps pushing more and more energy toward Michael. "Work, dagnabit!" The cry of frustration flies from Raphael's lips before the energy stream cuts off and he punches the ground. At some point, Gabriel arrived and positioned himself on the ground. He's bent over Michael's head, cradling it in his arms, and he whispers words that only he can hear.

Desperation crackles in the air, palpable to all. The sounds of the battle fade as the truth sinks in: Raphael can't heal Michael.

"Take him and go!" one of the centaurs shouts, and reality sets back in. Gabriel pulls his brother's body over his shoulder and starts running toward the Gate. Although the centaurs' clash with the harpies mostly emptied the clearing of souls, there is still a line of them trying to make it through the Gate. They're frantic, but we're even more so.

We push our way through the crowd blocking access to the Gate. They can wait an extra second or two. Our need to pass through is far more urgent.

We crash into Deception, racing through the barren forest that greets us. Raphael leads the charge, his long strides rapidly devouring the distance between us and the next Gate. As we pass through the outskirts of a town, souls pop their heads out of their small wooden shacks, watching our group sprint through their lands.

A tribe of fauns detaches from the camouflage of the sparse trees interspersed among the homes. They surround us as we race through the eighth circle, offering both guidance and protection. Their cloven hooves pound against the hard, dusty ground, creating a rhythmic battle call that raises clouds of dirt with its force.

I don't fully understand Michael's current state. I don't know what it means that Raphael can't heal him. But Michael hasn't vanished in a flash of light like Ariella and Kemuel did, so at least I know he hasn't passed on yet.

When we reach the gate to the ninth circle, the fauns melt back into the trees without so much as a backward glance. Raphael rushes through the Gate, Gabriel close on his heels. I pass through last, almost stumbling when I collide with Haniel's back on the other side.

Several battalions of sphinxes stand assembled before the Gate. Tension coils through my muscles as I scan the massive brigade, wondering how in the world we are going to fight our way through so many. Fear clouds my vision, narrowing it to a pinprick as my eyes dart over the mass of troops before us.

One of the sphinxes steps forward, tipping her head respectfully toward Raphael and Gabriel. "Divine ones, Lucifer has sent us to escort you safely to the castle. We are honored to assist you on your journey."

"Thank you," Raphael replies. "We must make haste. Michael doesn't have long."

Raphael's words hit like stones, heavy and inescapable. I had gathered that the situation was dire, but hearing it spoken aloud makes it all too real. The sphinx nods in understanding, then turns to address her forces. "Security formation. Clear a path."

Her subordinates spring into action, forming a straight corridor through the center of the gathered troops. Gabriel shifts Michael's weight into Raphael's arms, his exhaustion evident in the strain on his face. Without hesitation, Raphael accepts Michael's bulk and launches into a sprint, completely ignoring the sphinxes that flank us.

We're coming, Brie. Just hang in there for a little bit longer. We need you. *Michael* needs you.

Chapter 43

LUCIFER

When Brie started hiding books in her piles from the library, I knew she was going to flee the castle—it was only a matter of when. I called Dee into my office and asked her to keep me apprised of Brie's progress. I also ordered her not to interfere.

I knew if I didn't allow Brie the opportunity to try escaping, she would never stop trying. It was something she needed to do for herself, and I hoped it would lead to her accepting that her future was here. Dee kept me updated on Brie's plans, even before Brie involved her in them. And when Brie did bring Dee into her plans, it made thwarting her escape all the easier.

We faked my reaction to the toxins Brie had asked Dee to add to my breakfast. The guards were instructed to act as though they were searching for Brie, but not to apprehend her. I needed her to believe she was evading them on her own, to build up her hope—so that I could crush it completely, ensuring she wouldn't attempt to escape again.

Dee's betrayal of both me and Brie was unexpected, but not entirely unanticipated. I knew she was a kuntilanak when I hired her to be Brie's lady's maid, and one can never fully trust a kuntilanak. They're devious creatures. The very epitome of deception.

It broke my heart to see the betrayal on Brie's face when I arrived to retrieve her, but I thought it was necessary. Now, looking at her newly blackened wings, I know it's my fault she's fallen. If not for my scheming, she would still have her light. I'll never forgive myself for damning her to this life of darkness—a life like mine.

I wish I could go back in time and do things differently. I would change everything. I would have left her to live happily with Michael, even if it meant my sanity withered away here in Hell. Because her light is so much more important than mine. Her light is everything that is good and pure in this world—or at least it was.

My mind can't fully grasp the extent of my failure this time. I've made countless mistakes throughout my existence, but this is the worst by far. I've never felt as ashamed of myself as I do now.

Love is supposed to be unselfish, beautiful, and magical. But I've managed to corrupt even that. I twisted my love for Brie into something vile. I tainted it, sullied it, and defiled it. And Brie is the one paying the price for my sins.

How can I ever look her in the eye again, knowing her soul is stained because of *my* actions? I knew what I was doing was wrong, but I was so consumed by it I couldn't stop myself. Now, I'm immersed in such thorough regret, it envelops me like a suffocating shroud, choking me.

Brie is so broken and defeated that she doesn't shed a single tear for all she's lost. Her soulmate bond is gone, and she simply stares at her reflection with a blank expression. She's become a hollow shell of the angel she once was. This is my doing—I've destroyed everything I loved about her.

Boagdan bursts into the room, panting heavily. "Your Majesty...the guard...sent word...the...angels...are...arriving," he wheezes, bending over with his hands on his thighs. Why is he so out of breath? He only had to run up four flights of stairs.

Brie turns toward Boagdan with vacant eyes. Her expression doesn't change in the slightest, concerning me even more. She should be happy they are here—or at the very least, relieved—but she shows no reaction at all.

From the moment Brie arrived in Hell, I knew I had gone too far. As soon as I learned the angels had entered Hell to retrieve her, I ordered the guards to grant the angels safe passage and accompany them when possible. It wasn't safe for Brie to leave on her own, but I trusted Michael to get her back to Heaven safely. It seems they've arrived too late though. The damage has already been done.

"Brie, come with me downstairs. It's time to greet your rescue party."

She doesn't respond but tucks her blackened wings closer to her back to navigate the spiral staircase more easily. I lead her down the stairs and through the throne room to the entrance hall. Mere seconds pass before the castle doors burst open and Raphael storms in, cradling a comatose Michael in his arms.

"Brie!" Raphael booms. "You need to save him." He places the unconscious warrior at Brie's feet, but she just looks down at her soulmate dispassionately.

"Save him!" Raphael yells again. "You're the only one who can."

"I can't do anything. Our bond no longer exists," she responds, her voice devoid of emotion. And in this moment, I see the full extent of the damage I've inflicted upon her. I've truly broken her.

"Brie, you need to try," I urge. "You can't let him die. The bond can be restored. Just because it's broken doesn't mean the foundation isn't still alive within you. Think of the good memories you share with him. Remember what he's meant to you."

"Yes!" Raphael agrees emphatically, placing his hands on her shoulders. "Think about all the training he put you through, the meals we shared, the battles you fought together. Remember how he encouraged and supported you. Appreciate the faith he had in you when you didn't have faith in yourself. Bring up every good memory you have of him and push that energy into him. Do it now."

Brie closes her eyes and furrows her brow. She drops to her knees beside Michael's body. His breathing is shallow, and his light dims with each passing second. His superior healing has kept him alive this long, but it's fighting a losing battle. If Brie can't reestablish their bond and transfer some of her energy into him, he will surely perish before the hour is out.

Her wings spread wide, drawing audible gasps from the other angels, but she doesn't open her eyes. She remains focused on her task. As she recalls the good memories she has of her soulmate, a single gold stripe appears on a single feather amongst the black of her wings, and I stifle my own gasp. Perhaps it's not too late after all. Perhaps they can both still be saved.

Brie channels a ball of energy into Michael, and when I focus closely, I find a single dark green thread weaving through the darkness. Her memories of Michael, and her love for the archangel, have brought her out of the darkness and redeemed a tiny sliver of her soul. There's hope for her yet.

Michael's body rejects the darkness, but that single thread of healing magic pierces straight into his soul. His body latches onto it, using it as a tether, and amplifying its energy. Like a chain reaction, his healing accelerates—doubling, then tripling. He'll need time to recover, but he'll survive. Thanks to Brie. She saved his life. I was so wrong to take her from him. They need each other. I see that now.

"So, are we all just going to ignore the fact that Brie's wings are black now?" a feminine voice chirps, shattering the moment. The tone is far too chipper for the gravity of the situation, and a growl rumbles in my chest at her audacity.

"Did you seriously just growl at me?" the angel asks, popping her hip and placing a hand on it as she stares me down. I don't recognize her, and her disrespect sets my hackles rising.

"Yes, I growled at you. Your impudence is disgusting. Haven't you learned to read a room? Who even are you? I know them," I say, pointing at Raf, Gabe, and Han, "but I have no idea who you are, so you're clearly not important enough to speak in my presence—let alone so brazenly."

"Well, excuse me, Mr. King of Hell who's been holding my best friend captive," she snaps back. "Let me just muster up some respect for the failure of a being that got two of my friends killed. Oh, wait, I don't have any."

My jaw drops. How dare she speak to me like that?! No one speaks to me like that.

"I am the King of Hell, and you will apologize for your outburst, or I will feed you to my hellhound." I won't actually feed her to Cerberus—he wouldn't so much as nibble her, even if I tried—but she doesn't need to know that. It's a good threat, and Cerberus can pretend to be aggressive when he wants to be, even though he's a softy at heart.

"Cerberus, come eat this impertinent angel!" I call loudly.

Cerberus comes loping into the room with a carrot hanging out of one mouth, tongues lolling out of the other two, and his tail wagging. He looks like the least intimidating dog in all four planes at the moment, and I want to slam my palm against my forehead. "Cerberus, act intimidating," I whisper to him.

The infuriating angel looks at me like I've got a few screws loose, "You do realize I can hear you, right?"

I bristle. No, I didn't realize she could hear me. I thought my whisper was quiet enough.

Raphael clears his throat, "Well, as entertaining as it is to watch you two bicker...Luc, we have some things to discuss."

I nod my head. We all know I messed up. Now it's time to pay the piper.

Chapter 44

BRIE

As I reflect on Michael's honor, compassion, and patience, the tiniest sliver of light pierces my soul. The thread it forms is thin and ragged, looking like it would break apart with a soft wind. But it's there. And it's reaching for Michael's soul.

I hold my breath as I watch the thread traverse the distance between us in my mind's eye. Then I exhale a steady breath when the thin thread latches onto the light in his soul. Hope slams back into me for the first time since Dee's betrayal, feeding the thread of healing energy that Michael's inert form is accepting.

The dark part of my magic bounces off him as though he's wearing a shield. I hadn't even considered that my magic, now corrupted, could hurt him. I mindlessly trusted Raphael and Lucifer when they said I could save him, and I'm relieved my oversight didn't worsen his condition.

Tuning out the bickering between Callie and Lucifer, I glance up at Raphael. "He'll live?" I ask, needing confirmation.

"He will," Raphael replies. "You two will need to restrengthen your bond. It will take a lot of work, time, and energy, but I believe you *both* can fully recover."

I shake my head, doubt weighing heavily on me. "I'm too far gone. I fell when our bond broke."

"The fact that you were able to give him any energy, no matter how little, tells me you aren't," Raphael counters. "The mark he placed on your soul still exists. It might be strained and faint, but your love for him endures. And as long as that remains, you'll never be too far gone. He will always be able to pull you back and remind you of who you are at your core."

I offer him a faint smile. "I hope you're right. I hope there's still some piece of myself left in my soul." I don't feel like there is, but I trust Raphael to be honest with me.

Cerberus nudges one of his noses against my neck before settling on the floor next to me. I didn't notice him entering the room, but I'm grateful for the comfort he brings. Keeping one hand on Michael, still trying to reinforce the bond between us, I run my other hand through Cerberus' soft fur.

When I hear Raphael addressing Lucifer as "Luc," I finally tune into the conversation happening around me.

"Obviously, Brie is leaving with us," Raphael states sternly, leaving no room for argument.

Lucifer is silent for a long moment before he finally speaks. "I can't rule Hell without a source of light here to maintain my sanity."

"Why should we care about your sanity?" Callie cuts in with a tone I've rarely heard before. She's pissed.

"Because, little baby angel," Lucifer replies tauntingly, "when my sanity is not all it should be, certain things can be...overlooked. Like Hell Gates opening on the earthly plane, for example."

Callie wrinkles her nose, glaring at him, but she can't rebut his statement. She knows he's right. Raphael starts to speak, likely to propose a solution, but Callie beats him to it.

"Fine. Then I will volunteer to stay here in Brie's place," she says firmly.

"Callie, you can't!" I cry, wanting to scramble to my feet but unwilling to withdraw my hand from Michael's chest.

"Oh, so this is the infamous Callie," Lucifer sneers, looking her up and down, and making sure she knows he finds her wanting. "You've caused a lot of problems between Brie and me. Now I understand why, given how...difficult...you are."

"Lucifer!" I gasp. "That was unwarranted. None of this was Callie's fault."

"That's true," Callie adds smugly. "From where I'm standing, everything that has gone wrong was your fault," she says, staring Lucifer down without a hint of fear. Then she gives him the same, dissatisfied once-over he gave her. I'm not sure I've ever seen her so riled up before. Something about Lucifer is definitely pushing her buttons, and I suspect it isn't entirely about me.

"Brie."

The deep baritone of Michael's voice draws my gaze down to him. Hearing him say my name is such a welcome relief, tears of happiness pool in my eyes. I swipe them away and whisper, "Michael."

"I love you too," he says, his hand lifting to cup my cheek. His thumb brushes away more tears. "Don't ever leave me again. My soul won't survive without you."

"I promise I won't. As soon as I jumped, I knew I'd made a terrible mistake. I'm so sorry. I can't even express how sorry I am. Can you ever forgive me?"

"There's nothing to forgive. You did what you thought was best, and you did it with noble intentions. Just don't do it again."

"I won't," I promise.

"How very touching," Lucifer mocks loudly. "Michael, I see you've recovered enough to show us all your mushy side."

Michael sighs. "I don't get a break from your attitude even after nearly dying?"

"Oh, I'd have given you a break if you'd actually died," Lucifer counters with a devilish smile. "But while you're still living, it's my duty to hold you to your accustomed high standards."

"Should we give you two some privacy?" Callie drawls. "I thought we were negotiating how to prevent you from ruining multiple planes of existence for the second time."

Wow, she's genuinely upset with Lucifer. He did trick me into sacrificing myself, so her anger is warranted, but it still surprises me. Callie was the most bubbly, upbeat person I knew. While this darker side of her could be a result of my captivity, I wonder if the violence of her death at Chad's hand is also contributing to it. Traumatic events like that leave a mark on one's soul.

Her soul is still pure, of course. Otherwise, she wouldn't have ascended. But perhaps her soul is a little bit scarred now.

"I am glad to see that you're recovering, Michael," Callie says, her tone much softer. "But as I was saying before, I volunteer to stay in Brie's place."

"Callie, you can't. It would destroy you. Look at how I've lost my light since I came here. I can't let you go through that because of me."

"Not to mention, I don't want you here," Lucifer proclaims. "Request denied!"

"She would need to spend time on the earthly plane or the heavenly plane every so often to detox from the darkness," Michael suggests. "That would prevent her from losing all of her light. We'd need to find the balance for her to safely maintain both light and darkness within her soul." In keeping with his habitual role as the voice of reason among us, his contribution is eminently sensible.

"But the pain! I could never accept that she'd experience the pain I did when my body was trying to metabolize the darkness. That was excruciating."

Lucifer waves me off. "We'd just need to maintain a certain threshold of darkness within her. The pain would only affect her once. As soon as she reached that threshold, we'd ensure she didn't let her darkness fall below that point." He looks over at Callie and does a double-take before adding, "Hypothetically speaking, of course. Not that it will be an issue, since she won't be staying."

"It could work," Raphael muses.

"No!" I shout. Why are we even discussing this? "Callie, I could never let you do this. I made the mistake of coming down here in the first place. I can't let you pay for a mistake that I made."

"Brie, you are always the one making sacrifices for everyone else. For once in your life, be selfish. Sometimes, putting yourself first does more good than putting everyone else before yourself. Think of all the angels in Heaven who look up to you, who are inspired by you. If you're down here, who will inspire them? Who will step up the next time they need someone to show them how to be strong? Haniel told me a little bit about how you volunteered to be sent to Earth. He said that the other angels wouldn't have volunteered if you hadn't done so first. You need to be that leader for them. Staying here isn't a selfless act if it will negatively affect everyone else. You're needed in Heaven. You need to regain the light you've lost and become the leader you once were. That is the most selfless thing you can do right now. And me? I can do this for you. Accept my help and go home with your soulmate. He needs you."

"Your life was cut short once before because of me. I can't do that to you again."

"But it's not really your decision, is it? It's my decision to make. I'm not asking for your approval. I'm asking for your understanding."

"Callie." My voice breaks. She's made up her mind, and there's nothing I can say to change that. I know the guilt of this will eat me from the inside out, but in the end, I need to respect her decision. If she feels like this is something she needs to do, I'll accept her sacrifice and be grateful for it. Because she's right: I can do more good overall by being selfish this one time.

"So, I get no say here? Sure, let's all decide which angel is going to move into Lucifer's home without giving him any input in the matter," Lucifer says, throwing up his hands.

"How old are you? Five?" Callie snipes back with an eye roll.

"Cerberus, attack!" Lucifer yells, pointing at Callie. Cerberus rolls onto his back, legs in the air and tail wagging.

"Cerberus," Lucifer groans, scrubbing a hand over his face. "You're making me look bad."

"I don't think you need the dog for that," Callie mutters.

Lucifer ignores Callie's latest gibe, instead addressing Michael. "Why don't you all stay the night and recover? I'll have the guards escort you through the circles on your way back so you don't have any problems."

"Thank you, Lucifer. Maybe we can catch up in the meantime? I've never forgiven myself for the way our friendship ended, and it seems like maybe this could have all been prevented if we were still talking."

Lucifer looks shell-shocked, hesitantly admitting, "I think I would like that. I've missed all of you. It's very lonely down here. I was angry with you for so long, but seeing the effect my actions had on Brie—I understand now how toxic I've been. I want to change that."

"Aw, group hug!" Raphael shouts, trying to drag Michael and Lucifer together.

I laugh as both males rapidly pull away from Raphael's attempts.

"Too soon?" he asks me with a wink.

"Too soon," I confirm. But hopefully, that won't be the case for long.

CALLIE

"**B**rie!" I squeal.

"Callie!" she squeals back, pulling me into a hug. "How are you?"

"Ugh, that male is insufferable!" I tell her, hooking my thumb over my shoulder to point in Lucifer's direction as we ascend the few stairs of the entrance to The Plaza Hotel.

"I heard that!" he yells.

"You were meant to!" I call back.

"I swear, Michael, she's most certainly a demon masquerading as an angel. I'm thoroughly convinced this whole situation was engineered by the divine spirit as a new method of punishment for my transgressions."

I roll my eyes. "He's so melodramatic."

Brie's tinkling laugh is music to my ears. "How are you doing?" I ask her.

"My soul grows brighter each day. And my bond with Michael is returning quickly. We've been spending a lot of quality time together cleaning up the lingering infestation of darkness on this plane. It's slow going, but we're making progress."

"I'm so glad to hear that. I've been worried about you." I really have been. There was so much that was left unresolved when she left Hell. Lucifer had told me that he received confirmation that all of the angels had made it to the astral plane safely, but I couldn't believe it until I saw Brie and Michael whole and healthy with my own eyes.

"That reminds me," Brie says, pulling an ornate handheld silver mirror from her white clutch. "Gabriel made this for you and Lucifer, since he shattered his watch face. It will allow us to chat with you regardless of which plane any of us are on."

I take the handle from her grasp carefully. The metalwork is beautiful, with little dragons and flame insignias artfully framing the looking glass. "This will be a lifesaver. Thank you, Brie. Even though we can travel through the astral plane to meet you on this plane, Lucifer is worried about leaving Hell for extended periods of time. There has been too much turmoil amongst the souls lately and he's worried that an uprising is brewing, but he also refuses to let me leave Hell without him. He keeps grumbling about me getting hurt."

"He'll learn to recognize your strength soon enough. I'm sure he's already aware of it and just doesn't want to admit it."

"I don't care," I shrug. "I tell him that if I don't return to Hell, it will be because I fled his attitude. Not because I'm injured. That really winds him up. It's fun to watch his face get all pinched as he tries to figure out how he should respond."

"You're enjoying this," she observes.

"Yes, yes I am," I say truthfully. "He deserves some pushback after everything he put you through."

"He wasn't in his right mind," she notes, with forgiveness.

"That doesn't excuse what he did," I say, taking her hands in mine. "It doesn't make it okay. He hurt you—to the extent that you are still recovering. He needs to understand that his actions have consequences."

"He does understand that, and he has apologized to both me and Michael dozens of times. He feels true remorse for everything he put in motion. We can't go back. We can only move forward, and part of that is forgiving him and acknowledging that he wasn't fully in control of his actions."

I let out a long sigh. I love Brie like a sister, but sometimes I think she's too forgiving. I can't let go of the past so easily. "Have they told you how long they think it will be before you can enter Heaven again?"

"It's hard to tell. We have to wait until my soul is purged of nearly all the darkness. Michael said it's fine if there's a little bit left, but if there's too much, it could contaminate the plane. Maybe spring? That's just an estimate though. Gabriel is going to reintegrate my angelic memories on Monday. They think that might speed up my recovery."

"I'll hope it does. Just don't change too much. I like my best friend just the way she is." Brie smiles over at me with such love, it nearly makes my steps falter. I'm glad she's getting her happily ever after. She deserves it, especially after all she's been through.

"Are you ladies ready?" Michael asks as he and Lucifer join us.

"Ready as I'll ever be," Brie responds softly, looking up at him like he hung the moon. The angel did walk through Hell to save her and nearly died on the way, so I guess she's not that far off.

"We'll see you in there," Lucifer says, motioning me through the doors of the grand ballroom. We slip in and scurry to our assigned seats at the head table.

"Nice of you to join us," Raphael whispers, punching Lucifer in the shoulder. Gabriel takes that as his cue to stand, the room instantly quieting. "Thank you all for making the trip to be here today," Gabriel begins. "Please rise in appreciation of our guests of honor."

We all stand. Brie and Michael enter the ballroom hand-in-hand. Brie looks radiant in her sparkling white ball gown, her rich brown locks hanging over her shoulders in soft curls. The angels applaud the couple as they approach our table, standing behind the two empty center seats between me and Gabriel.

"As you all know, Brie selflessly sacrificed her memories before embarking upon her last mission," Gabriel continues once the applause has quieted. "And it is important to Brie and Michael that they recommit their lives to each other before her memories are reintegrated. They want to make it clear that their love for each other transcends their forms or their purities. And that even if they had no memory of each other, they would still find one another and fall in love again, because their souls will always be two halves of a whole."

"With that in mind, let us renew their vows. Brie, do you acknowledge Michael as your soulmate, the one being throughout the four planes that completes you and makes your spirit sing? Do you promise to support him and believe in him, no matter the obstacles you encounter? Do you promise to trust in his devotion to you and give him the whole of your heart and soul in return?"

"I do."

"And do you, Michael, acknowledge Brie as your soulmate, the one being throughout the four planes that completes you and makes your spirit sing? Do you promise to support her and believe in her, no matter the obstacles you encounter? Do you promise to trust in her devotion to you and give her the whole of your heart and soul in return?"

Michael pulls a gorgeous diamond, sapphire, and aquamarine engagement ring out of his suit pocket before answering. "I've been carrying this ring in my pocket since we left the airport in Nicaragua to close the Hell Gate in Masaya. It was our anniversary, and I had planned to propose to you once we'd sealed that last Gate. I'd thought it was perfect timing. A divine coincidence, one might say. But then I lost you, and I walked through Hell—literally—to get you back."

Lucifer flinches next to me, but I pretend not to notice, focusing on Michael as he continues, "I have fallen in love with every version of you a thousand times over. And every time, just when I think that I can't possibly love you any more than I already do, you surprise me in the best of ways and my love grows deeper. So yes, I most definitely do, and I am humbled to be able to *finally* put this ring on your finger."

THE END

Author's Note

Thank you so much for reading <u>Encompassed By Darkness</u>. I hope you enjoyed reading it and were satisfied with Brie's and Michael's HEA. If you did love the story, please consider leaving a quick review on Amazon or Goodreads. It helps authors out so much!

While this is the end of Brie's and Michael's story, the *Savior of the Light* series will continue with Callie's and Lucifer's story in <u>Beguiled By Darkness</u>.

Again, I truly hoped you enjoyed this story! More adventures await.

To stay up-to-date on future releases, join my newsletter at https://algordon-author.com/ or follow me on social media @algordon.author

About the Author

A. L. Gordon is an American author and self-described book addict. On the rare occasions when she is not reading or writing, you can usually find her making some of her own adventures with her dog.

If you want to stay up to date with A. L. Gordon's new releases, sign up for her newsletter at https://algordon-author.com/ or connect with her on social media.

Instagram: https://www.instagram.com/algordon.author

Facebook: https://www.facebook.com/author.algordon/

Facebook Readers Group:
https://www.facebook.com/groups/algordon.author

www.ingramcontent.com/pod-product-compliance
Lightning Source LLC
Chambersburg PA
CBHW071358300726
48976CB00006B/1917